*Advance Praise for Battles Forgotten*

"*Battles Forgotten* is a taut, dramatic, historical novel, that as the name implies, sheds light on an important period of human conflict. Despite the serious nature of the subject matter, Mr. Vardaman injects his unique witticism to amplify the characters. He draws on his Scottish roots to accurately depict not only the local language, but the morals and integrity of the era. While the brogue can be challenging, the authenticity is indispensable. The protagonists, although inimitable in their own right, are woven together in such an engaging manner that the reader wants to keep turning the page. Mr. Vardaman recognizes that the brave sacrifices of young men and women in places other than the Hollywood, iconic pages of history books, should never be forgotten. And so should we.*"

— Robert "Bob" Glickley, BA Psychology, C.P.M. Certified Purchasing Manager from Institute for Supply Management, American Honda Motor Co., Inc./Assistant Manager, Corporate Procurement

"*Battles Forgotten* is a unique historical novel about life in the United States during the Great Depression and World War II. The author takes the reader on an engaging journey into the social, financial, moral and military lives of an extended family of that era. It also provides a thought-provoking commentary on the issues of poverty, race, religion and freedom that provided the exceptional foundation for the 'Greatest Generation.' This book bolstered my understanding of my own early grade-school years. I recommend this book as an enjoyable read for all ages to appreciate how 100 years of our history can help us today.*"

— RW Harsh, 1st Lt. US Army
Retired Professional Engineer

# BATTLES FORGOTTEN

## NORTH AFRICA

### BOOK ONE

# DEDICATION

*Battles Forgotten* is dedicated to my parents' Greatest Generation, who fought and won World War II. We are not likely to see their strength and wisdom again.

Thank you to everyone who selflessly served our Republic. Sacrifice is part of God's loving plan.

# BATTLES FORGOTTEN

## NORTH AFRICA

### BOOK ONE

## GEORGE VARDAMAN, JR.

SHAMLAIGH MEDIA, DENVER, CO

*Battles Forgotten: North Africa*

Copyright © 2021 by George Vardaman, Jr.

All rights reserved.

No part of this book may be reproduced or transmitted in any form or by any means, electronic or mechanical, including photocopying, recording or by any information storage and retrieval system, without the written permission of the author, except where permitted by law.

FIRST EDITION

ISBN: 978-1-60414-045-3 (hardcover)
978-1-60414-905-0 (paperback)

Published by

Fideli Publishing, Inc.
119 W Morgan St
Martinsville, IN 46151

www.FideliPublishing.com

Produced by

# Shamlaigh Media
Denver, CO

*This is a work of fiction. Names, characters, businesses, places, events, locales, and incidents are either the products of the author's imagination or used in a fictitious manner. Any resemblance to actual persons, living or dead, or actual events is purely coincidental.*

**Cover art:** USAAF Engineer clearing out the wreckage of a Luftwaffe aircraft at an ALG, with a P-38 Lightning flying overhead on landing approach, 1945.

Source: The Air Force Engineer. Army Air Forces Engineer Command, MTO (Prov). Permission: USGOV-PD.

PRINTED IN THE UNITED STATES OF AMERICA

# TABLE OF CONTENTS

# CHAPTER 1

# WHOA, SANTA!

Christmas Eve, 1927, a Saturday night. The family walked five miles and back to eat the First Baptist Dallas Texas Church's Christmas supper, and the boys were in bed early with wary anticipation of sitting in the front row to hear Pastor Dr. George Truett's Christmas message the following day.

As they lay together in their skinny twin bed under Aunt Bea's warm quilt, the brothers listened attentively for the sound of sleigh bells. It was an abomination too. Before bed, Mary Mother had smacked both of them squarely upside of their heads for mentioning Santa Claus on the night of their Dear Savior's birth.

"Do you hear anythin'?" Callum whispered.

"Shush! How can I hear when you're talkin'?" Gordy replied. His name was pronounced "JOR'dee," his Mary Mother Ward's Scottish endearment for young Gordon.

"I was whisperin'. You're whisperin'. Wasn't 'talkin.'"

"Quiet!"

As usual, Father was away somewhere while Mary Mother was down in the kitchen listening to Uncle Laurence whine. "I'm a might bound up, Sister! Maybe dem turnips we ate at the church supper?" He glanced at her, rubbing his slightly bloated stomach.

"Well, Laurence, if you'd listen to me, you'd eat something more else than rice and beans. Isn't natural not to eat meat. You're as skinny as a rail!"

"Funny, sister, you disparagin' the railroad. Helps us pay for this place, and rice and beans suits me jus' fine! Still, not feelin' meself…"

Luckily, Mary was a well-known home remedy genius, blessed with years of experience. For a sore throat, a swallow of raw alum (used for dyeing or tanning). For an earache, a cooked-cabbage-leaf-and-carrot poultice inserted deeply and forcefully, their overpowering, noxious smells making anyone forget their pain. For constipation? Her go-to remedy was NR (Nature's Remedy) all-vegetable tablets for "defective elimination." The fact was Laurence—who possessed a prolific gag reflex—was a poor pill-swallowin' candidate. Still, she felt compelled to help.

Mary Mother knew Laurence was a sweet potato varietal connoisseur—Garnet, Hannah, Jewel, or Vardaman. If it were sweet and a potato, Laurence craved it. Several jewels were lying in wait in the vegetable bin. Crushing eight NRs (the normal dose was two) into a fine powder with her mortar and pestle, she mashed the jewels into silky paste in a mixing bowl. When mixed with buttermilk and poured into a tall ice-cream glass, the concoction took on an unappealing brown-orange, sludge-like appearance. Even so, it wasn't hard to convince Laurence of Mary Mother's preparing a thoughtful before-bed Christmas Eve surprise "just for him." He relished every ounce to the bottom of the glass.

Meanwhile, time was a-wastin' upstairs. No sleigh bells. No reindeers' hooves upon the roof. No "Ho-Ho-Hos." Still listening carefully, it wasn't long before the boys heard the familiar hinge of the outhouse door shut with a screech, pop, and a crunch. Within its confines, the loo was dark and drafty, and despite regular lye poo maintenance, the smell was breathtaking. So, the boys expected the normal quick turnaround squeal and slam of the door within moments. Instead, their intense listening for Santa was rudely interrupted.

"Whoa-uh!" Seconds passed. "Whoa-aaaaah!"

Now, it wasn't uncommon to hear Father or Uncle Laurence vocalizing their satisfaction with the completion of their duty, but that night it seemed as if it were way more than usual—more pathetic. Things were not well in the crapper! "Whoaaaaa-a-a-a-ah...whoa! Whoa-a-a-a-ah-ah-ah!"

"Is that Uncle? Is he dyin'?" Callum asked, obviously frustrated. Before Gordy could answer, another woeful wail came forth. "Whhhhoa-a-a-a-ah! Whoa-eeee-uuu!" It was a new ending with a pitiful soprano punctuation, octaves and volume climbing higher with every movement (not that of a symphony).

"You think we should go down there?" Gordy asked, his voice a whisper although he didn't know why. No one within a mile was getting any sleep anyway.

"No, sir! I don't wanna see Uncle's dead body in the privy! You go!"

"He wouldn't be wailing like that if he were dead! and no! I'm not goin'!"

Unfortunately for Laurence, such histrionics continued for the larger portion of the long, starry night.

Finally, in the blessed break of morning light upstairs, silence was laced with the lingering regret of missing the opportunity to hear—or perhaps see—Santa. There was little doubt; Uncle Laurence, living or not, was a Christmas spoiler!

Callum lay fast asleep as Gordy climbed down the steep stairs to the kitchen to get a glass of water. There, slumped in a chair, sat Laurence, depleted, sighing, and moaning. Gordy attempted to turn and run back upstairs, but before he could...

"Boy, come down in here!"

Pretending he didn't hear, Gordy crept up a couple more steps.

"Boy, come down here—now!"

Obviously, there was no means of escape. Moments later, Gordy became a reluctant captive, alone with his uncle in the kitchen.

"Boy, you come on over right here. Sit!"

With trepidation, Gordy obeyed, plopping onto the chair next to him. Silence descended upon them. Gordy thought about asking his uncle if he was all right, but before he could, Uncle Laurence declared, "Boy let me tell you somethin'. You listenin'?"

"Yes, sir."

"Are you sure you're listenin'? 'Cause this right here an' now is real dang important, boy."

Gordy sat up straight. "OK! Yes, Uncle. I'm listening!"

"Boy, don't you never drink sweet potaters and buttermilk. Never ever!"

Mary Mother, perhaps within earshot, wasn't anywhere to be seen—mayhap getting ready for church?

Her prescription would never to be known to Laurence—never, ever revealed.

Thus ended the "Whoa, Santa!" episode, one of life's most potent and crucial lessons.

****

It wasn't until fifty years later at Mary Mother's (a.k.a. Mary Clover Ward) graveside service when Uncle Laurence peered down at the plot next to her, designated for him amongst the thirty plus she had purchased for the entire family at Oak Park Cemetery. "I ain't dead sure I want to be buried there," he declared with profundity. Was it the sweet potatoes and buttermilk or perhaps his keen biblical erudition concerning eternity? We shall never be dead sure. He was, however, buried at Oak Park next to Mary Mother.

# CHAPTER 2

# "BE NOT DRUNK WITH WINE…"

## or "Do not drink old, moldy, corked and contaminated wine"

**LATE JULY 1942**

Given Gordy's tech sergeant training with aircraft, he was obsessed with the enemy's planes almost as much as he was with learning French, German, and Italian phrases, memorized by asking friends or native speakers for help with pronunciation. He studied German, Japanese, and Italian fighters and read everything he could about them.

Of course, with such studious tendencies, his knowledge of the US Curtiss Wright P-40 Warhawk as well as the Lockheed P-38F Lightning was legendary. He could break down both planes' original respective V-12 radial and Allison V 1710-horsepower engines in his sleep. In fact, he dreamed about both, reinforcing hours of memorization before bed. His vast knowledge enabled him to service the only remaining P-40 on the US West Coast after Pearl Harbor, literally the *only* operational fighter to oppose a potential Japanese invasion. Pilots trusted his knowledge implicitly, and Gordy was responsible for every detail from his post at March Field in Riverside, California.

Ultimately assigned to the newly formed 48th Training Squadron at Hamilton, CA, the unit was composed of P-38Fs, his squadron patrolling the West Coast to guard against a Japanese attack. In August 1942 the squadron hopscotched from California to Michigan and then to Maine. Thanks to the addition of drop tanks to their P-38Js and six accompanying B-17 Flying Fortresses, the renamed 48th Fighter Squadron (FS) went on to Iceland and Prestwick, Scotland, finally heading to Shrewsbury (Atcham) in northwest England. As a part of the ground echelon, Gordy shipped out to England, arriving in mid-July to participate in the build-up of American troops and weapons in Operation Bolero (staging for European Theater operations). Worried about his young pilots—some were inquiring about the controls on their P-38s—more training took place throughout October. The plane was much more complicated to fly than the P-40, and Gordy was grateful his comrades had more flight time to and in England. Although the squadron flew protection for several bombing missions, it remained unchallenged in combat. That, however, was about to change.

Within eleven days of the successful Operation Torch—the invasion of North Africa at Casablanca, Oran, and Algiers occurring from November 8–16, 1942—Gordy was ordered to Algeria. He and his ground crews arrived in a B-24 Liberator—dubbed the dreaded "flying coffin" because of its difficult controls and single escape exit—from England through Gibraltar.

Then on November 11, they proceeded to Tafraoui Airfield near Oran and finally, to Maison Blanche (French for "White House"), Algeria. Prayers for safe passage were answered with his own P-38s as escorts from "the Rock" south to Algiers, arriving on Wednesday, November 16, 1942, his other ground echelon comrades making passage by sea.

Gordy's first assignment at Maison was an all-important flight-readiness check of the newly arrived P-38s. As was tradition in the Air Corps, tow trucks lined the planes up in stiff, precise rows only feet apart. Gordy, however, was aware of the consequences of such a routine. At Pearl Harbor, under General Walter Short's orders, rigidly aligned aircraft on the tarmac were easy, consecutive targets for Japanese dive-bombers.

Requesting permission to stagger the P-38s into pods of four or five planes each with a gasoline truck for each pod, he also requested extra jeeps mounted with .50 caliber guns for mobility of defensive fire as well as consent to test-fire the guns. Partly successful, Gordy received permission for the pods and four gas trucks but not for the jeeps. Five new M15 half-tracks provided anti-aircraft artillery (AAA) close cover for the camouflage-netted Lightnings and the runway.

For Gordy, the P-38s' presence was a point of pride—only about one hundred were built by 1941. Unbeknown to him, eventually, they would account for 1,300 air victories against the Germans and the Italians over North Africa and Italy. His 48th Fighter Squadron would score the 14th Fighter Group's leading 153, and Gordy kept them flying.

Already exhausted from the journey and his duties, he was also a mentor to his squadron counterpart, Tech Sergeant Wilson "Willie" Edson. Willie turned to him for tips on tuning the often-temperamental P-38 1710 Allison engines during training in Shrewsbury. A tall, outgoing, and affable twenty-year-old Alabaman with handsome good looks, Gordy couldn't help wondering how well Willie was trained given his youth. However, the question could easily be asked, was Gordy trained well enough? Was he qualified with his six years in the service?

"Hey, Ward! Let's explore Algiers!" Perhaps it was Willie's youth, but there appeared to be a palpable excitement as he shouted to Gordy.

"We just got here!" Gordy shouted back with a barely discernible grin. "We're not getting off of this airfield. We still have more checks to do. There may be sorties tomorrow."

"We deserve a break, Sarge. How many more checks can we do?"

"You can never be too sure, Willie. Never forget one thing! The best way to do that is to check, double-check, and triple-check all of these planes. Their pilots are our responsibility."

"Yeah, I know. But ya know what they say, Sarge. All work and no play..."

"OK then, let's have some fun. You see that sad sack asleep on top of the M15?" Gordy pointed to a private stretched out on the hood of the vehicle, a stocking cap and helmet covering his face. Stealthily, he crossed over to the soldier. "Private! Atten...shun!"

The soldier jolted upright, rolled off the hood, and hit the ground hard. Dazed, he picked up his cap, helmet, and rifle, then stood at attention.

"Are we taking a nap, Soldier?"

"No! I mean, No, Sergeant!"

"Are you on watch, Private?" Gordy paused as he eyed the M15. "Is this vehicle your responsibility?"

"Yes, Sergeant. I mean, yes, I'm on guard. Uh, guarding this M15. I just dropped off for a minute. So sorry, Sergeant! It was a long trip from England."

"A long trip, huh? What's your name, Private?"

"Private Enzo Rossi, Sergeant!"

"Well, Private Enzo Rossi, Tech Sergeant Edson and I wish to keep you off report for falling asleep on duty. Would that be OK with you, Private Rossi?"

"Oh, yes, please Sergeant!"

"So, Rossi, you're Italian, right? Ciao?"

"Buongiorno." He smiled, sheepishly. "Really...so sorry. Yes, but not from the old country. My family's from Brooklyn. You know, New York, in the USA. Tried-and-true Americans!"

"Of course, you are, Private. What we'd like to propose is you need to pee. You need to pee now, you need to pee a lot, and you can't hold it. You need to go to the latrines now!"

"Pardon, Sergeant? I need to pee? Oh! Oh! I need to pee a lot right now! I need the latrine right now!" Rossi scanned the area. "Sorry again, but which way are the latrines?"

Gordy pointed. "They're way over there at the other end of the field. But before you need to do that, you need to show us your M15."

"Pardon again, Sergeant, but this isn't my M15. It's an AAA piece, and its crew is assigned to this airfield."

"Where are they, Algiers? Rossi, we're the guys responsible for the Lightnings under those camo nets. I need to see the M15 long enough to be familiar with its guns, just in case."

"Sorry, Sergeant, in case of what?"

"In the unlikely event you fall asleep again, the gunners don't return from Algiers, the Luftwaffe pays us a visit, and we need to man them to save you, us, and our Lightnings."

Rossi showed Gordy and Willie the guns, but he had no idea how to work them.

"Private Rossi, I think you need to pee now. Right now!"

"And how long do I need to pee?"

"About fifteen minutes. Starting now."

"Fifteen minutes. That's a long...that's a lot of pee, Sergeant!"

"As you've said, Private Rossi."

The private turned, then hurried toward the opposite end of the airfield as Gordy and Willie climbed up the back of the M15's turreted and armor-shielded guns—two .50 caliber Browning machine guns. Between them was a 37-mm (1.5-inch) AAA cannon that usually required a crew of four.

"Well, I do declare, Gordy, we need to check the ammo and guns!" Willie said.

"And so we shall, Sergeant!"

Test-firing Brownings or a 37-mm cannon wasn't a field manual requirement, but there were stories throughout the Army about "gremlins"—old, corroded, and degraded ammunition—or incorrect ammo leading to misfiring and jamming. There was also a rumor that the 37-mm was useless against German armor, all good reasons for Gordy to double-and triple-check.

He allowed Willie to fire the tracers on the .50 toward the barren desert landscape surrounding the field, following with one blast from the 37-mm cannon. If anyone else had been sleeping, they weren't anymore.

It was a good play too. Gordy and Willie used the "You need to pee" ploy four more times that night, never suspecting their actions proved prescient.

That same evening, Private Rossi delivered a bottle of aged Tuscana white wine as a gesture of thanks. Given to him by his uncle, he had lugged it all the way from Brooklyn to Gordy and Willie's tent. Hard to believe after transport over thousands of miles, but the wine was tainted, corked, and moldy. Also astonishing was Rossi's cooling it in a cesspool-like puddle behind his tent!

The good sergeants reported to sick bay early the following morning, experiencing their own "I think you need to pee but from another orifice" moment.

Dysentery. Amoebic dysentery.

As Gordy took his first-ever sip of alcohol, he remembered Ephesians 5:18, "And do not be drunk with wine, wherein is filled with excess; but be filled with the Spirit." *What part of unsanitary, unholy Little Italy did Private Rossi come from?* he wondered when the consequences became obvious.

Moreover, Gordy finally understood Uncle Laurence's angst so many Christmases ago.

****

Flight Surgeon Dr. Samuel Bosnick was quick and sure with diagnoses, his preferred tactical treatment for everything being to paint the throats of his patients with iodine regardless of whether they complained of a sore throat or not. Besides producing horrendous gagging, the procedure resulted in an inability to focus on anything other than constant, choking irritation. Who knew fulminating, bloody diarrhea could be supplanted—at least in thought—by elongated, orange-colored cotton swabs?

Willie and Gordy spent the next day conflicted as to which ends of their digestive systems were inflamed worse, both considering they were blessed to have a day to recover.

Being disabled in any way wouldn't be an option for what was coming next.

# CHAPTER 3

# DEATH OF A SALESMAN

Jeremiah was his father's name before him, and Enoch and Elijah were the only two prophets not to die in the Bible. Therefore, his parents chose their names as his first and middle—Enoch Elijah Ward. He hated both, but he went by Eli. He had been raised on a farm near Scyene, Texas, east of Dallas. His father prepared his brothers and him to become his successors, and as the eldest, Eli acquired an aptitude for the business side of things. He maintained the books and encouraged his dad to invest in new equipment and cooperatives to generate greater profits. Even so, the dutiful son had plans for his life other than crops. His interests?

Property and investments.

Studying sales correspondence courses in the evenings, he practiced techniques on neighbors, friends, and farm clients. Blessed with being a good listener, he also had the gift of gab.

At twenty years old in 1898, Eli traveled to Dallas every Friday, going from office to office seeking a sales job. A new concept of life insurance was in vogue—insurance for farmers—pitched to provide for survivors of the one in thirteen people who would contract cancer at the time. New York Life (NYL), founded in 1845, was one of the most prominent purveyors of said insurance, and Eli found the Dallas office teeming with activity and potential. To his delight, there was a spot for a NYL sales representative in West Texas. Upon passing a sales aptitude test, he was on his way to New York City to complete his training. No more peanuts, beans, or cotton for Eli Ward!

Back then, trains were few and far between from Dallas to West Texas, but Eli found his way to Wichita Falls, Lubbock, and Amarillo. Farmers and ranchers were prime targets for NYL policies, and Eli sold the benefits to all who would listen.

In early 1900, he found himself in Floydada, Texas, traveling by buggy to the family ranch, and it was there he met sixteen-year-old Hana Mills. Being a man of words and action, he asked Mr. Mills for permission to court her, and within two months, Eli sold him and every rancher in the area a NYL policy.

Then he asked for Hana's hand in marriage.

As fast as the couple were hitched, within the year, their firstborn, Job, graced their lives.

Eli continued selling policies, purchasing distressed properties of the decedents of some of his clients, prompting him to pursue a real estate license, all while he continued to travel. A year later, his daughter, Beatrice, was born, and by 1904 Eli Ward was the father of two and an empresario. Things were grand!

Sadly, however, tragedy struck. Hana contracted scarlet fever, succumbing in December. Shortly after, Eli moved back east of Dallas to the Ward farm to seek the family's help in raising Bea and Job. In his mind, there were still fields to be plowed, and potential deals to be done there. Because Eli's work required weekly travel, his sister, Telsie, took care of the kids.

Luckily, it turned out his NYL and real estate businesses were complementary. When a distressed property became available as a result of a rancher's passing, Eli was there to help buy or sell. He did so not out of greed but rather out of biblical sympathy for widows and orphans. He knew and had experienced loss. He helped grieving people move forward with their lives.

So, Eli eked out a living, sending money and savings back to Telsie for Bea and Job's care. His prized possession was his Model T, and he was known to provide rides to strangers for free, his character reflecting his parents' strong Southern Baptist training. Though his travel often kept him on the road, he enjoyed attending the First Baptist Church Dallas (FBCD) whenever possible.

It was at a Wednesday night prayer meeting where he met Mary Clover MacDougal. A second-generation Scot and slight of build, she was stern in bearing with bright gray-green eyes. Her eyes and her shy smile captured Eli's attention. She impressed him further with her biblical knowledge, enough so that after the meeting, they shared punch and cookies.

That was the beginning.

Their courtship lasted nearly a year. They memorized Bible verses together, meeting only at church. However, Eli didn't tell Mary Clover about Bea and Job. He was enjoying her company, and he was uncertain of how she would react if she knew he was a widower. When she suggested he meet her parents, he felt compelled to inform her about Hana and his kids.

"God willing, and with my father's permission, I would love to meet your children," she said, weeping for his loss.

A proclamation dear to Eli's heart.

****

Mary Clover's father, William "Mac" MacDougal, was direct from Glasgow and spoke with a harsh brogue. An engineer who emigrated to America to build bridges in Texas, his wife, Mariam, was the daughter of a Kirk Presbytery Minister, also from Glasgow.

When Eli first met Mac, there was little doubt where Mary Clover's striking eyes and stern demeanor came from. Mac was an irascible, crusty, old Scot, his piercing stare accompanied by a jaw-clenching frown.

They met over dinner at the MacDougal house. "Father, this is Enoch Elijah Ward," Mary began. "He goes by Eli. He's from Scyene, and his father is a rancher."

"A farmer, sir. He's a farmer near Scyene," Eli clarified. "Beans, cotton, and—"

"Hoo's that?" Mac MacDougal interrupted, scowling. "Where? Nay heard of it. Wh'd'ya do, lad? You sow bread an' blankets, th'n?"

"In addition to running the financial affairs of his father's farm," Mary Clover broke in, "Eli is a successful real estate and insurance salesman, Father. He travels all o' the state."

Stunned, Mariam remained silent.

"Aye, an' I'm a priest in the Kirk then! Shall we take up a collection fur insurunce, prop'ty, chaff, and cottun, then, aye?"

"Father, please! Eli is a widower. He lost his wife, Hana, to scarlet fever. He has a daughter, Bea, and a son, Job. He supports them in Scyene. He sends them money every week. He's a fine man, Father. He's a Baptist—"

"Aye, and I'm a Presbyterian, Lassie! A dunkin' in the river alone does not a fine man make, aye?" He paused. "What be yur intentions thun, lad?"

Finally, Mariam stood up. "Mac, be kind." Then she turned her attention to her daughter. "What would you like to say to us, Mary Clover?"

"Well...I wish to ask you, Father, for your permission to meet Bea and Job this week. I wish to be married to Eli and be a mother to them."

Well, that was a shock! Not only to Mariam's parents but also to Eli! He hadn't asked Mary Clover to marry him. In fact, he hadn't thought that far ahead. It was, however, his hope and his prayer.

"Ye askin' him to marry ye? Isn't tha' his job, Lassie?" A crimson flush began to creep up Mac's neck, reaching his face. If it were possible, steam would have poured from his ears, and his bald spot would have exploded off the back of his head.

His reaction didn't go unnoticed by Eli, who stood up. "Sir, I am asking for your permission to have your beautiful daughter meet my children. I am also asking for your permission to marry her!" Eli turned to Mary Clover and knelt on one knee. "In the name of Jesus, our Lord and Savior, and by the Spirit, and in the name of our Father, Mary Clover MacDougal, will you marry me?"

Stunned silence followed, Eli silently praying for an answer.

"Aye, you're askin'...and if you're askin' here and now," Mac blustered, "you either be in love with me daughter or a lunatic, eh? If you're that buggered up, tell me bonnie Mary Clover, 'Aye love ye!' You may have me permission then."

"Mary Clover, I love you. Mary, my bonnie Mary, will you marry me?" Eli looked up at her, still on one knee.

Mary Clover welled up and cracked a broad smile. "Aye, me love," she said slowly and confidently. "A lou-ve you, Eli. Yes, I will, Eli. I will marry ye! Yes!"

"Yes!" Mariam cried, echoing her daughter's acceptance.

"Auch! Aye," Mac grumbled, lighting a cigar.

****

Enoch Elijah Ward and Mary Clover MacDougal were married in the First Baptist Church in Dallas, Pastor George W. Truett presiding. Before they were pronounced, Dr. Truett referred to one of his past sermons: "There is no failure in God's will and no success outside of God's will..."

Eli was impressed. He was successful and a man of God. He felt his marriage to Mary Clover was God's will. In turn, Mary Clover was certain God had sent Eli, Bea, and Job to her as her greatest blessings.

The couple settled in a small house at 927 Oak Park in Dallas, which Eli got for a steal because there was no indoor toilet. Bea and Job moved to Dallas, and within a year of their marriage, Mary was pregnant. In August 1920, she delivered Gordon Truett, she and Eli agreeing to have Dr. Truett included in the name. It was practically biblical.

Eli's work still took him away from home. When he was there, his biblical "go forth and multiply" approach to life continued. A year later, in early 1922, Callum David came along, and after a four-year respite from raising four children, Miriam Anabelle was born in 1926. In June 1927, Isaiah Ephraim joined the clan. Finally, shortly thereafter, Mary became pregnant with a fifth child in late February 1928—Timothy James, named in honor of their favorite New Testament books.

With seven mouths to feed, Eli's work became increasingly crucial to providing for the family. However, unbeknown to he and Mary Clover, the Great Depression was looming. His work took him farther away— Texas was a vast expanse of opportunity but also a huge place to cover. West Texas oil fields also offered great new earnings potential, and Eli continued to sell life insurance as well as buy and sell properties to keep their heads above water.

Throughout 1928, he was driving his Model T all over West Texas, and from June to October he didn't return home, wiring money to Mary Clover to keep her in good stead. He didn't sacrifice his meals, however. Food was his comfort when away from his family, and he was a welcomed customer at diners and homes along the way. A man who could "put it away," his large waistline was a true sign of success. At 5 feet 9 inches, he weighed nearly 300 pounds.

At each meal, he prayed and read his Bible, often out loud. Joking about his weight, he referred to Genesis 1:29, "Everything that lives and moves about will be food for you. Just as I gave you the green plants, I now give you everything." So, it was biblical to eat just about everything. After all, he was in cattle country, and the best steaks abounded—the best pies too! He may have forgotten Mathew 4:4, "Jesus answered, 'For it is written: Man shall not live by bread alone, but on every word that comes from the mouth of God.'" He was pretty sure he was OK with the latter part of that scripture though. Most of his meals were fried in lard.

****

By late October, Eli headed home for the holidays. As he neared Fort Worth, driving from Midland/Odessa, he felt a sharp pain below his ribs on his right side. He stopped to walk it off. Standing up seemed to help, and after a while, the pain subsided, and he continued to drive. Twice more, however, he experienced the pain, which became increasingly severe. *Perhaps I should stop at a doctor friend's house in Ft. Worth,* he thought, but he was eager to be home with Mary and the children. With only thirty miles to go, he kept driving.

Seeing his children and Mary Clover was therapeutic—he was finally home! November would bring rest and relief.

Early in the month, he visited the Dallas NYL office for a sales meeting. Then, on November 7, his gallbladder ruptured, and he was admitted to Parkland Hospital.

After surgery to remove the organ, there was promise of recovery, but it was too late. Sepsis set in, and without antibiotics, Eli passed away on November 9 or 10, 1928. His death certificate read the former, his headstone reflected the latter. Regardless, Mary Clover was devastated.

In the days following, it became certain that Eli, while successful at selling life insurance, had neglected to buy any for his family. In those days, there was little that could be done, so the First Baptist Church of Dallas took up a collection, its value meager. Eli's friends at NYL also contributed, but the funds dwindled quickly. Laurence, Mary's brother, also helped with the situation, but as a worker on the Southern Pacific Railroad, he earned very little.

Fifteen days after Eli's passing, Mary delivered Timothy James. Sadly, Miriam Anabelle and he would have little or no memory of their father. Upon Tim's birth, Laurence dubbed Mary Clover "Mary Mother" for being full of grace, a moniker not to her liking. Catholics were persona non grata in her good Baptist house. Nevertheless, it became her identity even if only behind her back. Laurence had unwittingly created an untoward nickname that stuck for the ages.

Mary Mother was strong in her faith as much as she was a petulant Scottish lass. Seeking practical solutions to raise her seven children, through First Baptist and with the help of Dr. Truett, she secured a job as the proprietor of the Oak Park Cemetery. She sold flowers to the bereaved at the cemetery, sometimes reselling them if they were fresh enough.

She paid herself to dig graves, enlisting Gordy's help, and she coordinated with local mortuaries to send clients to Oak Park. A special arrangement with two local gravestone carvers to provide their headstones at a discount provided her margin to help her family. She had witnessed Eli making deals, so she became her own dealmaker, and making ends meet seemed possible.

In their early twenties, Bea and Job had dreams of college, but they needed to find jobs to support themselves as well as the family in addition to helping with the youngsters. At eight, Gordy was the eldest of the younger batch, and he became the man of the house, doing some kind of job while the other four children were too young to help.

A year later, on October 29, 1929, the US stock market crashed, signaling the beginning of the Great Depression, no one considering the possibility it would last for nearly a decade. Oak Park felt its impact immediately, and by Christmas, it was apparent work would be hard to find and keep. Job worked for the church, but his stipend was suspended, and Bea's waitress job was also soon gone. Mary Mother's parents had been heavily invested in the market and were now broke, choosing to return to Scotland. Within moments, the Wards went from poor to the poorest of the poor.

In 1930, the family would make the five-mile trek to the First Baptist Church of Dallas (FBCD) twice a week. Job and Bea clothed and carried the babies, and Gordy would dress his younger brothers. In the heat of a Dallas summer, "the march," as Callum called it, was brutal. In keeping with Mary Mother's demands as well as the threat of being whipped with a switch, the Ward clan arrived early, sitting in the front row to listen to Dr. Truett.

There was one other important reason for their attendance: food. In the coming months and years, the FBCD provided the only meals the Wards ate in a week. Soup kitchens became another "only" option.

Gordy continued to help at the cemetery. *At least these people won't be eating food anymore,* he thought as he shoveled dirt for a new grave. *None for them means more for us.* A morbid thought, to be sure.

By the end of 1931, it was apparent to Mary Mother that something had to change. Through a contact at church, she learned of a wealthy member, retired Army Colonel Samuel Bass, who had helped found San Marcus Baptist Military Academy in 1910. He gave two scholarships to FBCD as a donation every year, and the candidates for 1931 hadn't been nominated yet. So, Mary Mother had a friend of the colonel put Gordy and Callum forward for consideration.

With the friend's influence, they were accepted—a blessing they would be housed and fed. The boys would be located between Austin and San Antonio, where the family moved briefly before 1920. In fact, Gordy was born there.

Miriam Anabelle, Isaiah, and Timothy, however, were still destitute, but what could Mary Mother do? With no other options, she returned to the church, inquiring on their behalf. A woman referred her to Buckner Presbyterian Orphanage, which offered a unique program that allowed poor children to be cared for without the possibility of relinquishment.

Mary Mother walked to the orphanage that same day, praying for guidance. She grieved for her children—for Bea and Job—but she did the only thing she believed she could do. *They all will be fed and safe,* she thought as she walked. *Better off than living with me...*

For all of them, it was a pain never to be erased.

Gordy and Callum took the train to San Antonio and were picked up and driven to the Academy. Miriam, Isaiah, and Tim were delivered to Buckner by an associate pastor at FBCD, their goodbyes gut wrenching.

The greatest enemy of a fragile heart remained the fear of abandonment...

# CHAPTER 4

# NOT CASABLANCA, ALGIERS, BUT...

## *"Go ahead and shoot—you'll be doing me a favor"*

November 17, 1942, arrived cold and dreary at Maison Blanche, Gordy not believing they were in the desert. He'd been in the California desert before, it was hot—nothing like Maison. Algiers was freezing-butt cold.

The Army had mistakenly provided briefing booklets about Morocco to the Air Corps combatants in Algeria, mentioning the existence of fifty species of resident scorpions—*arthopoda scorpiones*. From an expletive-laced, painful, railing rant in a nearby tent, Gordy and Willie learned quickly either not to take their boots off or to hang them high and upside down by their laces in their tent to avoid adding a venomous sting to their already rumbling lower tracts.

Dr. B would likely paint their tonsils for that too.

Thanks to Private Rossi, Gordy and Willie were up early—and often—sprinting to the latrines, neither of the sergeants getting any sleep. Plus, their voices were squeaky high, their throats parched from wine and iodine.

"Can't eat or talk, Gordy! How am I gonna brief my crews?" Willie squeaked. "I sound like somebody dumped a dirt road down my throat."

"From the sound of both of us, must have been at least forty miles," Gordy replied, his voice a raspy squawk.

By the time they were ready for their day, work consisted of starting and tuning the Lightnings' engines as well as checking the oil pressure. The cold weather didn't help, but they were grateful for the low ceilings, limiting the likelihood of a German air raid, and it meant the P-38s were grounded for the day, allowing time for pilots' final briefings before their first day at war.

****

Among Gordy's trained maintenance crew was a Polish mechanic, Lech Marcin. His parents had been Jewish educators in Kraków. In 1937 they saw the war coming and sent their thirteen-year-old son to Chicago to learn automotive repair from a cousin. Turned out he was a natural.

Always looking forward to hearing from them, letters from Marcin's parents ceased when Germany invaded Poland on September 1, 1939. Krakow surrendered in six days. Six days later, it became the German administrative capital of Poland. Marcin wanted to go back to find his parents, but his cousin refused permission to do so without hearing from them first.

After Pearl Harbor, Marcin lied about his age—then sixteen—passing induction into the US Army despite his heavy Polish accent as well as his limited ability to speak or read English. Because of his mechanical acumen, he was assigned to the Air Corps even though his understanding of the P-38s' manuals was nil. But his ability to troubleshoot their engines was unsurpassed due to his training at Hamilton Field in California before shipping out to Shrewsbury.

Naturally, Marcin suffered merciless ribbing for being a Pollack, but Gordy would have none of it from his crews. He felt responsible for the kid because he needed his aptitude to quickly repair his Lightnings and keep them flying.

In addition to their flight-readiness checklists, Gordy and his crew focused on two critical design issues with their P-38s—engine problems caused by high oil consumption and leading-edge inter-cooler failures at high altitudes. Marcin was Gordy's triple-check guy for such problems as well as testing the needed pure-fuel mixture in all four gasoline trucks. Gordy, however, personally inspected the twin tails and their horizontal superstructures. Their duties also included briefing crew chiefs, assistants, and armorers, who all carried out the final steps to gas and arm the Lightnings. By dusk on November 18, 1942, all twenty-five new P-38Fs were flight ready.

Gordy worried about the crowded conditions at Maison Blanche—a beehive with hundreds of drones. It was one of the few Allied hardstand (concrete) runways, commanders using the field-stage C-47 transports for paratroop raids on German lines. P-40 Warhawks were on the tarmac with B-24s already stationed there in anticipation of early bombing missions.

The field was an emergency landing area for British Spitfires and P-38s—not to mention the huge number of personnel, paratroopers, and pilots on the ground. It was, indeed, a target-rich environment. Again, Gordy prayed for protection.

The heavy cloud cover and cold drizzle finally gave way to clear skies and a waxing moon, completely illuminating the airfield. As exhausted crews headed to their tents just before midnight, air raid sirens blared.

"Battle stations! Man your positions!"

Six rhodium parabolic-mirrored spotlights popped on, their generators creating a loud, humming accompaniment as their bright beacons bounced skyward. Shadows of men running to their AAA guns resembled mice being discovered in a dark kitchen at the flip of a light switch, their frenetic motion accompanied by slide clicks and the loading of magazines.

Clicks and double-clicks.

Then the sound of hell from the heavens—aircraft engines.

Gordy took cover in a sandbagged pillbox crammed with ground crew and support personnel close to his tent. As beams from the searchlights bounced and overlapped, he heard a different siren—the German Jericho-Tompete (Jericho's Trumpet). It was unlike the one setting everything in motion moments prior, allowing no time for pilots to scramble to their planes, sounds of war filling the air.

From above, a Ju 87 Stuka dive-bomber plummeted down, flashing through one of the spotlights. Two M15s fired .50 cals while 37-mms blind-sighted at the fighter, to no avail. The screeching siren grew louder and louder.

As the bomber appeared in what appeared to be a death dive, at the last moment, the pilot deployed his dive brake and leveled out, releasing a 550-pound bomb, scoring a direct hit on a pod of P-38s just off the end of the runway. Shrapnel pierced the tank of the nearby fuel truck, and a huge secondary explosion erupted, sending burning pieces of the truck in every direction.

The Stuka climbed up and out. Then there was another siren. Another Stuka. In an almost ninety-degree dive, it repeated the first's bomber's maneuver, its bomb striking the staggered pod across from the first hit. Again, the fuel truck exploded, even though it wasn't located as close as the first, and so it continued—seven more times.

Fire hoses were deployed and manned. Then Gordy heard what he feared at the appearance of the first Stuka—the droning hum of Junkers Ju 88 night bombers. Louder and carrying up to 5,500-pound bomb loads, he knew they'd wait for the Stukas to clear before dropping their payloads.

The larger AAA batteries positioned outside Maison Blanche opened up, black puffs of flak filling the air, the rhythmic boom of their firing continuous. With only one P-38 pod left completely undamaged, a Ju 88 was in sight.

Almost at once, the whistling of bombs began. Initially, the Ju 88s' targets seemed not to be the airport as explosions lit up farther away, closer to Algiers. One of the airfield's perimeter AAA batteries took a stray hit, and then the Ju 88s' formation of six bombers flew closer to the airfield. Flying low, they tried to stay below the flak to take out the runway. At that moment, however, Gordy noticed the M15 half-track closest to him and next to the undamaged pod was unmanned. "Willie!" he shouted. Then they both sprinted to help bring it to life.

The first 88 approached, aligning with the runway as a second bomber followed with about five minutes of separation from its leader. Gordy and Willie opened up, aiming at the first Ju 88's nose. With ten bursts from the .50's tracers and eight booms from the 37-mm, the *nachtjagdgeschwader staffelkapitan's* (night-bomber squadron captain's) port engine cowling blew off, bursting into flames. Its left wing separated with a jolt, and the bomber rolled violently right, crashing and exploding just beyond the airport's east border.

Was the shoot-down thanks to Gordy's and Willie's practice accuracy? Unlikely.

The following pilot pulled up hard and left to avoid the flames and smoke from his *kapitan's* crash into dense bursts of flak. Willie and Gordy fired in concert, and immediately, a bright flash in front of the cockpit signaled a direct hit. The plane nosed into the desert almost opposite of its leader, just missing the end of the runway.

As Gordy and Willie listened to the screams of the dying in the burning bombers, the remaining Ju 88s aborted their formation, turning up and hard away. They did, however, drop their ordnance around the field and near Algiers. The last glimpse of a trailing Ju 88 was seen smoking as it disappeared over the horizon. Then the all-clear was given.

Willie ran to his pods to help with the fires, Gordy heading to his. There, at the only unscathed pod, lying under a gasoline tanker truck as cover, was Lech Marcin, curled into a ball.

"Lech!" Gordy shouted. "You're not doing much to remove that Pollack label we both hate so much by taking cover here!"

Marcin uncoiled and jumped to attention, his legs shaky. "Nou! Nou! 'Won't, Sergeant!"

Gordy grasped him by the shoulders. "No you won't! What were you thinking—glad you won't *ever* do that again, right, Private Marcin?"

Marcin nodded weakly. Then he passed out, collapsing into Gordy's arms.

****

The defense of the Maison Blanche airfield cost the enemy two Ju 88 bombers and their crews of four each. Of the twenty-five (one in reserve) P-38s on the ground, five had been destroyed, and four were badly damaged. A crew chief, a pilot, and a gunner had been killed, and nine ground personnel sustained injury.

After the raid, the squadron's full fighting strength was cut by a third the night after its arrival, and the 48th Fighter Squadron's first taste of battle on November 17, 1942, wasn't a glorious victory. It was a terror-ridden loss.

That night, the leaders of the squadron at Maison Blanche weren't heroic P-38 pilots. They were green non-coms on the ground working with their subordinates despite their fears, protecting one another so they could survive to run again.

Run again they did—all of November and December.

****

The American press was restricted from revealing battle locations, deployments, or any service designations specifics. On November 21, a small front-page column in the *Dallas Morning News* detailed the downing of two enemy planes in North Africa, the hero of the engagement heralded only as a local boy from North Texas.

However, when Gordy received a clipping of the news enclosed with a letter from his mother a month later, he was furious so much had been published.

His two comrade heroes were buried in the desert.

# CHAPTER 5

# DEPRESSION (OF THE) IN-MATES IN TEXAS

**P**rior to the 1930s, many orphanages in Texas referred to their orphans as "inmates." Given the conditions and the abuse at some of them, a better label might have been "prisoners." Fortunately, Buckner Presbyterian Children's Home (BPCH) was much better than some.

Beulah Marker, headmistress of BPCH, advised Mary Mother not to visit her three children for the first month after placing them. "They'll need to become comfortable with their new environment," she informed her, "without expecting a possibility of returning to you soon." She paused. "In fact, the longer the better."

Frustrated but not wanting to make things worse, Mary Mother didn't visit for two months. When she finally did, she was surprised to find baby Timothy cranky and crying when she held him. Isaiah was indifferent to her, and Anabelle turned, shying away from her. Not what Mary Mother expected.

Callum and Gordy settled in well at San Marcos, thriving when Mary Mother visited them six months into the academic term. Their uniforms made them look much older. Both were excelling academically despite their short time there. Gordy, ever the bookworm, had read thirty books since his arrival, and Callum was a math and science whiz. Both were stars of Sunday school and Bible studies because of their early exposure to the gospels.

Although they were doing well, they missed their siblings terribly. They asked about their welfare as well as the address of Buckner, so they could write to their sister and brothers. Privately, Gordy contemplated how he might get them out of BPCH.

By the end of 1931, Mary Mother was squeaking by financially. Although she did not have to care for her children, her brothers, Laurence and Connor ("Conn"), were still living with her in Oak Park. Laurence's job with the Southern Pacific Railroad helped, in a small way, with living expenses. Conn, on the other hand, had been committed to the former North Texas Asylum for the Insane (NTA) at Terrell, Texas, in 1915 at the tender age of twenty.

Despite the NTA's control being handed over to the Texas State Hospitals and Special Schools in 1920, he was there until 1930, when he was thirty-five. Government funding for the NTA was dwindling with the onset of the Great Depression, and Conn was deemed "not threatening to do harm" and "capable of fending for himself." The truth was, in those days he would've been labeled the "village idiot." He was harmless and lovable, but Conn was incapable of taking care of himself or anyone else.

On November 8, 1932, the Democratic Governor of New York State, Franklin D. Roosevelt, was elected the thirty-second President of the United States, defeating the Republican incumbent, Herbert Hoover, in a landslide. FDR's victory on the promise of a New Deal for America created hope for the impoverished and the unemployed. He had been in charge of New York since the 1929 crash, promoting government programs to combat poor economic conditions.

The Wards were "all in."

At twelve and eleven years of age, respectively, Gordy and Callum were excelling beyond their fellow cadets, the youngest to earn special status with the Reserve Officer Training Corps at the academy. Both were superb athletes and almost as tall as most seniors, dominating at football, which they played as sophomores. In 1933 they played basketball and baseball and were also on the wrestling team. They were not looking forward to summer vacation.

During spring and summer in 1933, Texas weather was severe. In late April, a tornado in Texarkana killed five people. Three days later, an enormous dust storm in the panhandle and south plains darkened skies to an inky black, extending north from Sweetwater to Kansas, west to New Mexico, and east to Oklahoma.

The Dust Bowl had arrived in Texas.

A tropical storm in July dumped up to twenty-two inches of rain, and on July 30, a tornado hit Oak Park, killing 5 and injuring 30, caused $500,000 in damage. At 927 Oak Park, the Ward's property, the only casualty was the privy.

"It blew the crap out of the outhouse," Laurence declared in a serious manner as Gordy and Callum mentally prepared for clean-up. There was a lot of crap to remove.

****

As one might imagine, Gordy and Callum were looking forward to returning to the academy. Between the heat and no running water—thanks to the tornado—August was nearly unbearable, the boys walking three miles each way to haul water to the house. Then, more bad news...San Marcos Baptist Military Academy canceled all scholarships for financial reasons. Gordy and Callum were on their own. That meant public school and relying on First Baptist for biweekly meals.

Gordy, however, didn't rest on his laurels. He had friends at San Marcos whose parents were in the oil business, and it made perfect sense to write to them, begging their help to find a job. One of them, Junior Jim Gilder, responded quickly. Luckily, his father had holdings along the Mexia Fault Zone in the East Texas Salt Basin near Tyler.

With his reply, Junior included an important letter of recommendation to Gilder's field foreman for a roughneck apprentice job. So, the "man of the house" packed a bag and hopped a train to Tyler with two things in his favor—he looked eighteen, and he was skinny-strong as well as deceptively tough. Both traits were requirements to endure work in the oilfields. If necessity truly is the mother of invention, then for Gordy, his survival and that of his four siblings was the father of dogged perseverance.

On his first day at Gilder Oil, Gordy was introduced to the art of the spinning chain on a drilling rig. His driller, Leslie "Lefty" Burress, had the grizzled, tough look of a roughneck that belied his soft southern drawl, and he always kept his right hand in his coveralls pocket. A tall man, Lefty looked enormous to Gordy, who didn't tip in at six feet.

They met on a sweltering day, Lefty asking Gordy to read his letter of recommendation aloud because Lefty couldn't read.

"OK, sir. From the Office of James T. Gilder, President, Gilder Oil Company—"

"I recognize the company symbol on the page, son," Lefty interrupted.

Gordy glanced at Lefty, then continued. "To Leslie Burress, Driller, Gilder Oil—"

"Skip the formal stuff, kid," Lefty interrupted again. "And, never, ever call me Leslie again."

"Sorry. You want me to give you the gist of the letter then?" Gordy focused on him, waiting for an answer.

"Whatever 'gist' is, just give me the facts."

"This is a recommendation to you from Mr. Gilder," Gordy summarized, "to make me an apprentice roughneck."

Lefty snarled, taking his mangled right hand out of his pocket and thoughtfully placing it under his chin. "I won't make you nothin', boy," he said, staring at Gordy's hands. "But, you, boy, you, and those hands will!" He paused, sizing up his new roughneck. "We'll start you out at fifty cents an hour."

"Thank you, sir! I'll work hard!" Gordy immediately calculated that twelve hours a day at fifty cents an hour worked out to six dollars per day, a fortune compared to fifteen to twenty cents a day for digging graves!

"You'll earn every penny of it, and likely you'll wonder if it's worth it." Lefty laughed, offering his mutilated hand in congratulations.

Gordy hesitated, not wanting to hurt it. Lefty noticed his apprehension. "Go ahead, son, shake it! Ain't felt nothin' in it for years!"

"Proud to be in your employ, Mr. Burress, sir!" Gordy vigorously shook his withered hand, at the same time wondering how it had been mangled.

"Boy, never call me 'sir' again.

"And never call you 'Leslie,' sir! I mean, Lefty..."

"Amen."

With that, Lefty turned and motioned for Gordy to follow him to a nearby drilling platform. Tough lessons were about to begin.

That afternoon, Gordy learned how Lefty got his nickname. He watched as his mentor used his left hand to spin the chain, wrapping it around the drill casement to extend the setting of a new length of casing quicker than turning it by hand. A marvel to behold, Gordy also realized how Lefty had injured his right hand—any miss could cost a finger or worse.

"Watch, son! Never take your eye off the drill casing, the chain, or your hand!"

Gordy spent that night—and every night for three weeks—on a drilling platform with Gordy attempting to throw the chain to wrap it around the casing, Lefty coaching him to remain focused at all times.

Then his time came.

With Lefty barking orders, Gordy spun his first chain perfectly. Time after time, with Lefty by his side, he repeated the process. By the end of the day, his arms and shoulders were mush. His wrists were aching from the twisting motion of throwing the chain, the days following were painful, but Gordy was determined not to show he was hurting. Having just turned thirteen, he was proud to be the youngest roughneck ever with Gilder Oil.

****

Gordy wired money home that week and every week, but doing so didn't seem to impact his younger sister and brothers' predicament. He was determined to get them out of the orphanage no matter how long it took, and he wanted Callum to join him to make that happen.

# CHAPTER 6

# MUD, STINKING MUD, DEADLY FOG, AND MORE DAMNABLE FOG

November 18, 1942, dawned dim and dreary at Maison Blanche. Pouring rain was a blessing and a curse—foul weather decreased the potential of another Luftwaffe air raid, but also prevented the 48th from flying sorties. Clean-up from the attack the previous night was slowed due by having to move heavy equipment away from the airfield, which was mired in mud. Gordy and Willie concentrated on their surviving P-38s, again performing their flight-readiness checks on the operational fighters while crews helped clear bombed debris.

Commanders of the 12th Air Force debated where the first air raids would be conducted against the Afrika Korps and the Luftwaffe. After the successful bombings of Tokyo by B-25 Mitchell Bombers, led by General Jimmy Doolittle, he was quickly moved to the North African theater upon the success of the Operation Torch landings. Doolittle recognized the strategic importance of Bizerte and Tunis to air superiority in the Mediterranean. Controlling those bases allowed the bombing of Sicily plus air protection for Malta.

Airdromes provided potent bases of operation for Luftwaffe bombers and fighters, and time was of the essence. Axis forces were reinforcing troops and aircraft to defend Tunisia. Then, on November 18, Doolittle ordered B-17 bombing raids on Bizerte and Tunis in anticipation of the Allies' first Tunisian ground offensive.

At 1600 hours, orders came in for the 48th to send its P-38s to fly cover for the bombings in Tunisia. All but four of the squadron's operational fighters scrambled, joining eight B-17s of the 97th Bombardment Group from Algiers. Required to fly anywhere from 115 to 140 miles to their targets, Gordy prayed for his Lightnings' safe return—a crapshoot because of the raid's late-day timing.

Of course, the Luftwaffe was prepared for probable attacks, fortifying Bizerte and Tunis airfields with approximately forty Bf 109 Messerschmitts and a few Focke-Wulf Fw 190 fighters to engage the Americans.

It was the first test for the P-38s. Everything went well as they approached their targets. Thirty or so miles out, the bombers split into two sets of six for their runs, four Lightnings per set as cover. The Luftwaffe was already airborne with only about twenty miles to engagement.

At Tunis, the Bf 109s dove at the B-17s outside the range of the bombers' formation, firing at will. The 109s stayed well off, as if testing the planes' capabilities and limitations. The German pilots were surprised by the Lightnings' size and that the P-38s weren't taking their bait to dog fight.

German pilots later reported they'd encountered a plane with superior firepower in its nose. One pilot limped back to his base, a gaping hole through his tail from a 37-mm cannon hit. Not only that, the B-17s delivered their payloads on the port, damaging ships and docks where German reinforcements and supplies were accumulating.

Similar encounters occurred at Bizerte, during which the only hostile fire came from a Fw 190s that damaged a Lightning's right boom. The pilot didn't realize he'd been shot up until he returned to base because he couldn't see the boom from the cockpit. Again, B-17s hit their port and naval targets, and again the German pilots tried to bait but couldn't fully challenge the Lightnings.

At both locations, the Luftwaffe's hardstand airfields were undamaged. The P-38s did well not to sustain losses in their first air battles, and the 48th scored its first Lightning victory in North Africa when Lieutenant Carl T. Williams, Jr. shot down a Bf 109 that was diving away from the bomber formation over Bizerte.

It was then that the legend of Der Gabelschwanz Teufel—the Forktailed Devil—was born, but not in a legendary way. It didn't originate with German fighter pilots. The *Frontschweine*—Poor Bloody Infantry—ground troops coined the moniker later, fearing its deadly accurate low-altitude bombing and strafing. American propagandists learned it from captured German soldiers and used it to boost morale.

The relative success of the first Tunisian bombings was eclipsed by the consequences of the raiders' late return. At Maison Blanche, the P-38s hit fog and darkness. Early P-38s weren't designed as night fighters, and two Lightnings were lost on approach due to fog obscuring the runway. The 49th Fighting Squadron at Tafaraoui Airfield lost four pilots because of similar conditions, but ten of Gordy and Willie's pilots landed safely.

"Begin damage assessments!" Gordy shouted to Marcin, both of them intending to perform their duties to perfection. On the inside, Gordy screamed for the loss of his two pilots.

# CHAPTER 7

# AND THE BEATINGS SHALL BE BEGOTTEN...AND CONTINUE

Gordy's hard work at Gilder Oil was paying off. He wrote Callum to join him to fulfill his plan to rescue his siblings. Like Gordy, Callum could take a term off from school, and the wages would be enough to save the family. Before Gordy could mail the letter, a tele-

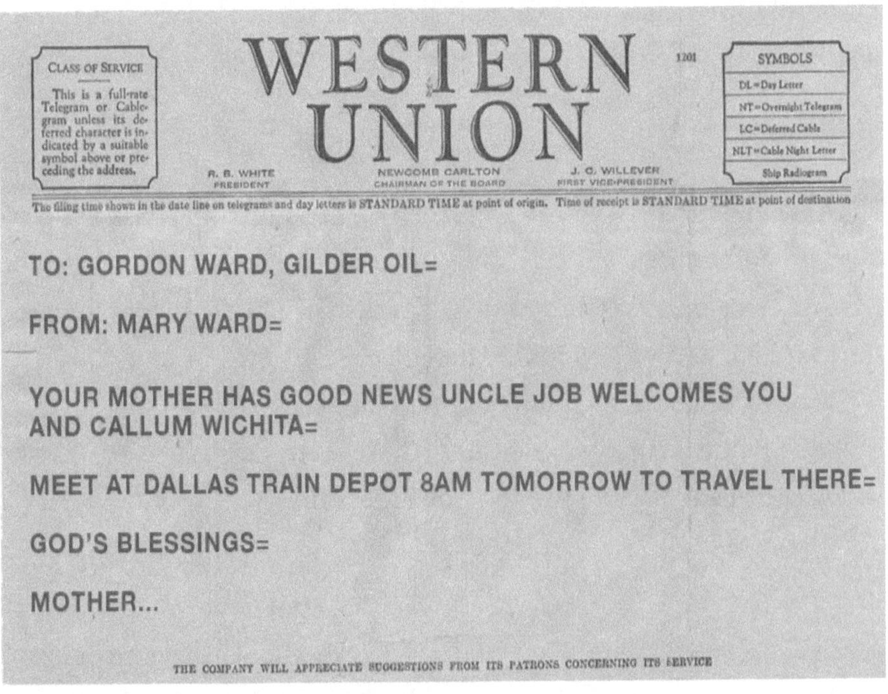

gram arrived at the oil field. Too often such communication meant dismal news.

"What? No!" He reread the message. "First she throws us out. Now she parcels us out!" He sank to his knees. "Please, God, no!"

But that was that. At 5:00 a.m., Lefty delivered Gordy to the Tyler depot to connect to Dallas, sorely saddened to say goodbye.

"Lefty, thank you. I'll miss you," was all Gordy could muster, his voice cracking.

"Gordy, everything happens for a reason. It's true. I'll keep you in my prayers. You keep workin' hard!" Lefty reached out his shriveled right hand, but Gordy leaped passed it, hugging him hard and tight, weeping in his arms. "So sorry, kid! I'm so sorry for you." Lefty said, also welling up. "Remember, you're a roughneck, and roughnecks is rough and tough! Go on now, and be tough!"

Gordy swiped his tears with his sleeve, then boarded the train. *I'm a man!* he thought. *I've got to be a tough young man...*

****

Arriving in Dallas, Gordy met Mary Mother and Callum on the platform, and then the three of them waited for the next train to Wichita. Glaring at his mother, Gordy listened as she tried to explain. "This is for the best," she said. "It's all for the best..."

What could be best about Wichita, Kansas?

"Keep God first in your heart." Those were her last words as she shook their hands before they boarded the train.

****

Ever curious, Callum seemed to ask Gordy about every tumbleweed on the way to Wichita. "What do you know about Uncle Job?" he asked finally.

"Technically, he's your half-brother; we just call him Uncle. To answer your question, not much. He's a preacher, and he trained with Dr. Truett. He speaks like him, but he's not him."

"What do you mean?"

Gordy eyed Callum. "You know how Uncle Laurence and Conn are silly and kind?"

"Yeah. I like both of them."

"You love them both! But Uncle Job is solemn and hard."

"What do you mean by 'solemn'?"

"Remember at father's burial? Pastor Truett's words were hopeful and comforting. But when asked to speak, Job reminded everyone of the perils of hell. It was like he was the opposite...solemn."

Callum thought for a moment, then changed the subject. "You always know about words, Gordy. I know how things are put together. We're a good team."

"Yes, we are, brother! I just wish I knew how sending us to Wichita will be best or if that's even the right word for it. You know, how it will be put together."

"We'll be together, and that'll make it the best!"

"Amen, Cal. Amen!"

As the train chugged on, Gordy recalled an encounter with Job at First Baptist. Gordy had taken down a book by Dr. Truett. While waiting in the church library alone, Job entered the room, enraged that Gordy had removed the book without permission. For that transgression, Job slapped Gordy hard across the face. Gordy had never been hit that hard by Mary Mother—ever.

The boys arrived on time on a Wednesday afternoon and were met by Job's wife, Natalie. As they walked to the Baptist church, about two miles away, she asked about their time at San Antonio, what they liked for supper, and how they liked the train ride. She was gentle. She also asked about them.

Finally, they were escorted to a small house behind the church, Natalie explaining it was the former pastor's house, though he had passed away earlier that year. Because Job was his associate pastor, he had been assigned as his successor until the elders decided whether he would become the lead pastor. In the meantime, the house was theirs, given the pastor's wife moved back to Tennessee after her husband's passing.

Located on three acres of farmland, the church property included chicken coops as well as a lean-to shed for several sheep and cattle. It also had a small pond with ducks and geese. A garden and an acre of wheat and corn were planted, and there were two acres of pasture for the animals. The church stood at the front of the property, appearing as if it had been built before the turn of the century. It was sorely in need of a paint job.

****

Natalie escorted the boys to a small bedroom with two twin beds—their own beds for the first time! When suppertime came, Natalie prepared fried chicken and mashed potatoes. Later, everyone enjoyed ice cream at the Wednesday night prayer meeting. All seemed well in Wichita!

The next early morning brought a list of chores for the boys—make their beds, feed and milk the cows, clean out the cattle stalls, feed the chickens, collect the eggs, and clean out the coops. After that it was raking the garden and reporting for breakfast when Aunt Natalie rang the bell promptly at seven. The boys were happy to help, even though Uncle Job said he'd be inspecting their work. They didn't have much experience with tending to animals, but how hard could it be?

Beds made, they headed for the lean-to—for only two cows, the stalls were a terrible mess. Callum sat with a pail to milk Bossie, and Gordy was surprised to see he knew what to do. "When you went off to Gilder," his brother explained as he repositioned the milk bucket, "I helped Conn do odd jobs. There was a dairy that paid him a nickel to milk some cows. He could never remember what they taught him, but I did."

"You mean you did it for him?"

"Yeah, I did—he couldn't remember. Besides, after I was done, he bought me ice cream or candy with the nickel."

The stalls took longer to clean than anticipated, forcing them to hurry with the chicken coops. Cal grabbed the basket to gather the eggs while Gordy carefully swept the bottoms of the coops, then scattered the feed. Then it was on to the garden.

Aunt Natalie's rows of vegetables were well in order. They couldn't find a rake, so they used a hoe to smooth the ground, pulling the weeds with their hands.

Just as Gordy pulled the last weed, the dinner bell rang, its clanging urging them to hurry. "Breakfast, boys!" Aunt Natalie yelled, watching them run toward her with the milk and fresh eggs. At the door, they smelled biscuits in the oven and bacon frying in the cast-iron skillet. They couldn't believe their noses! At Oak Park, hardtack and coffee were standard fare if breakfast were served at all. At Wichita, there were fried eggs!

Job sat at the table reading his Bible, the specs on the end of his nose making him look much older than his twenty-six years. He looked up, rubbing his balding head in contemplation. "Who was Solomon, boys?"

"He was the richest and wisest man in the Bible," Gordy answered. "The son of King David."

"Was he, now? Which books of the Old Testament are his works?"

"Proverbs and Ecclesiastes, Uncle," Callum offered.

"'He that spareth his rod hateth his son; but he that loveth him chasteneth him betimes.' Where is that from, boys?"

Gordy hesitated a moment, finally answering. "Proverbs, Uncle?"

"Yes, Gordon. Proverbs 13:24. Do you understand your mother sent you both here to be chastened?"

Neither of the boys answered. *What does he mean, and why is he calling me "Gordon"?* Gordy wondered, keeping his eyes on his "uncle."

Before he could come up with an answer, Natalie placed their plates on the table—the best breakfast ever. "Let us pray," Job said, everyone joining hands. "For this fruit you have provided, we are blessed, Lord. You have given us bounty, and we are thankful. These boys are your creation, Father. Make them your worthy, faithful workers. For you are our Lord and Savior, and by your blood only are we saved. Amen."

They'd never eaten so much or so well! Or been so confused...

****

Weeks passed, and Gordy became increasingly frustrated. Although he and Callum weren't starving, they were working on the church farm daily. Not only that, by Uncle Job's mandate, they were deemed "service volunteers" to work on parishioners' lands for no pay.

The day after their arrival, they experienced Job's wrath. Apparently, their using the hoe rather than the rake in the garden enraged him. He ordered them to the shed, where he beat them with his belt. "Spare the rod, spoil the child!" he screamed repeatedly. Gordy remembered Job's admonition about being "chastened." They had been hazed and disciplined at the academy but never like Uncle Job's version of discipline. In an instant, he became the boys' tormentor.

At night, in the privacy of his and Callum's room, Gordy wrote Mary Mother, asking about his siblings—always hoping.

****

On Wednesdays and Sundays they helped prepare the church for service, dutifully cleaning up afterwards. Whenever there was a church supper, they served and bussed tables. Because of his penchant for numbers, Callum was assigned the duty of double-checking Job's counting of the tithes for delivery to the bank on Monday. His accounting was spot on. Gordy also double-checked the double-check so as to not raise his uncle's ire if there was a discrepancy.

It wasn't until several weeks inched by that Gordy found a two-cent deficit between Cal and Uncle's ciphers. He re-ran the accounting twice, then informed Cal of the error. "But I've already told Uncle Job we're right," Callum exclaimed, a familiar angst beginning to rise.

Before Gordy could show Callum the error, Uncle Job interjected. "Who told you to help with the books, Gordon?"

"I...we just wanted to help—to make sure, Uncle!"

"You weren't assigned to the church's books!"

"Sorry, Uncle Job. I'm sorry!" Gordy's voice trembled, as did every inch of his being.

"Did you take out two pennies for candy, Callum?"

"No! No, Uncle! I wouldn't—I didn't!"

Even with such protestations, Uncle Job's punishment was swift. Quickly and forcefully, he trotted both boys—pulling Callum by his ear—to the shed to endure another rage-filled beating of their backsides. "Never assume anything, never!" Job's mantra gained strength as he inflicted bloody damage on the boys with a branch switch. They cried out for mercy, but no one heard, and no one came to stop the beatings. Somehow, from the depths of his soul, Gordy remembered one of his favorite Bible verses: "Do justly, love mercy, walk humbly before your God" (Micah 6:8).

As great as it sounded, the boys were fearful of their Uncle's "justice." They thought they knew about love and mercy, but they weren't becoming humbler. Instead, their resentment of Job was building to a fever pitch.

****

What was the purpose for Gordy and Callum's staying in Wichita? They were pledged servants to their half-brother without a sworn promise.

Beaten almost on a daily basis, they worked out of fear rather than of their own accord. Their only solace came from Natalie, who showed them love and fed them but wouldn't intervene on their behalf. So, as disappointing as it was, it seemed there was no negotiation to change their situation, a situation they both endured for nearly two years...

****

On a trip to the post office, Callum noticed recruitment fliers for the Kansas National Guard pinned on the announcements corkboard. Carefully, he removed one notice, quarter folded it, then stuffed it in his pocket. It wasn't until he was on his way back to the church house that he took the time to read it carefully.

## MEN! SERVE KANSAS! SERVE AMERICA!

*Recruiting new members for immediate enlistment —*
*A representative will be here Wednesday, November 18!*

Meet a National Guard soldier who can answer your questions!
Meet your service obligation for only two weeks a year,
and four weekends!

On his return to the church home, he sought out Gordy and led him behind the now infamous shed, showing him the flier. "What do you think? We could run away from here and join!"

Gordy was quiet for a moment, thinking about the possibilities. "I don't know, Cal. I'm barely sixteen, and you're only fifteen. I think you have to be eighteen to join. Besides, the military is pretty tough."

"How much tougher can it be than being here?" Callum's eyebrows headed north as he stared at his brother.

"That's true, but where would we live when we're not on duty? We'd have to come back here."

"Please, Gordy? I don't want to be here! I can't be here much longer, or I'm gonna die!'

Gordy nodded. "I know. I feel the same way. But we can't let on we're thinking about such a thing! Let's see the recruiter on the eighteenth and see where it leads."

Callum glanced again at the paper, then at his brother. "I'll be prayin' we're led away from here. Livin' in a shantytown outside of Kansas City can't be worse than this!"

"Amen, brother..."

****

On November 18, 1936, the boys met with Sergeant Cliff McCann. Gordy thought it was a good thing he was a Scot.

"Men, there's no finer unit in all the National Guard than Kansas and the 137th Infantry Regiment. Our farm boys are tougher than most. We hold the highest citations from the command, and because we're a smaller unit, there's more training and opportunity for advancement."

Gordy liked the sergeant's calling them men. "Sir, we're originally from Texas. We attended Baptist Military Academy there until the Depression ended our scholarships. We were both at the top of our classes." He paused. "Can you tell us more about the training and potential for advancement?"

Sergeant McCann liked his question. He liked the boys too. "Our training is six weeks of basic and two weeks of advanced—that's when we give you a skills test, introducing you to more specialized work." He hesitated, glancing at both boys. "For example—if, after basic training, you show aptitude for mechanics, you would work for two weeks in that skill. After that, if you work out well, there's up to another six weeks in that area of expertise. If you complete that sequence, you can specialize for ten weeks in tanks or aircraft."

Gordy and Callum looked at each other, their imaginations soaring. Both thought about the timeline. If they qualified, they could be away from Job for six months. They could be on base away from his beatings.

"Where do we sign up? When can we start?" Callum exclaimed.

McCann smiled, "Not so fast, men! We need you to take a physical exam and pass it. You both look strong and fit, but we also need you to take a basic entrance exam. You need to verify your ages. All standard procedures and requirements must be met."

Gordy's heart sank. Their birth certificates would give them away as underage. Callum, however, wasn't quite so ready to throw in the towel. "We have birth certificates," he said. "I'm turning eighteen in January, and Gordy just turned nineteen!"

"We'll need to see them, but I'm sure you'll be fine. Let's start with the basic exam, shall we?"

Gordy glared at Callum. "Yes, let's start with that!"

****

The results? Perfect scores.

"Amazing!" McCann exclaimed. "Congratulations, to both of you! Never has anyone gotten a perfect score before."

*What kind of moron couldn't pass that test?* Gordy wondered as the sergeant reread their scores.

"Need to schedule your physicals," McCann continued. "When can you get me your birth certificates?"

"Well, sir, the thing is our birth certificates were badly damaged in the tornado of 1933 at Oak Park, Texas. Our mother stored valuables in the outhouse, and..." As much as Callum wanted to glance at his brother, he didn't dare.

"What?" McCann eyed Callum. "Why would anyone store valuable documents in an outhouse, son?"

"Our mother is quite eccentric, sir," Gordy explained. "She lost Dad when I was eleven. Sadly, she became distrustful of our uncles, who were living with our three siblings as well as a half-brother and sister. She hid important documents behind the crapper's ceiling supports, so when the tornado hit, the documents were mangled and defaced with the contents of the privy."

"There were eight of you living together...in one house?" McCann asked. Gordy and Callum nodded. Sergeant McCann heard some stories in his day, but that one was a dilly. Holding back a smirk, again, he eyed Callum. "Seriously, son, is that what happened?"

"Oh, yes, sir. We had to personally clean up the mess! Our Uncle Laurence complained the tornado blew the crap out of the outhouse, sir." A lie for which Callum asked forgiveness.

Busting a gut, McCann clutched their test scores in hand. "You...you boys...are the best recruits I've ever had!" He paused, thinking of what to do next. "Bring what's left of your birth certificates..." He chuckled. "On Tuesday we'll get you your physicals!"

So, with the promise of a new life puffing their chests, Gordy and Callum left, required forms in hand. Both knew they were going to hell for lying, but the hell they were headed for couldn't be worse than the hell they were enduring in Wichita.

At the perfect moment when both were granted a modicum of privacy, Gordy and Callum retrieved their birth certificates from a box in the church house kitchen where Natalie kept them on a shelf. Aging the documents by wadding, tearing, and stomping on them in cow manure, they carefully altered the numbers to fit the necessary days, months, and years of birth to appear barely legible.

Mission accomplished.

The final straw? The following weekend.

Job advanced Callum and Gordy twenty-five cents each for working on a neighbor's windmill and well, Gordy's roughneck experience coming in handy to help bring the well back to life. After walking six miles each way to and from the church member's farm, by the time they returned to the church house, the boys were exhausted. Hungry, too.

That Saturday night they "volunteered" at the church supper, Natalie and the First Baptist Women's Ministry preparing an unrivaled feast. Callum and Gordy were obliged to fill up to bulk up for their anticipated entry into the Guard, so sneaking leftover biscuits into their overalls and pockets seemed like a good idea. After all, they wanted to be strong and ready if Sergeant McCann inducted them the following Tuesday.

Early on Sunday morning, they were preparing the sanctuary for services, as usual, and ensuring the hymnals were in place in the pews. They checked and double-checked the post boards for the correct hymns and scripture readings, making sure everything was ready for the service—until a powerful, resounding crash interrupted their duties.

The side door flew open. Uncle Job stood in the doorway, fuming, with a look on his face that Callum and Gordy knew well. There was however, a slight difference. That day it was a glare beyond fury.

"You boys are heathens!" His voice boomed as if he were the Almighty himself. "God will smite you for this!"

Gordy thought he saw the vein in Job's neck begin to pulse, their silence serving to enrage him further.

"You stole from God's holy bounty!" he shrieked as Gordy braced for the onslaught. "Fall on your knees! Now!"

Both boys landed on their knees right where they were. "What did we do, Uncle?" Callum whimpered.

"What did you do? You stole from God's bounty last night!"

"We...we took some leftover biscuits, so we could eat them on Monday while we worked," Gordy said.

"You stole from God's bounty!" Job paused, gaining strength. "Both of you stole from God's bounty!"

"We're sorry, Uncle..." Callum's voice was barely a whisper.

"What did you say? You're sorry? Have I not taught you boys anything? You ask for forgiveness but do not repent! Every time you do not repent!" Job stared with a searing, soul-slicing gaze. "There is no forgiveness without repentance. That should be clear to both of you!"

With that, Gordy was done. Enough was enough. He stood. "The biscuits were left over! We didn't steal them. They were left over! We didn't steal anything! We saved them, so we could take them to work—the work we do for you!" Clenching his fists until his knuckles were white, Gordy had no intention of backing down. "And Jesus's forgiveness isn't conditional!"

Job stared in disbelief, stunned any child would speak to him in such a manner. Leaping toward Gordy, his eyes bulged with rage. "I'll show you who Jesus is, you heathen! You'll not speak to me so!" Job clenched his fist and swung, striking Gordy full force in the jaw, launching him between two pews.

Callum jumped to Gordy's defense, only to be pummeled like his brother, blood trickling down his chin. "Jesus's love is unconditional," Gordy mumbled as Job kicked him in the side.

Despite the incident, services began right on time. There was, however, an unusual twist. At the front of the sanctuary, the two boys knelt with a quarter laid in front of them to be put in the offering, Gordy with a shiner and Callum sporting a swollen lip.

The congregation filed in, but before the organ began to swell, Pastor Job had an announcement. "These two sinners before you have stolen from God's bounty. They will kneel and pray for the duration of our service in penance for their sins."

The service was long and arduous, its message not lining up with the title printed in the bulletin. Pastor Job spoke on Luke 16 and Matthew 25 for almost an hour. After the service, the beatings continued in the shed for almost as long, Callum and Gordy having no idea how Uncle

Job found out they took the biscuits. All they knew was the reality of their Wichita hell.

****

On Tuesday the boys met with Sergeant McCann, and despite their illegible birth certificates, both were accepted into the Kansas National Guard. McCann didn't comment on their injuries, perhaps assuming they were the product of a brotherly scrap. Gordy and Callum were, however, more than a little dismayed to learn it would be another two weeks before basic training began.

That night they packed their meager belongings, sneaking off the church property. Gordy had secretly saved enough for their train fares to Dallas. The Wichita station master, Dylan Jones, a member of the First Baptist Church Wichita, had witnessed the atrocities dished out at Job's hands. Knowing God's love is, as Gordy said, unconditional, he hid the boys in the station until their train departed the following morning.

When they were gone, Jones penned separate letters to the Southern Baptist Convention and its past president, George Truett, as well as Pastor Job Ward. Jones resigned his membership with the church and the Convention but not before detailing his knowledge of the abuse of the Ward boys. Still, as he wrote, he knew what would happen. There'd never be a formal response from the Church. He was right. Job pastored First Baptist Wichita for the next thirty-six years.

****

Stunned to see Callum and Gordy back in Dallas, Mary Mother reprimanded them for returning without consideration for the family's ability to feed so many empty bellies. She demanded they return to Wichita immediately, but Gordy replied on behalf of both boys. "We will never return to our cruel half-brother, Mother. If he represents Jesus, then we're all damned!"

"Wash your mouth out! Job is a man of God!"

"He is the devil, Mother. Look at Callum's fat lip! Look at my black eye! Look at my side!" He lifted his shirt to display bruises below his ribs, his heart racing as he spoke. "He beat us continuously, and he's an angry, hateful tyrant. We will not go back there!"

From outside, Laurence overheard the conversation, instantly stepping up to Gordy's defense. "Stop, sister! Dem boys have been good to you. Dey don't deserve this." He pointed to their injuries. "Lemme go there! Give me ten minutes with Job. I'll whump him good!"

"You'll do nothing of the sort, Laurence. You'll not 'whump' your half-nephew." Mother Mary stopped and pondered. "Oh, my! What to do…"

"We joined the Kansas National Guard, Mother," Gordy said. He hesitated, gauging her reaction. "We report to Topeka in two weeks!"

"You what?" She glanced at Laurence, then again focused on her children. "You insolent boys! How? You're too young! I'll write a letter to the commander. You will not!"

In that moment, Gordy's backbone straightened even more. "No, you will not, Mother! We will report to Topeka, and you won't stand in our way! We need to do this for us! For the family!"

"Dees boys are men, Mother," Laurence said. "They ain't boys no more; they're men. The Army is men, Mother! They're men. Lettum go! They're men!"

Suddenly, Mary Mother's voice lowered, her tone stern. "They are not men, Laurence! They're children."

But Laurence wasn't dissuaded. "Dang, woman! Dis here ain't right, and you know it! Dees boys ain't got nothin'! I ain't got nothin'! You ain't got nothin'! We ain't got nothin'." He paused, focusing on his nephews. "At least in the Army, they'll have somethin'."

"Stop using 'ain't,' Laurence! You know how that vexes me!"

"Alright…we got nothin'. Nothin' is nothin'…"

# LIGHTNING STRIKES TWICE

Through late November and December 1942, Americans, Brits, and the French swept across Algeria and deep into Tunisia, coming to within twenty miles of Tunis on the ground. They put enormous pressure on General Irwin "the Desert Fox" Rommel's infamous armor, ground forces, and supply lines.

On Hitler's orders, Axis reinforcements and supplies flooded in. Twenty to fifty JU 52 transport flights were sent to Tunisia daily. With a range up to 1,300 miles and a cruising ceiling of 44,000 feet, the P-38 became the logical choice to interdict the airlift. The 12th US Army Air Force expanded the 14th Fighter Group's breadth of North African operations to patrol the southern Mediterranean Sea targeting enemy transports. The 48th Pursuit Squadron Lightnings were soon deployed to do so. Their opposition remained the Focke-Wulf Fw 190 and Bf 109 Messerschmitt fighters flying cover.

When matched against their German counterpart fighter aircraft, the Lightnings had two advantages. First, firepower. They had four .50 cal. machine guns and a 37-mm cannon direct-fired from the nose (versus guns mounted on the wings at converging angles), a formidable and deadly combination. Vision to their targets was unobscured, resulting in accuracy up to 1,000 yards. Second, climbing power and speed. P-38s could quickly move higher, roll, and rapidly turn a defensive climb into an offensive advantage. With their turbocharged Allison engines, they could cruise quietly high above the enemy and then dive down at an optimum attack angle for surprise.

All fighters in North Africa had performance limitations at higher altitudes. Pilot experience and endurance were critical to success. Gordy and Willie managed the increasing pressure to keep their Lightnings flying well. The compressibility issue that had been experienced in early P-38s was remedied with dive flaps that were deployed in a steep dive. Marcin monitored those on F models that had required retrofitting. It was bad enough to lose a pilot in combat, worse to lose one because of mechanical failure.

Night loss of pilots and planes did not go unnoticed. The 12th Air Force began a series of protective moves to and from bases in North Africa. On November 20, 1942, the 48th was ordered to move to Youks-les-Bains Airfield northwest of Tébessa. While this would seem a daunting task for most units, Gordy and Willie performed the move with aplomb. Transport of their equipment and tents, not so much. Willie was not happy about the airfield's remote location, but he made sure there was coffee in their tent for an early morning conversation.

"Lordy, Sarg," Willy exclaimed. "This is a godforsaken place! What was the brass thinkin, Gordy?"

"The brass has its reasons, Willie. This puts us tactically closer to Bizerte and Tunis. I will say it's not protective for us though. We're closer to the enemy's air-strike capabilities. We need to be extra vigilant to protect our assets here."

Willie laughed. "Now, you're talkin' like the brass! Ya think we're gonna be in Bizerte soon? Hear that we're cuttin' Rommel off by takin' Gabes."

"I don't think so, my friend," Gordy replied, his face serious. "I'm worried that we've stretched our supply lines too thin. Just prayin' that our infantry and armor haven't moved too far too fast. Logistics wins battles. You have to feed your army and provide them the necessary weapons to win."

Willie chuckled, "What? You *are* the brass! Ha ha ha! Who made you a general?"

"I didn't say that," Gordy replied. "General Eisenhower did." He went on to quote him. "'You will not find it difficult to prove that battles, campaigns, and even wars have been won or lost primarily because of logistics.'"

"Well aren't you the smart guy!" Willy chided. "You read that in one of those books or papers I see you studyin' under your blanket by flashlight in our tent every night?"

"As a matter of fact, I did. Now, s'il vous plais, we need to get back to work."

"Wha...wha'd you say?"

"It's French for 'please.' Now, can we get back to work?"

Willie laughed, "Mercy buccups, then."

"Merci beaucoup," Gordy corrected.

"Uh-huh. Just one more thing," Willy said, not ready to give up. "We hold the high ground along the Dorsal Mountains. Isn't that a good thing?"

"OK, just one more thing then," Gordy replied. "The Dorsals have three passes. Each is wide enough to drive a full-on armor counterattack through. Rommel can move his tanks quickly. They have airpower to support a thrust—a blitzkrieg. I fear that because we're spread thin guarding the passes, that's a real possibility. Think like your enemy."

"What about—"

"What about our pilots, Willie? We have sorties to prepare for. Get your crews together for checks."

"I know, checks and double-checks."

"Esattamente."

"Wha? Esatta who? OK then."

Their P-38s were armed and off to escort regular B-17 bombings of Bizerte and Tunis and eventually to patrol the Mediterranean for enemy air transport targets of opportunity. As they watched the aircraft speed over the horizon, Willie and Gordy prayed for them all (Please, God!) to reappear.

****

On November 18, 1942, six Lightnings were lost on their return from the raids on Bizerte and Tunis while attempting to land in heavy rain and fog. To compensate, 14th Air Command ordered the 49th Fighter Squadron to Youks-les-Bains to join with the 48th from November 21–22. Callum remained in Casablanca. Losses were mounting. Gordy, Willie, and Marcin were stretched to the limit to keep their planes flying. The addition of the 49th crowded the airfield, and mud and mire slowed delivery of support equipment.

Lieutenant Mark Shipman of the 48th claimed a victory over an unidentified Italian twin-engine aircraft (likely a reconnaissance Ca.309 Ghibli "Desert Wind") on November 22. Early dogfights against the Axis fighters didn't go in favor of the Lightnings. German and Italian fighter pilots were more experienced, and they took advantage of a soon-to-be-recognized flawed US Air Corps tactic of weaving above the bombers and staying close to the formation. American P-38s were not yet in a position to establish air superiority. There were too few Lightnings and heavy pilot losses. There also was not enough production of P-38s stateside to support both the Pacific and the European theaters, certainly not enough to keep up with demands of four squadrons comprising the 14th Air Corps in North Africa.

The enemy still had strength in numbers with tanks and anti-tank weapons in strongholds east of the Dorsals. Winter had forcefully set in. Heavy rains and mud remained the nemeses of any immediate Allied victory in Tunisia.

# CHAPTER 9

# YOU'RE IN THE CCC NOW, WPA AND NORFOOTE, WHO?

In late January 1937, before Callum and Gordy's Kansas National Guard (KNG) inductions, they applied to the Texas Civilian Conservation Corps (CCC) and Works Progress Administration (WPA) in Dallas. Ongoing projects were close by, but they required an obligation of six months to a year, which would conflict with their commitments to the KNG. They employed their barely legible birth certificates again to meet the age requirements.

At the CCC camp, Callum and Gordy approached the forwardmost tent marked "CCC Headquarters." Gordy entered first and knocked on a wooden beam. When the only occupant turned around, he was surprised to see his old oil field driller friend, Lefty Burress! Lefty was dressed in a Texas National Guard uniform, his mangled hand peeking out of his right sleeve.

"Lefty!" Gordy exclaimed. "Um, I mean...sir!"

Lefty struggled to put on a pair of glasses and then looked at Gordy, astonished. "Boy, it's so good to see you!"

The two awkwardly began to embrace, then shook hands.

"Blessed to see you, boy!" Gordy's eyes welled up with tears. "You back from Wichita, then?"

"Sir, this is my brother, Cal...I mean Callum." Callum stepped forward and uncomfortably shook Lefty's mangled hand.

"No worries, Cal! Gordy can explain. Pleased to meet you!" Callum stepped back, embarrassed as to whether he should have shaken hands at all. "You boys back from Wichita, then, huh?"

Gordy tried to hide the tears welling up in his eyes, avoiding Lefty's question. "We're here to apply for work, sir."

"You call me Lefty, son, remember? I'm always Lefty to you! You too, Cal!"

"We're down from Kansas for the next two weeks. We've been accepted into the Kansas National Guard. We're committed to basic and—"

"You two boys are in the National Guard?" He stopped to assess Gordy's age and knew Callum had to be younger still. Instead of questioning them about that he exclaimed, "I'm in the Texas National Guard!"

Gordy looked at Lefty's hand and wondered how he'd ever passed a physical.

"This?" Lefty said as if reading his thoughts. "This here is *not* a problem! Junior Gilder got me in—don't tell no one. His dad had connections through Colonel Sam Bass with the Guard. Sam had connections, and his ol' doc buddy did my physical. And, well, I'm in! Yup, I'm in!"

Gordy didn't have an immediate response. He looked in his old friend's eyes and for a moment was lost in memories of Lefty's kindness to him. "We have two brothers and a sister at home in Dallas," he blurted. "They're starving! We need work to buy food for them, our mother, and her brothers!"

"They assigned me to be the commander of the CCC camp here," Lefty said, thinking out loud. "Guessing they thought I couldn't be a regular soldier. I can *shoot* a rifle, you know...left-handed. So, you boys need work? You ready to work?"

"Yes, sir! Please, sir!" they shouted in unison.

"Lefty, boys...it's Lefty! I can't officially sign you in for short-term work. Let's see what we can do though. We have two projects, one in

Cleburne and the other in Tyler. When you get on the truck, just tell the other guys you're new. Say nothin' other than you're new, OK? When you come back for your pay, come and see me here, savvy?"

"New, yes, Lefty," Gordy replied. "We'll tell 'em we're new! We'll come back to see you for our pay." Callum nodded in agreement.

As they left the camp for the dusty ride to Cleburne, they looked back at the CCC camp. "We're new...just new," Callum said to a fellow worker, "and we're grateful!"

"Who ain't?" the fellow replied.

****

As Callum and Gordy's CCC truck arrived at Cleburne, smoke and limestone dust covered a plain of frenetic activity. A dam was under construction to form a reservoir and a spillway. Everywhere, men were swinging pickaxes or shovels. A few steam shovels pushed soil up to form the earthen dam. The barrier towered thirty feet over the land below and looked to stretch for two or three miles. Men were tamping the sides with flat shovels. At one end of the dam, a bridge was under construction. Men were moving rocks by hand to form its structure.

As the truck pulled up next to a large tent, they jumped down and were ordered to form two lines. Callum and Gordy both stood in the same line. An impressive man emerged from the tent dressed in an army uniform and adorned in a pith helmet. "My name is Norfoote Goggins Woodwark," he said. The boys' jaws dropped, and they stared at each other in disbelief. (Who would name a person so? Their family should talk.) "I am the Commandant of CCC Camp Cleburne. I was discharged from the Army five years ago. I run this place like a military man, thus my old uniform. I am a landscape architect. My objective is to complete this project within six months. Whether we meet that objective is up to you. You are divided into two lines for a purpose. One line will work on the dam, the other on the bridge. Your shovels and picks are there."

He pointed to a pile of tools. "You have arrived just in time for lunch. Remember the man in front of you, and after lunch, return to your line in order. We are building a new Texas state park. Pleasure to have you all here! Lunch is on the other side of this tent. Good luck!"

Woodwark half-saluted and then returned to his tent. The scramble began to line up for lunch. The other workers were still in the field, which left the newcomers with first dibs on food: hardtack, chipped beef, and coffee. Hungry men stormed around the tent. The new workers feasted before the steam whistle blew for the bridge builders. As they flooded in, the boys dutifully returned to their respective lines to pick up their tools. Callum noticed he and Gordy were in the bridge line. He whispered to Gordy that it might be easier to work on the dam—the bridge involved breaking rocks manually and hoisting them up to the construction. Callum joined the dam line, and Gordy fell in behind him. No one seemed to notice they weren't remembering the man in front of them. Flat shovels on their shoulders, they followed the trail to the dam.

"You always seem to see an alternate path, Cal," Gordy remarked.

Callum chuckled. "You usually don't!"

Within a couple of days, their work on the dam included a test of the construction's water-hold worthiness. One side failed immediately, resulting in a rescue of three workers from being buried in mud and suffocating. Gordy and Callum pulled two from the collapse at their own risk. They were heroes of the CCC.

Two weeks of work earned the boys fifteen dollars each. On their return to say goodbye to Lefty, he reached into his lockbox and doubled their pay. He would allow them to do their Guard service and return at will. Callum and Gordy donated their wages to the family. Extra-special stipends went to Laurence and Conn for their sweet potato and ice cream/candy coffers.

# CHAPTER 10

# KANSAS NATIONAL AND NOT SO MUCH GUARD

The brothers reported to the Topeka headquarters of the Kansas National Guard (KNG) on Monday, March 8, 1937. They completed more health checks and were inoculated for smallpox. Then they began two weeks of rigorous basic training, which they enthusiastically welcomed versus their experiences with their uncle. They ran circles around their fellow inductees with their athleticism, competing only against each other for top performance in their units.

What recruiting Sergeant Cliff McCann had told Callum and Gordy about the KNG wasn't a lie; it just wasn't necessarily the whole truth. The Guard had only recently been reactivated in January from the Home Guard, a state militia organization that had stood in post deactivation of the Guard at the end of World War I as a response to paranoia about potential German espionage and to quell labor disputes. The National Guard had authorized two Kansas regiments in 1918. After the KNG deactivation in 1919, the Home Guard was established. It was composed of men without previous military experience and had questionable discipline/order, which led to the establishment of the State Guard and much confusion

The 137th Infantry was "one of the finest," but it hadn't been officially active since the Great War. (The KNG commander, Charles Browne failed two physicals before WWII.) The KNG was revived in January

1937 when the State Highway Patrol was established. It was so formed because the State Highway Patrol could not "guarantee adequate assistance that the State expected." Those in the KNG were *not exempt* from any selective service obligations that would likely be invoked in the event of war.

Three weeks passed. In their barracks at night, Gordy studied languages with a flashlight while Callum pondered alternatives to their situation in Kansas. A colleague from the San Marcos Academy sent him a clipping from the *San Antonio Express* about the Air Corps Training Center at Duncan (Kelly #2) Field. The article reported ongoing flight-maintenance training for the Douglas O-43 and new experimental North American observation aircraft at Randolph Field. By contrast, the KNG had one Curtis B1 Robin, one Douglas O-38E, and one Stinson L-1, all soon to be obsolete.

Cal realized that if they continued with KNG, they would either be in the infantry or the artillery. KNG's aircraft capabilities were limited to only a few planes. He approached Gordy with his thoughts. "Brother mine, you know we've made a mistake."

"What?" Gordy muttered as he tried to concentrate on his German/English Dictionary.

"We have made a mistake!" Callum almost shouted.

"No mistake, Cal. This was your idea. And it's a good one. We're becoming soldiers. We're away from Job. You're going to be a great soldier!"

"No, no, no," Callum persisted. Please listen to me! If we continue with the Guard here, we're likely to become infantrymen. If we go to war, Gordy, we'll be on the ground, getting shot at."

"That would be our duty, Cal. What's wrong with that?"

"We'll have a much greater chance of getting killed."

"OK. What do you have in mind then?"

"Look at this clipping from the San Antonio Express News," Callum said, handing it over. "Junior Gilder sent it. We need to transfer to the Army Air Corps in Texas—maybe in a support role. We'd be much safer on the ground farther away from the front lines."

Gordy read the article, then contemplated its contents. "How would we do that? We've just started here."

"We complete our training here—we're almost at six weeks. We'll get a short leave soon. We go back to Texas and ask Lefty or one of Sam Bass's friends or the Gilders to help us to transfer to the Texas Guard. We'll ask to be attached to the Air Corps in maintenance or supplies. If the war comes, we'll be safer, don't you think?"

"I have to agree you have something there. I admit I've been wondering how we'd do when things became hot. Don't know I'd feel confident carrying a rifle or shooting off a howitzer."

"You're a great shot, Gordy. You'll have your marksman badge soon. I don't think I can handle the sound of the big guns—kills my ears!"

"Mine too. With training we could be mechanics or handle supplies. Tell you what: let's sleep on it."

"OK, but I'm going to pray about it! We've made a mistake, and we need God's help to fix it."

"OK, let's sleep and pray on it."

The next day Gordy was on the firing range with his bolt-action Springfield M1903 and scoring perfectly. Then one of his rounds backfired and bloodied his nose. Was it an old gremlin left over from the Great War? What if that had been real? What if the ammunition they gave them in the infantry was old or defective? What if that was the difference between kill or be killed? Why would anyone want to risk that?

# TRUST (NOT AT ALL) IN THE FAMILY

**TRUST:** firm belief in the reliability, truth, ability, or strength of someone or something, e.g., *"Relationships should be built on trust."*

On the home front in Dallas, Miriam (age eleven), Isaiah (age nine), and Timothy (just turned eight) were still at the Buckner Orphanage. They visited Mary Mother on some weekends, when allowed. She couldn't afford food or clothes for the kids. The orphanage was now overwhelmed with Depression "babies." There were large numbers of younger children in greater need. It was clear that Mary Mother's three youngest were not long-timers for Buckner.

Where to turn? The Presbyterian Homes and Children's Services had an orphanage at Itasca, Texas. Mary Mother applied for her children. She was surprised when they were quickly accepted. She had been made suspicious because of strong warnings from Buckner's Headmistress, Beula Marker. "For God's sake," she said, "find out everything you can about where your children will be."

After the peak of the Great Depression in 1933, orphanage populations grew to over 144,000 children in the US. Economic poverty created horrific evil. Orphanages in Texas and elsewhere became breeding grounds for abusers and sexual predators. One Texas state home near Waco was notorious for beatings and rape.

Mary Mother tried her best to investigate, but little information was available. After talking with the state, several parents, and the director of Itasca, she instead sent Miriam and Timothy to stay with family south of Fort Worth. Isaiah stayed at home to be the new man of the family.

The cousins were related to Stepdaughter Bea by marriage. They were members of the First Baptist Church Ft. Worth—Mary Mother took solace in that. They had one boy of their own, now nearly full grown. They were cattle ranchers. They even drove to Dallas to pick the kids up and prayed with her on their departure to back their ranch. At least Miriam (Miri) and Tim would be with blood relatives who could support them.

As the holidays approached, Mary Mother wrote them to bring the kids home for Christmas. There was no reply. She sent a telegram, no response. Then news came from Bea via letter. She was concerned for the kids' welfare. She believed their only boy was molesting Miri but couldn't confirm it. She had heard from another cousin that Tim was unkempt, unfed ("skinny as a rail"), and without shoes.

With help from another friend at First Baptist Dallas, Mary Mother traveled to the ranch and retrieved her children. Her rebuke of these "fiends" was a loud paraphrased rant of Mark 9:42, "You all have millstones upon your necks. You will be drowned in the sea! The devil and you all be damned forever!" Her screaming could only be heard at the ranch house. No one lived within twenty miles of there.

She tried to speak with Miri alone, asking her to confess what had happened to her, to tell the sheriff. Miri did not, could not respond. Tim sat silent in the car, emaciated and filthy and without shoes. On the way, Mary Mother stopped at a general store across from the Ft. Worth sheriff's office. She considered walking over to report what had happened.

Instead, she made a phone call, sent a telegram, and asked her friend to turn south toward Itasca.

Upon their arrival at the Presbyterian home in Itasca, Mary Mother began her conservation with the director, quoting Matthew 5:3, "Blessed are the poor, for they will inherit the kingdom of heaven." Miriam and Tim were back in an orphanage. The worst poverty was still the poverty of the soul.

# CHAPTER 12

# ESCAPE (AGAIN), MORE BEERS POUR MOI

Gordy and Callum returned to the CCC Camp to visit Lefty and to work. Their full pay as privates with the KNG was forty cents per day. They visited Mary Mother and their siblings in Dallas and Itasca.

They needed "big Texas help" to transfer to the Texas National Guard (TNG). Gordy sent a telegram to his friend, Junior Gilder, asking him to find an advocate for them within the TNG. Through Col. Bass, they were networked to a flight surgeon in San Antonio. The physician was the same doctor who had helped Lefty join the Guard and the catalyst as to why he ended up at the CCC. Dr. Samuel Bosnick was attached to the Texas Air Guard at Kelly Randolph/Duncan Fields. He helped with TNG's induction physicals for one dollar each. Given the 1937 Depression economy, there were plenty of exams to do. He knew a major at Kelly. Gordy and Callum were ecstatic to learn via telegram that Dr. Bosnick had arranged an interview for both of them with him in San Antonio. The boys took the bus (it hardly qualified as such) down to "Alamo City" to keep their appointment.

Major C. J. Laughlin was as round as he was wide and all of five feet six inches tall. He spoke with a heavy Texas drawl and chain-smoked Camel cigarettes. His "office" was in a tiny hovel next to a Mexican cantina. He looked much older than his forty years. He had a scar that ran from his left ear to his chin. His bushy eyebrows were as big a distraction as his completely overgrown ear hairs. His frown-fixed face made his appearance fierce and clown-like at the same time. Cal and Gordy stood before him at attention and with salutes.

The major put out his cigarette and clipped off a begrudging salute. "At ease, y'all. Sit." He glared at both of them. "What in tarnation?...You boys can't be more than fifteen or sixteen. Who put you in the Army, dang it?"

"We're in the Kansas National Guard, sir," Gordy replied. "And we're of age. We have our—"

"You're not ol' enough to be pickin' yur nose, son. You boys oughta be in school or out fishin' or playin' ball—*anywhere* but in this man's Army."

"Sir, we were inducted into the Kansas Guard and completed our—"

"Lordy, Lordy, recruiters in Kansas must be complete desperate jack-asses!" He began to laugh, sort of (it was hard to tell given his expression), and then belched. "So, where y'all from?"

"We're from San Antonio and Dallas, sir," Callum said. "Texas born and raised. We went to the San Marcos Baptist Military Academy close by here. Top of our classes, sir."

"Y'all got some cajones!" Gordy made a mental note to look that word up later. "Come with me." Major Laughlin guided them out the back door and then through the back door of the dingy cantina. "Can't talk w' outta beer, y' understand, to talk it over?"

They all sat at the bar. Neither of the boys had ever been in a bar, nor had they ever taken a drink.

The major ordered a Shiner. "Whad'll you boys, er, soldiers have? Y' know, on me, y'all?"

Gordy asked, "Sir, we...er, sir, should we be in a bar, sir?"

"This ain't a bar, son. It's a cantina. And cantinas are...they're for beer and Mexican food. Whad'll ya have?"

"Sir, we don't drink."

"Ha ha ha, neither do I! Bring my soldiers a couple of Shiners too."

"Sir," Callum interjected, "through Lieutenant Colonel Sam Bass, we were recommended to you by Doctor Bosnick, sir. We're putting in our papers requesting a transfer to the Texas Guard."

The beers were served. "Honest, fellas? Sam's a good ol' boy an' an old friend. The doc's also a friend. Drink up, boys!"

"Sir, we don't drink...in uniform, sir!" Callum pleaded.

"You don't? How 'bout outta uniform then?"

"No, sir, we don't. In or out of uniform, sir."

Laughlin put his hand under his bulging chin and scratched contemplatively. "No, n-o-o-o you don't. 'Course you don't!" He paused. "Here's the deal, boys...uh, soldiers: y'all drink yur beers, and you're in the Texas Guard."

More silence. "Sir, we can't do that, sir," Gordy replied. Callum scowled at him.

Laughlin returned to his feigned pose of deep contemplation, then snorted, raised his bushy eyebrows, and scratched his furry ears. "That's what I thought. And so...y'all are both in! More beers for me! You boys report here this week. Stay for a while. I need to debrief you."

The good major kept Callum and Gordy at the bar for two more hours in "debrief," regaling them with his stories from the Great War. He'd been a reconnaissance pilot with the 111th Observation Squadron over France. He'd survived two crashes, the second resulting in his disfiguring facial scar from a snapped wire wing brace that whiplashed him in the cockpit. What he didn't tell them was that he wasn't able to guarantee their attachment to the Air Corps. It wasn't his decision alone.

Thankfully, the transfer paperwork went through as promised. Was it Col. Bass, Lefty, the Gilders, Dr. Bosnick, or Callum's prayer? They would never know, but they were grateful.

Within the week, they reported for duty to Kelly Field at San Antonio. The airbase was famous for its innovations, such as the first formal "blind flight" instrument courses. The boys requested mechanic training and were accepted. Another incident of "dumb luck?" Perhaps so.

****

As World War II approached, the KNG was a mishmash of organized chaos. The Home, State, and National guards devolved into locally controlled militia units. There were even arrests of independent "fifth columnists" undermining KNG's 1st Regiment Commander Col. Charles H. Browne (appointed, despite being medically disqualified).

In an attempt to show the readiness of his unit, in April 1942, Col. Browne ran various rigorous training exercises. One at Lake Shawnee near Topeka was in cooperation with the Kansas Civil Air Patrol (CAP). The maneuvers were intended to refine aircraft rifle targeting by ground troops. On his own initiative, CAP's Capt. Elmo Else "bombed" the battalion command post with flour sacks. KNG ground troops, having failed to identify the plane as hostile, signaled the pilot to drop a message. Capt. Else obliged with one that read "Surrender at once!" Then "Dead Eye" Elmo dropped four more flour sacks that scored direct hits.

The press was merciless detailing the "loss" of Col. Browne and KNG assistant adjutant General C. I. Martin ("the best military minds in Kansas") to the flour bombings. What was Col. Browne's assessment of this? Riflemen would have been more effective than concentrated machine gun fire. "They [the riflemen] would fire into the engine; they would shoot the pilot in the cockpit." That explained it all.

Had Gordy and Callum stayed with the KNG infantry, they might have been shooting at engines, at pilots in cockpits, or getting flour bombed. Or maybe servicing Elmo's plane. They were blessed in Texas.

# CHAPTER 13

# PRAISE THE LORD, AND PASS THE PICKS AND SHOVELS

The Army Air Corps' 10th School (Advanced Flying Wing) was at Kelly Field #2 (Annex). Many of the renowned aviators in American history were trained there: Charles Lindbergh, Curtis Lemay, and Hoyt Vandenburg among them. Claire Chennault (WWII Flying Tigers) taught at the school. The 1927 silent film *Wings* was shot there. Jimmy Doolittle's 1922 transcontinental flight was pre-serviced at Kelly 1 (Randolph). His only stop was at Kelly 2 (Duncan).

As spring 1937 came and went, Callum and Gordy were in mechanics' training at Kelly 1 and 2. They tore down old Douglas O-Series bi-plane engines and reassembled them over and over. They worked hard to become the best of the best.

They alternated their TNG service (part-time always meant full-time commitment and concentration to them) with working for the CCC. The boys became regular working fixtures at the Cleburne, Tyler, and Austin camps. What monthly savings they could put together they sent back to the family in Dallas, and with Lefty's help and influence, they were able to establish themselves as supervisors.

****

At home, Isaiah became the new Ward family gravedigger at Oak Park Cemetery. He actually enjoyed the job. Of the boys, he was the true biblical scholar. He had read through the Bible four times in the last two years. After returning home he became Mary Mother's pride and joy. He asked deep, significant questions about the Bible and often searched it for answers. He always had a Bible close by, even at the cemetery.

One hot summer afternoon, he had dug a grave and was waiting to fill it. A small family of six gathered to grieve their loss and stood next to a pine casket. In his dirty coveralls, Izzie (Uncle Laurence coined it, it stuck; Mary Mother hated it—she always called him Isaiah) approached them respectfully and offered the widow, who was dressed in black, his hand.

"My name is Isaiah. Do you have a pastor to preside here?"

The woman shook her head no tearfully.

"May I offer my condolences and service, ma'am?" She was taken aback, probably wondering how old this kid was. Maybe ten?

"You're a pastor?" she asked.

"No, ma'am, I'm not. I'm not old enough. But I am a member of First Baptist Church here in Dallas, and I want to be a pastor someday."

"We could barely afford the coffin. We can't afford to pay you."

"It would be on me, ma'am. I would be honored to say a few words, by your leave."

"That...that would be wonderful, young man."

Izzie asked the decedent's full name and then asked each person if they'd be OK with him leading their service. They agreed.

"In the loving name of our Lord Jesus Christ," Izzie began, "we dedicate this time to prayer and in remembrance of Adam William Todd. Amen.

"The Lord said to the thief on the cross, 'Surely today you will be with me in paradise,' and Adam William Todd, having accepted Jesus as his Lord and Savior, rests in His loving arms today."

The family burst into tears. The mom, the four boys, and a little girl wept. The mother slumped into her oldest boy's embrace as Izzie continued.

"And the Bible says in Romans, 'Rejoice with them that do rejoice and weep with them that weep. And I say to you all, rejoice even though you weep.' Adam William is not in pain or suffering. He is at peace, and I believe he would not want you to suffer for him. That doesn't mean you cannot feel his loss. It means that Jesus holds you in your mourning and is wrapping all of you right now in His peace and His love." The silence was broken only by the sound of crying. "Does anyone want to say something?"

"I love you, Daddy!" the little girl burst out. "I love you! Daddy, please come back!"

Izzie knelt down and gently wiped her tears and lifted her chin, "You will see your daddy again! Jesus promised. You will! Anyone else need to say something?"

Silence.

"Then may the Peace of God which passeth all understanding keep your hearts and minds through Christ Jesus." Izzie tenderly looked into each of their eyes. "Peace I leave with you and you and you and you and you and you! Jesus's peace I give you: not as the world giveth give I peace unto each of you. Let not your hearts be troubled, neither let you be afraid. Amen."

Izzie waited for the family to depart the cemetery. After they did, he lowered the pine box into the hole he'd dug. He stopped to respectfully drop handfuls of dirt in the hole and pray. He had finished his job and his first graveside service.

****

Mary Mother hadn't told Gordy or Callum about the evil of their "cowboy cousins." She fully intended to keep it a family secret forever.

However, Bea had no intention of doing so. She surprised Mary Mother with a visit at her Oak Park Cemetery office and got straight to the point:

"Mary, have you called the sheriff in Fort Worth?"

"Bea, I told you never to speak of it again!" Mary Mother replied indignantly. "Nothing good can come of any of it. The children are safe now."

"They must be punished whether they're our relatives or not!" Bea objected. "They abused Miri and left Tim to starve. How can you ignore that?"

"I've not ignored it. I'm praying for Miri and Tim! Eli and I took you and Job in. Remember that? Of course I'm devastated for them. How will it help to bring it all back with the sheriff? How? 'Justice is mine,' sayeth the Lord."

"Mary, please! Your children are in an orphanage. What do they know of God's justice? They need their family. They need you!"

Mary Mother broke into tears of rage. "Stop! You don't know about me. You haven't had to be me! I've done what I had to do to feed my children and Conn, Laurence, you, and Job before them. I've done what I had to do!"

"But, Mary..." Just then there was a polite knock. The door swung open, and in the doorway stood Izzie. He looked perplexed and confused.

"Mother, Aunt Bea. I've finished the Todd grave."

"How long have you been there, Isaiah?" Mary Mother asked, panicked.

"Long enough to know that you and Aunt Bea have been arguing about Miriam and Timothy. I know God has been protecting them," he added gently.

Bea and Mary Mother were aghast and amazed at the same time. "How do you know *that*?" they asked in unison.

"Jesus told me. You know, 'Suffer the little children unto me...'"

Then Isaiah told them about the Todd graveside, how he'd spoken solace to the family. Bea teared up and hugged him tightly. Mary Mother stood there stunned. "My boy."

****

On leave from Kelly and after working for the CCC, Gordy visited Izzie at the cemetery late one Saturday afternoon and helped him dig another grave. As they did, Izzie told Gordy about the situation surrounding Miri and Tim. Gordy was enraged. Izzie prayed out loud for the kids and Gordy. Gordy's anger wasn't quieted by Izzie's supplication. "Mother! Why, Mother? Mother, why?" he screamed.

Izzie prayed silently for Gordy again.

# CHAPTER 14

# AIR WAR... STORMS OVER GABES

As 1942 came to an end, the Allies had much to be optimistic about in North Africa. Rommel appeared to be cornered in Tunisia, and the air war had expanded. The 48th Pursuit was a big part of the success with twenty-nine air victories. Those wins came at a terrible price though: four pilots killed in action (KIA), fourteen Lightnings lost, and one prisoner of war (POW) taken.

The mood at Youks-les-Bains was somber and intense. Gordy, Willie, and Marcin were working to find enough planes to fly sorties. They worked with their 49th counterparts to salvage parts and repair damage. Their teamwork took up the slack.

"Checked intercoolers on 817, sir. She eest goot," Marcin reported in his deep Polish accent.

"Eighty-second Fighter Squadron transfer, right?" Gordy replied.

"Yes, sir. Glad she eest to be here. No name. We need badly, jes?"

"Yes we do! Flight checks and put her on the line."

"Amorers goot too, sir?"

"Yes, and with our pilot, who do we have?"

"Eeest Harv," Lest said excitedly. "His plane, Tantrum, eest down. Replace fuel line, she next. I am doing."

"That's Lieutenant Harvey Smith, Lech," Gordy scolded.

"He say call him, 'Harv.' He said I best mechanical for him."

"If he said it, he meant it, and you are. Get him here. Ask him to clear it with his commander for the record. He'll flight check with me."

"Eeest goot!" Marcin said, a huge smile on his face. "I will do, Sergeant Vard!" He ran to the pilots' quarters.

Harv climbed into his 817, which was fully armored. His CC and Gordy performed final checks. Each of her Allisons puffed to life and then roared in unison. Thumbs-up and salutes were exchanged. One of Gordy's favorite sights was watching one of his Lightnings taxiing and taking off. "Godspeed," he whispered every time. Under Harvey Smith's control, she swept up perfectly and climbed out quickly, the squadron's best pilot at her helm. Two of his comrades were soon with him winging toward the Mediterranean to escort another bombing mission.

At 1400, air-raid sirens sounded. Flak began to go up as tiny specks sped toward the Youks base. Three Bf 109 Messerschmitts were on the way in to strafe and reconnoiter the field. Willie and Gordy ran to their battle stations. It was unknown if the 109s were the prelude to a bombing. As they came in succession, they opened up, targeting planes and personnel. Several rounds came close to hitting Willie, spitting off the ground. Then, as the field's AAA opened up, they heard a familiar sound—the roar of two Allison engines. A single Lightning was closing on the trailing 109. The two forward planes split up and climbed before they could make another run. The last was low, the P-38 on its tail, spitting fire from its .50s and its cannon. As the Bf turned away from the field, the pilot realized he was flying into flak. He turned back hard and down to the deck. Gordy recognized the P-38; it had no nose art. It was 817 returning with its three Lightning mates. Harv turned her on a dime and blew around to chase the 109 down, opening up his guns. As the Bf attempted twisting evasive maneuvers and raced outside of the airfield, he "blew hell out of it!" The record said exactly that.

The dogfight on December 28, 1942, was a surprise, although short-lived. "All clear," sounded, and Harv and his cohorts landed to cheers from those on the ground. The attack raised morale. While the mood at Youks-les-Bains remained tense, seeing one of theirs in combat up close and personal was amazing. Gordy, Willie, and Marcin were still scrambling to patch together enough planes to fly more sorties. The 48th and the 49th were now more of a team than ever. They had to be.

Two days later, on December 30, the ace of the 48th (with six victories), First Lt. Harvey Smith, a native of Texas, was killed in action (KIA), shot down at Gabes, Tunisia, near the Libyan border while escorting the 47th Bomb Group. He and his fellow pilots were jumped by Messerschmitts. The 48th lost two more shot-up ships on landing. One skidded off the runway; another belly flopped.

By the end of January 1943, the 14th Fighter Group had lost 60 percent of their 54 pilots. Only seven Lightings were operational in the Mediterranean Theater. The remaining planes were having mechanical challenges, such as the 49th FS Lightnings' tanks not feeding, resulting in their return to base, leaving their cohorts weaker in airborne strength versus the enemy. Something had to give.

****

The same day that First Lt. Harvey Smith was KIA, P-38 pilot Clark Smith (no relation) was also shot down near Gabes. When his Lightning caught fire, he bailed out. In his excitement, he almost forgot to open his canopy first. He landed close to a remote village. He suffered a broken ankle and a shrapnel wound in his arm. "Friendlies" provided him a donkey to ride outside the village, where they lit a fire to keep warm, which was probably why Smith was captured by Italian troops. He spent nineteen months as a POW in Sagan-Silisia, Bavaria, and Nuremberg-Langwasser Stalags. Asked what was the most beautiful sight he could think of, Smith responded, "Sherman tanks crashing through barbed wire." He flew twenty-eight missions in Tunisia.

# CHAPTER 15

# CALIFORNIA, THERE THEY WENT

Callum and Gordy were excelling at learning aircraft maintenance. As TNG members, however, they were limited in scope and pay. As the end of 1937 came, they were working the maximum allowed hours at Kelly and overtime with Lefty at the CCC for minimal pay in return.

Major C. J. "More Beers for Me" Laughlin caught Callum at the hangar at Kelly and asked for a moment. Gordy had run to the *gardez l'eau* ("watch the water," a.k.a. the loo).

"How're things for y'all here, soldier?" the major asked. "You gettin' on?"

"Sir, we're learning so much. Gordy and I are working hard to become the best aircraft mechanics ever!"

"Of course y'all are! You're both somethin' special. Proud of y'all. What'd you say to goin' active with the Air Corps?"

Callum frowned in confusion. "I don't—"

"Before you say no, think about your future here."

"Sorry, sir, our future?"

"Y'all are workin' on planes that we aren't even flyin' anymore. Y'all are sort of part-time here. Y'all can only be privates in TNG right now— privates for a long time. Y'all have gone 'bout as far as you can go here."

"And how would we change that, sir?"

"Please don't misunderstand," Laughlin said. "I don't want to lose y'all. I have respect for the both of ya. But there are more opportunities goin' active. We have new planes comin' in development. Experimentals. Because of limited fundin', they're not comin' to Kelly anytime soon."

"Where are they going then, sir?'

"California."

"California…Where in California?"

"Can't share that. Can't unless you're active."

Callum was becoming annoyed with the major's cryptic communication, almost as much as he'd been at the cantina nearly a year earlier. "So, if I understand you, sir, we can't know why you think we would be needed in California unless we are active in the Army Air Corps, sir?"

"Yup! You and your brother will rot here at Kelly tearin' down O-37s or worse. I have that on good authority."

Callum hated the condescending tone of Maj. Laughlin's language. Just then, Gordy returned from the loo.

Callum sprang into a summary of Maj. Laughlin's conversation. "Gordy, we need to go active duty."

"What? What'd you say?

"We need to go active with the Army! We can't continue to get paid practically nothing. Our folks in Dallas can't continue to get by on beans. The CCC and our TNG pay barely keep them from starving. We have to be either on base or at a CCC camp to eat ourselves! We're sleeping on a cot at the base or on the ground at the camps." None of that was in the major's talk. Also, none of what Callum referenced about the plight of the boys' family was known to Maj. Laughlin. His bushy eyebrows rose in surprise.

Gordy was confused. "Uh, yeah, we send some money home. We can eat at the base or the camps. Pardon me, but what have you and the major been discussing? "

"The major thinks we're needed in California. California's got new planes. If we go active, we can discuss all of this!"

"Say what? You've never made less sense, brother! I—"

"What Private Ward is tryin' to tell ya, Private Ward," Laughlin said, "is that y'all both need to go active. Yur not goin' nowhere if you stay here at Kelly."

"Excuse me, sir," Gordy said. "I'm trying to understand. Did we do something wrong? Why would you say we're going nowhere, here at Kelly?"

"Can't tell you that, Private, 'cause you're not active!" The word "obtuse" came to Gordy's mind.

"OK. Er, let's just say we went active, and California had new planes. Would we have the opportunity to work on those planes?"

"Can't answer that, y'all. Only you soldiers can decide to be better. I can say you're the best here."

"Can we take that under advisement, then, sir? Just we privates, you know, talk it over?"

"Y'all can, but do it quickly. Your active transfers to California are approved but only if you sign on, go active with the Army Air Corps t'day. At lunch y'all call me on the commissary phone with your decision." With that, Maj. Laughlin came to attention, as did they, saluted them, then turned and left.

Callum and Gordy were stunned. There would be no time to think this over. Was the major talking for someone else, someone more powerful than him?

"What'd you think?" Callum asked.

"I think we're active by this afternoon, brother."

During their lunch call, Major Laughlin asked them to meet him at the cantina after they finished work that afternoon.

Again, he sat at the bar with a Shiner spouting more reverie about his flying experiences in World War I. He talked and talked until Gordy interrupted. "Sir, can we talk about our active status, California, and the planes, please?"

"Was wonderin' when y'all'd get to that."

Gordy was wondering when he'd let them get to that!

"You men are Texans, th' best of Texas. Never forget that! We have new planes in testin' in California. Need you soldiers to learn 'em and work on 'em. Only have limited understandin' of 'em. Wish I knew. Wish I could fly one! Believe they're pursuit fighter aircraft, the P group. But then, what do I know? Believe th't you boys are among the chosen to make 'em fly. Air Corps needs you soldiers in California. No offense to Californians, y'all do Texas proud there!"

He gulped his beer, they finished their Dr. Peppers, clinked them together in a toast, and then the major reached into his pocket and pulled out corporal patches for their sleeves. "Just a little gift from an old grateful friend. They stood and the Major swore them in as corporals. Y'all be safe. Ain't in safe times now, men."

They all stood at attention and saluted. As they left the cantina, the boys put on their new Air Corps caps. They looked back. The major lit a Camel and then returned to the bar and ordered another Shiner. The old soldier pulled a handkerchief and quickly dabbed his eyes. That was not supposed to be seen.

****

The boys were given twenty-four hours to make their train to Los Angeles. A friend agreed to drive them to Dallas. On the way they stopped at Itasca to say goodbye to Miri and Tim. They were getting bigger. They were also reading poetry and history. Then, in Dallas, they met with Izzie and the family.

Mary Mother was unhappy with their decision to become full-time soldiers. She was fearful of having Callum and Gordy so far away. She was certain that having them in the Army Air Corps would have life-long spiritual consequences. "Jesus, Lord and Savior, protect Callum and Gordon from Satan's grasp," she prayed out loud. "Keep them in You at all times. Never let them forget that You are their God, that You are the Spirit dwelling within them. Let nothing calamitous befall them. Amen."

Gordy wondered what more calamitous situation could there be than being abandoned to Uncle Job or their sister and brothers being farmed out to orphanages and evil cousins. What more unfortunate circumstances could befall them in California than she had created for them heretofore?

Izzie also prayed. "These are my brothers, Lord. Bring them back whole and well. For you did not give us a Spirit of fear but one of power and love and a sound mind..." His voice broke. "Give them Your love, Your forgiveness, and Your protection. Let them know, through Your Holy Spirit, that my prayers for both of them go up every day. Amen."

On the train, Gordy broke out three language dictionaries: French, German, and Italian. He enunciated phonetically and memorized deep into the darkness, which was punctuated by the train's whistle. He took breaks by reading Homer's *Iliad* in ancient Greek (he had been given it for winning first place in the Texas State High School Oratory competition). Callum read his Bible, discarded newspapers, and a technical guide to aircraft engines, dated 1934.

He also continued to ask Gordy about words and more words. They quizzed each other on key components of the planes they'd worked on at Kelly.

They were still working and surviving. And forever, they were brothers—in fact and then in arms.

# CHAPTER 16

# MARCH FIELD...SANS MARCHING

**M**arch Field was established in March 1918 as Alessandro Flying Training Field, one of thirty-two such air training camps founded before the US entered World War I. One of the oldest military airfields in the US, it was renamed only a month after the son of Army Chief of Staff Peyton C. March, Jr., the second Lieutenant March (same namesake), who died in an air crash in Texas.

It took nearly three days for the train to arrive in Los Angeles and then one and a half hours from there to reach Riverside by bus. The boys' adrenalin carried them through the trip with no fatigue. They arrived at March at sundown.

The San Bernardino Mountains provided a purple background for the sunset. It was warm but not sticky like at home. It was almost too good to be true.

They hefted their rucksacks into a small barracks. Master Sergeant Xiao Wang escorted them on base, driving them to their quarters in a new jeep. Everything at March seemed new. Sgt. Wang was polite and welcoming. While clearly of Chinese heritage, he spoke without an accent.

"Be prepared for reveille at 0500. Your kitchen is separate from the general mess next to your hangar. Your hangar station is next door. You'll notice that you are alone here. You will be working incognito in Special

Projects. You're not to mingle with anyone here without my permission. I will see you for breakfast. Good evening, and rest well, corporals. You're not likely to get the opportunity to do so again anytime soon."

On each of their beds was a large three-ring binder and an envelope. Enclosed in the envelope was a letter. They opened the letters, which were identical, and read them together.

> Dear Corporal Ward:
>
> It is my pleasure to welcome you to March Air Corps Base. You have been chosen to work on the testing and maintenance of aircraft here upon my direct orders.
>
> Your work is classified TOP SECRET. You are NOT to discuss your activities with ANYONE other than Sergeant Wang and/or me.
>
> Your Orders:
>
> **COMPLETELY READ THE BINDER ON YOUR BUNK BY 0700.**
>
> Your work is critical to the 17th Pursuit Group's success.
>
> Sincerely,
>
> Major Lindell Pearson,
> Commander Special Projects
> US Army Air Corps
> March Air Field
> Riverside, California

The binder was another story. It was simply labeled "36HR." It contained over one hundred pages of schematics and instructions.

"It's nine o'clock, Gordy! How're we ever going to read all this, let alone understand it?" Callum wailed.

"We've got ten hours. Looks like everything in the binders are identical. We'll read it out loud to each other, and whoever isn't reading underlines in one binder."

"Uh...OK."

"You got a better idea?"

"No. No, I don't."

"Quick, run over to the kitchen, and see if there's a way to make coffee. We're going to need it." Callum wasn't a fan of coffee, but he did as he was told.

Callum was surprised to find a private on duty. The private snapped to attention. "What can I do for you Corporal, eh?"

"At ease." Callum was not used to saying that. "Why, er...Can you make coffee, Private?"

"Of course, Corporal. Here to please, don't ya know."

"What's your name, and how soon can you get that full tureen of coffee to our barracks?"

"Sorry, Corporal. My name's Erik Lundgren. And I'm not allowed in your barracks. The Major's orders, Corporal, eh."

"Then please make two tureens. Keep them hot, and Corporal Ward and I will run over all night long. Where's your latrine?"

"Yes, sir. Right away, sir! You have your own toalett, Don' ya know?"

"Huh? You mean, toilet?"

"No, Corporal. I mean, toalett, ya know, loo, sir. I'm from Minnesota. Swedish, don' ya know, eh Corporal."

"I see. I guess I noticed we have our 'toalett,' thanks."

"Sur, Ya sure. Du välkomnande. Njuta av din toalett. Um, that's, 'You're welcome. Enjoy yur toilet. You're gonna need it tonight, Corporal, eh."

"How do you say, 'thank you'?"

"Tack, Corporal. Tack, eh."

"Of course. Tack, Private, tack." *What a pair Sergeant Wang and Private Lundgren make,* Callum thought.

All night, Callum and Gordy alternatively read out loud to each other and underlined key portions of the text. The binder manuals seemed to be for the plane's engine. It was a radial star-shaped design. Gordy had read about them and thought they were great engineering.

Their only breaks were for coffee and toalett runs. When possible, even while in the loo, they continued to read and write. When they ran to the kitchen, they repeated what they'd read out loud and underlined to memorize as much they could. They "tacked" Private Lundgren every time. By 0230 they'd gotten through all 106 pages. Gordy suggested they continue their latrine/coffee routine, then quiz each other. Callum could not do so without some sleep.

At 0300 they were throwing technical questions at each other, first from the underlined binder, then from memory.

They showed up early at Private Lundgren's kitchen, right after reveille. The groggy private cooked up Swedish scrambled eggs. They'd never had eggs with cream cheese...delicious. They were still quizzing each other from their binders and on their second servings at 0600 when Major Pearson and Sergeant Wang arrived, as promised. The corporals stood at attention and saluted Pearson. Then they all sat down.

"Did you rest well, gentlemen?" the major asked.

"No, sir. We read and studied the binders, sir," Gordy replied.

"All night? Did you now. What's the difference between a radial and piston engine, then?" Wang asked.

"Pardon me, sir, but that's a trick question," Callum replied.

"How so?"

"Sir, a radial engine is a piston engine," Gordy explained. "The difference is the pistons reciprocate around the crankshaft rather than being in line with it."

"And what's the advantage of a radial engine?" Pearson asked.

"There are actually two advantages, sir," Callum said. "First, the cylinders are evenly exposed to air cooling. Second, because of air cooling, the engine can be made lighter."

Sgt. Wang began to ask another question but was interrupted by Maj. Pearson, "I've heard enough, Sergeant."

Callum and Gordy exchanged worried looks. Was that a bad thing?

"Corporals, welcome to Special Projects," Pearson said. "You both are clearly serious about your work. Let's talk about next steps. Let's see… Oh, I forgot, the pay grade will be three additional years beyond both of your cumulative active service at $72.60 per month (unheard of for that time). That'll work for you, right?"

"Yes, sir! Thank you, sir!" the boys blurted almost in unison.

"You're going to earn every penny of it, corporals."

In the hangar next door was a disassembled P-36 Hawk Fighter. Next to it was an Allison 1710 engine. Surely, the major knew that the 75 Hawk/Mohawk wouldn't accommodate the Allison?

"Gentlemen," Maj. Pearson began, "we need you to reassemble this fighter as completely as possible and as quickly as possible. If you need assistance, Sergeant Wang is at your disposal." He nodded at Sgt. Wang.

"And, we expect you to tear down the engine to its bolts," Wang added. "Understood?"

"Yes, sirs," the boys responded.

"You should begin with the Curtiss Hawk first. We'll be timing you both." Wang pulled out a watch and noted the time, 06:30. "Begin."

The Curtiss P-36 Hawk was one of the first all-steel American fighters. Hefting the wings and fuselage would be aided by several chain lifts strung over the hangar's high structural beams, a job for strong young men. Callum and Gordy began with the tail section and moved forward.

"Sergeant Wang, sir?" Gordy said. "What about the metal skin attachment rivets, sir?"

"Suspend the major parts via your hoists. We have a factory riveter on base to complete your work. Fit her together, Understood?"

"Yes, sir!" they replied.

Nine and a half hours later, Sgt. Wang checked in. All was in order from tail to nose. The engine and crankshaft hung below waiting, the fuselage and the rest suspended above it. The retractable landing gear was installed under suspended wings and the small tail-dragger gear under the tail. The engine cowling and the propeller were aligned under the nose on the ground.

"Well done, corporals. Time for some chow." Gordy and Callum hadn't noticed they'd worked straight through to 1600 hours.

At dinner, Sgt. Wang began the conversation. "You're probably wondering about my heritage and presence here at March." Actually, they weren't, but Wang explained he was a native of Taipei, Formosa, China, where he was an acolyte of Sun Yat-Sen, the Kuomintang (Nationalist Party of China) and Chaing Kai-Shek. He had come to the US at age four. His parents were brilliant. His mother was a physicist, and his father was an electrical engineer who worked with Thomas Edison. Xiao graduated from high school at age fourteen and then attended Princeton University for two years, where he studied mechanical engineering. His passion was aeronautics. Princeton had no aero curriculum at the time, so he took flying lessons.

At age sixteen, he was recruited by Curtiss-Wright. His work on several iterations of aircraft and his mathematical genius drew the attention of US cryptologist Herbert Yardley (who helped the Chinese nationalists break Japanese diplomatic coding). Despite his aptitude for the FBI's intelligence wing, Wang chose to enlist in the US Army Air Corps. He spoke and wrote English, Mandarin, and Spanish.

Gordy and Callum were amazed by Sgt. Wang's background. Why was he working with them? More to the point, why were two corporal mechanics working with him?

After dinner, they went back to the hangar and began to tear the Allison engine apart. By midnight, the manifold sat centered around concentrically arrayed parts and bolts.

The boys were starved. They stopped by the kitchen to be welcomed by the most wonderful smell: Lundgren's simmering Swedish meatballs.

"Wondered when yu'd be here. My meatballs are probably soggy by now, don't ya know?" He served their plates to overflowing.

"Tack, Lundgren. Tack," they replied.

What an unusual group of people Callum and Gordy were working with. Were they all a part of some bizarre plan? What had old Major "More Beers" Laughlin gotten them into?

****

On April 26, 1937, Heinkel HE 111 and Junkers Ju 52 bombers attacked the town of Guernica in northern Spain. Dubbed by the Germans as "Operation Rügen," it openly exposed their secret Luftwaffe Kampfgeschwader 53 "Legion Condor" air support for Generalissimo Francisco Franco's nationalist movement in the Spanish Civil War. The northern Spanish Basques were republican loyalists and obstacles to Franco's dictatorial takeover of the country.

The bombings killed at least 200 civilians. It was an early demonstration of German air tactics, a grim precursor of the brutality to come from their "lightning war" (blitzkrieg) technique. The Luftwaffe's development of new aircraft had been prolific in the 1930s despite the Versailles Treaty's ban on offensive air weapons. They and the Italians were already prosecuting war in Europe and the Mediterranean.

After the Japanese invasion and occupation of Manchuria in 1931, their aggression continued into northern China. By 1933, a truce between the Kuomintang government of China and Japan was tenuous at best. By 1937, Japan had 15,000 troops in China. A July 8 dispute on the Lukouchiao Bridge ("Marco Polo Bridge") sparked more conflict. Complicating the fighting was the presence of the Communist Chinese Revolutionary Army, which refused to join a truce. All of this led to the Japanese shelling of Wanping and eventually to a second all-out Sino-Japanese war. By July, Japan had 180,000 troops near Beijing.

About the same time, the Chinese Republic Air Force had 645 aircraft, about 300 of which were fighters. The Japanese had about 400 aircraft in China. Many of the Chinese planes were US-designed Curtiss Goshawks and Boeing P-26 Peashooters. In August 1937, America's foremost advocate for pursuit fighter intercept, Claire Chenault, became an air advisor to Chaing Kai-Shek to train Chinese pilots. He soon became the leader of the "Flying Tigers" and the Republic of China's Air Force.

The importance of air supremacy was finally being recognized by most combatants. In World War II, the deadliest conflict of all time, it would be critical. Staying ahead of the enemy would be imperative in aircraft innovation and manufacturing, pilot training, strategic planning and tactics, maintenance, and logistics.

It was apparent to Callum and Gordy that they were at March Field to be a part of something bigger. Defeating three Axis enemies in two theaters of war seemed more formidable than they'd ever imagined. They were determined to do their best and to work beyond expectations to help win.

# CHAPTER 17

# THE AULD TEXAS HOME

It was two months before either Gordy or Callum wrote home. They were vague about their location (the letters were postmarked Riverside, CA). When they finally did write, it wasn't to Mary Mother. Rather, they sent notes or books to Izzie, Miri, and Tim. It wasn't odd for them to send pages of the same questions to their siblings about their activities without mentioning anything about how they were. They truly wanted to know about their siblings' lives back in Texas.

For Miri, the boys sent notes from their memories of poetry and literature lessons:

"He hath a heart like a bell ringing."—William Shakespeare and
"Love is the energy of Life." —Robert Browning

To Izzie they sent three books of Dr. George Truett's sermons, entitled *Salt and Light*, that Mary Mother had given them, one from Gordy and two from Callum: "To know the will of God is the greatest knowledge! To do the will of God is the greatest achievement."

To Tim they sent notes and clippings they'd kept on military history and about the Kansas National Guard. These included notes on Waterloo and Civil War battles they'd studied at the San Marcos Baptist Military Academy and clippings from friends still in the KNG describing the "flour bombings" and a *Sabetha Herald* newspaper article detailing chemical warfare exercises (complete with phosphorus explosions and gas masks) led by a KNG corporal who was a local high school chemistry teacher.

Miri and Tim replied in perfect cursive script with well-written letters, exhibiting their intelligence and their teachers' coaching at Itasca Presbyterian.

Izzie had less time to reply. In addition to his grave responsibilities at Oak Park Cemetery, and thanks to a letter of introduction to Lefty from Gordy, he was able to work with the CCC. He did take time to write in excitement about having found fossils at one of the sites. He said he wanted to become a biblical archeologist to prove the divinity of Christ by doing digs in the Holy Land.

All of the siblings were focused on their love of learning. They were, despite their situations of separation and scarcity, achieving academic excellence. This was a source of pride for Callum and Gordy. They expected nothing less from the Ward clan.

As for Mary Mother, she was still working at the cemetery and taking care of Conn and Laurence. She continued to find new "cures" for whatever ailed them. After the "Whoa Santa" incident, Laurence was less inclined to ask for or accept her help. Conn, however, was another story. He never heeded (or more likely never understood) Laurence's warnings about sweet potaters and buttermilk. Conn's maladies were many: gout, heartburn, frequent throat (tonsil)/ear infections, rheumatism, and ingrown toenails among them.

Mary Mother had a source for every one of her home remedies. She obtained cow urine (Gomutra) from the local dairy. She distilled it in an old "collection system" (a still) she'd inherited from her Scottish relatives from Kentucky. The family accepted her explanation that it was a holdover from the house's previous owners.

When Conn complained again about his "throat ache," she was ready. She prepared a "tea" for Conn. Perhaps it was a leak in the distillery thumper attachment, but the rancid odor was not that of tea. Conn, in his nightshirt and bare feet, was having nothing of it. She forced the concoction into his deteriorated mouth (neglected for years at the asylum) and held it shut. Conn half snorted it out through his nose, swallowed some of it, and spit the rest all over Mary Mother, himself, and the kitchen.

"Now, aren't you ashamed of yourself?" Mary Mother chided.

Conn displayed his almost toothless smile. "Nope."

"You'll feel better soon!" she encouraged.

"Nope and nope!"

"You will!"

"Nu-uh!"

Although not known then, it was proven later that the urea in cow's urine had, among other medicinal qualities, antimicrobial properties. So, it was not surprising weeks later that several of Conn's mangled toenails were markedly improved. His throat was also better, as was his indigestion, and his gout subsided—another cure! Mary Mother's "science" marched on in triumph. As an added bonus, the distilled urine also proved to be the best floor tile cleaner ever.

****

Uncle Laurence "loved him" some trains. As a boy, he ran from the MacDougal house to the tracks whenever he heard a locomotive whistle. Upon arrival, he'd stand on a rail to feel the vibration of the wheels turning heavily on the rails and listen to the clickety-clack sound of them hitting the rail gaps. As the puff of smoke from the engine rose nearer, and the train rounded a curve hidden by a large stand of live oak trees, he would wave his arms wildly, which incurred the ire of the engineer, who blew the whistle as much as possible. Thus came the elation of meeting his goal to completely annoy the engineer. To Laurence's delight, it happened each and every time!

At age fourteen, he volunteered to help with an engine water stop nearby. He often played hooky from school to do so. After helping with the fill, he'd swing out on the spout high up from the tank until the brakeman dutifully removed him. During one of these episodes, he sneaked onto the train engine for a look around. The engineer returned and set the train in motion.

Laurence was afraid he'd lose his "job" if he was discovered, so he hid in the coal car but was found despite his best efforts. He begged the engineer not to kick him off. The train was now more than a mile from the water tower. The engineer obliged to stop and let him off under one condition: Laurence had to bring him some of his mother's fried chicken (a legend around Dallas) the next day or else.

When Laurence returned to the house, it was apparent to his mother, Mariam, that he'd been up to some mischief. He was covered in coal dust from head to toe.

"Laurence, wha...Hoow...Xplin' yeself!" Her Scottish brogue made the admonition seem even fiercer.

"Màthair (Mother), I will not lie to ye. Fell from the watir tower spoot rith' inta' the cuul ceur," he replied. Laurence loved her accent and mimicked it well when in trouble.

"Whoot? And hoo *black* ye are, aye! Goo outside and strip...Ull oof it. Ull!"

"I think I brook me buns! Ye knoow, me bottom." He was working it.

"Ooooh, dit' ye neuoow? Strip if ull ooof, and git on cleeen britches. Neoouw!"

He went outside, tore off his clothes, and grabbed the only pair of coveralls from the clothesline. He ran back into the house sporting nothing but the dungarees.

"Ooooh, yooou canno be kiddin'...doo ye nut knoo thoose overalls are your dadaidh's (father's)? An' he'll be right fiadhauch (angry) yoo poot yer bare boottum in tooch wid 'em." Goo an' find soom britches oof yur ooown, Neoouw!"

Laurence knew his mother could not stay mad at him for long. Mary Clover was another story. He dressed and noticed Conn in the yard. He would enlist him in his chicken-fried conspiracy.

"Brother Conn!" Laurence called. "'Need your help to git Màthair to fry up some cluck for supper. Can I count on ye?

"Ya need wh't? Mother's in th' kit'chin."

Laurence was used to this sort of conversation with his brother. It wasn't always easy to get through to Conn. "No, I know she's in the kitchen. Ya know how much you like hur fried chicken? Ask her to make some for supper, OK?"

"Chicken? Not chicken. Who you callin' chicken?"

"Er, no, brother! No, not callin' you chicken. You want some cluck for supper?"

"I love Màthair," Conn said. "I love her...love fried bird. How's 'bout you?"

"You love it, and I love it too. Who doesn't love it? You want some for supper?"

"Why? Are we havin' cluck for dinner?"

This talk could go on forever if Laurence allowed it.

"We should have cluck for supper, don't you think? I think you should ask Màthair to cook cluck for us, don't you?

"Oh then, you think we could have cluck for supper? Should I ask her to cook cluck?"

"Yes, brother, yes! Why don't you go on in now an' ask her to cook it?

"Yeah, maybe I jus' will! Jus' will." Conn ran toward the house.

In the kitchen, Mariam was just putting a batch of biscuits into the oven. She turned around and gasped at Conn's standing outside the doorway, his nose bulging the screen in. "Oh, you sturtled me, Connie!"

He stood still like a deer in headlights, staring through the screen, smiling toothlessly.

"Cum in, cum in, thun!" He nearly broke the screen, but he found the handle and bolted inside. "Connie, wha'd ya wunt thun, my fine boy?"

He wasn't sure he knew. His brother had him on a mission. What was it? He searched the kitchen for a reminder. Then he saw the painted wooden rooster on the windowsill. "That," was all he said.

"The rooster, the ròc? Ya'canno 'ave it! It's decura-shun. Your sister, Mary Clover, guv to me for me burthday."

"That!" Conn said again.

"Me bonny lad, it's not yurs. It be mine."

"Cluck."

"Cluck...cluck? Oh, you want cluck, Connie?"

Conn nodded vigorously. "Yes, ma'amma!"

"You want fried chicken, me funny, bonniest boy? I don't have any, dear man of mine."

"Cluck!"

"Fried cluck for supper?"

Conn jumped up and down in delight. He'd remembered (with the help of the window ròc). "Cluck for supper! Yes!"

Mariam grinned. "Al rit, thun. Tell yur brother to kill a couple of hins and pluck 'em."

"Cluck...pluck!" (Connie had an innate penchant for "Poet, didn't know it" impromptu verse.) He ran out, again almost forgetting the screen. "Laurence, cluck! Cluck...pluck, Laurence!"

Laurence was already outside the henhouse at the chopping block, having beheaded two chickens and working on number three.

"Two, two!" Conn shouted when he reached him.

As Laurence dropped the hatchet on the third hen, he quickly helped Conn understand. "Three, Conn, three! You want to be able to eat *all* the cluck you want, don't you?"

"Three! Yeah, three! Want more for me. Three! More for me!"

Supper, it seemed, would be great. When Mac MacDougal returned home from work, he was excited at the smell of Mariam's fried chicken wafting from the kitchen. He wasn't pleased, however, when he found his coveralls on the porch turned inside out and blackened with soot.

Mary Clover had overheard the whole "cluck setup" while reading her Bible in the living room. She was suspicious of Laurence's motives, especially after Conn had been the conduit for the supper plans. She'd helped Mother prepare the meal. Then everyone sat down at the table for the blessing.

Immediately, Mary Clover noticed Conn was missing for the serving of his "favorite food."

"Where's Conn? He'd never miss this!"

Just then a cacophony of cackles and squawks erupted from the hen-house. High-pitched shrieks were punctuated by thuds, interrupted by more screeching. Mac and Laurence ran out to the coop. There, as if in a trance, was Connie, whispering to himself as he killed the last of the twenty-six hens, "Mary Clover, you are over. Mary Clover, you are over!" The hutch was splattered in blood, as was Conn. Dead hens littered the dirt floor. Only the prized rooster remained, crowing and poking the ground outside.

"Conn, Lad what 'ave you doon?" Mac cried.

"Mary Clover is over. Laurence said three...more for me!"

"Put the hatchet down, Conn!" Laurence pleaded.

By then Mariam and Mary Clover had arrived at the door and were looking in. Seeing the carnage, Mariam screamed. Mary Clover retched and vomited.

"Connie, me bonny bouy," Mariam implored, "poot doown the ax, fur your màthair!"

Conn smiled and flipped the ax in the air. As it tumbled down, it narrowly missed Mac's outstretched hand.

"Bollucks! Yoou pissin' ant, ye coolt of coot off me hand!"

"Dadaidh! Ye neigh not vex hem moore! Please! Me bonny boy, coom whid me!" Mariam said.

"Mary Clover is over! There's more than three for me!" Conn said as he walked out with his mother.

Inside, Laurence retrieved a curiosity from the bloody floor—the wooden rooster from the window sill. It was decapitated, just like the hens. "Whut be that, Laurence?" Mac queried as they went out.

"It's Màthair's carved rooster from the kitchen. It's been whacked too!" Indeed, it was a headless cock.

Mary Clover was close by and heard Laurence. "That's whut he said, Dadaidh! Did you not hear? 'Mary Clover is over!' He kept saying that, Mary Clover is over! Dadaidh! He meant that for me!" She pointed to the remains of the carving.

Mac was enraged and confused. Was his gentle boy a psychotic menace? Was he a potential murderous danger to the family? He ordered Laurence to clean up the mess in the coop. Laurence didn't object.

Mariam already had Conn in the trough that doubled as the men's bathtub around the side of the house. Conn was silly with delight to be taking a bath. He continued to whisper the mantra, "Mary Clover, you are over," over and over.

Mary Clover slept on the floor in the bedroom with Mac and Mariam that night. The next morning the sheriff arrived and put Conn in the car to drive to the Texas Asylum for the Insane. Mariam cried and begged Mac not to send him.

Mac did not listen. Mary Clover was relieved for him to go.

That day Laurence performed his duties at the water stop, as usual. He was overloaded with fried chicken for the engineer. He would become his apprentice, and he would never return home again.

# CHAPTER 18

# THET OL' CREOLE MUSIQUE

As spring of 1938 came, Gordy and Callum had built and torn down the Allison 1710 engine countless times. They worked on multiple P-36s as they migrated through March Airfield. They were still isolated from their fellow soldiers, often working nights and weekends. They saw the planes arrive and heard them take off. The same aircraft never returned for maintenance or teardown. Now trusting their skills, Sgt. Wang was often gone for days. They believed he was flying some of the Hawks and some Peashooters in and out. The planes were ultimately destined for China and the Philippines.

As time went on, whatever they were asked to do, the brothers completed, including working on several Northrop A-17A dive-bombers. They were doing safety inspections on the newly developed retractable landing gear. There were 129 A-17s in service. Again, the aircraft were deployed to parts unknown.

When Sgt. Wang was with the boys in the hangar, he seemed obsessed with the Allison. As things were getting darker in Europe and China, the search for a US fighter that could compete with the Messerschmitt Bf-109, Focke-Wulf Fw 190 and the Mitsubishi A6M Zero became critical. Unknown to Callum and Gordy, the good sergeant was in close contact with Lockheed in Southern California. He had procured the 1710 engine through a cousin who worked there in February and had it delivered in early March.

"How long are we going to continue to work here, Gordy?" Callum asked in frustration. "How many times can we tear down and build back this stupid engine?"

"How long, you ask?" Gordy snarled, "as long as they tell us to, brother! What, are you unhappy with, the pay? The Swede's cooking?"

"No, not at all. I just would like to know where this is going."

"We do and don't know, Cal. Germany's annexed Austria without a shot and under threat of a Luftwaffe blitz, and the Japanese are killing thousands in China. I fear their air force will dominate the Pacific. What we don't know is who we'll be fighting. What we do know is we'll be working—working to keep our planes flying. Working to keep our family fed. Working, as you planned, to stay well behind the front lines."

As they continued to toil for Maj. Pearson and Sgt. Wang, the diversity of aircraft struck them. The P-26 Peashooter, the P-36 Hawk, the A-17s, even some Martin B-10 bombers and the Allison engine seemed like transitions to better fighters and bombers but not necessarily the answers to the enemies' aircraft fleets.

By October, just as Callum's exasperation piqued with the monotony of the engine work, yet another variable was introduced when they heard three loud bangs at the hangar door. "Open up, corporals, it's Sergeant Wang!" They dutifully flung up the huge heavy door. There stood Sgt. Wang behind a hand-lift pallet, a large tarped lump upon it.

"Corporals."

They stood at attention.

"At ease, corporals. I'm here to deliver your next challenge." Sgt. Wang pushed the lift into the hangar. "Close the door, gentlemen." Together, they pulled it down.

Pulling the tarp off, Sgt. Wang revealed another engine. "Corporals, meet our friend the Pratt and Whitney Twin Wasp!" He seemed as excited as a kid opening Christmas gifts.

"Radial. Nine cylinders, air-cooled, sir!" Gordy exclaimed.

"You gentlemen are, as usual, on top of it," Wang said. "But look closer, corporals. This one has two rows and fourteen cylinders—a twin wasp!"

Callum couldn't help himself. "Pardon me, Sergeant! What good is another engine without an aircraft?"

"Why do you ask, Corporal Ward?"

"Begging your pardon, are we expected to tear down and rebuild this engine too?"

"That is correct, Corporal."

"But pardon me, we don't know which plane this goes with, Sergeant."

"Indeed you don't. You might have an idea, but you shouldn't guess at this point."

"We've worked on numerous Peashooters, some Hawks, and a Douglas O-38 with radials, sir," Gordy said, attempting to salve Callum's frustration.

"Yes you have. And it might be a good assumption that it's an upgrade for a P-36, but not so. They're retooling to Allisons. You remember I worked at Curtiss, right? With the exception of the Rolls Royce Merlin, you have the two most capable pursuit plane engines in your possession!"

*What's with this guy?* Callum wondered. Is he trying to prove he can procure aircraft engines at will for kicks or just to continue to aggravate us?

"Yes, Sergeant," they answered in unison.

"Well, I've said too much. Get back to work."

Callum was angered by Sgt. Wang's cryptic statement and breathed an irritated sigh.

Wang turned back. "What was that, Corporal?"

"Nothing, Sergeant. It was nothing."

Callum needed to be more careful. March Airfield was the general headquarters of the US Air Force. Who knew what power Sgt. Wang and Maj. Pearson actually possessed?

The rest of the year continued to be tedious. An early design P-36 came in for retrofitting of an Allison engine. That, at least, required a new binder and more interesting precise work. Again, Sgt. Wang flew away, this time for even longer. Gordy and Callum speculated he was helping to train and further build the Chinese Nationalist Air Force.

For the better part of two years, Callum and Gordy tore down and rebuilt the Allison and/or Curtiss engines. They continued to be tested (and surpassed expectations) to adjust as improvements and different versions of aircraft and engines quickly advanced. They began to train other mechanics brought in from other bases in California at March. They enjoyed the challenge of training but noticed that only a few students shared their passion for perfection.

Training was always conducted outside of their "inner sanctum" hangar, sometimes in the blistering heat. Callum was a whiz at the technical side of the engines and the controls. He had a way of translating complicated information into simple steps. Gordy liked to use similes, though he never called them that. "The Allison's oil pressure is like an old lady's temper. One minute she's running even, the next moment she's through the roof!" They were both looking for signals that something different was to happen. Extensive squadron training with full ground crews and armorers was yet to come.

****

In the wee-hours of the morning in early September, Callum awakened to the unique sound of Wright radial engines overhead and listened as they feathered on landing. He didn't think much of it because Douglas B-18 Bolo bombers were deployed at March and often ferried between there and Hamilton Field in Northern California. Within moments, he also heard the buzz of a Pratt & Whitney R-1535 Twin Wasp, likely an old Northrop A-17. That too was not unusual.

However, at breakfast, feasting on Pvt. Lundgren's Kanelbullar rolls, he and Gordy were surprised to be joined by Maj. Pearson. He praised their work and then ordered Callum to fly up to Hamilton immediately. Callum knew not to ask why because the major's favorite reply was "For me to know and you to find out." Cal was not excited to do so, but of course, he obeyed. Further orders would come at Hamilton.

A pilot arrived to pick him up at the barracks and quickly took him out on the tarmac. To Callum's surprise, he spoke with a French accent.

"Je suis Lieutenant Amos Jean-Louis. I am a Haitian pilot, and yes, I'm a Negro. And yes, I am a pilot and eest an excellent one. Rumor has it you ur from Texas. Tha-et won't be a problem, I assume-a?"

"Uh, how would that be an issue, Lieutenant?" Callum asked.

"Vous people from Dixie are zee th' problem."

"Sir, I believe you have mistaken me for someone else. I am a proud United States Army Air Corps soldier from Texas. I am *not* about Dixie. Besides, sir, you outrank me, regardless."

"Abien. Allons-y."

Callum wished Gordy was there to interpret the French and witness the encounter. Even though the boys had relatives in Mississippi of "unfortunate Klan affiliation," they both were sons of Texas. Mary Mother had unsuccessfully tried to convince them that the South would rise again.

Callum realized they had arrived at the plane. It was an old A-17 Nomad two-seater with fixed landing gear. He thought, *What? Am I flying in this old thing? Lord Jesus, protect me!* He needed still more divine intervention. He couldn't bring himself to tell Lt. Jean-Louis that he'd never flown before, and he was about to do so with someone who suspected he was a bigot.

Panicking in the moment, Callum blurted-out, "Where'd you get this bucket of bolts?"

Lt. Jean-Louis was duly insulted. "Uh, mais no! You joost di'nut cull Manman ("Mom" in Haitian Creole, his nickname for his Nomad) le bucket de bolts!' Let me tell you soma-thing, Coporale Monsieur: this a-thi-ang eest my fighter trainer. I am toop of muh class, eh! I was awarded her fur dat! Get in, and strap oop!"

Wondering what "Manman" meant, Callum climbed into the observer seat. "I am *so* sorry, Lieutenant Jean-Louis, sir! I am sorry! Please, sir, I've never flown, sir!" The sputter and howl of the Twin Wasp engine drowned out his pleas. The chucks holding the plane were removed by the ground crewman, and they began taxiing. Callum frantically looked for a Douglas B-18 and pointed at it. "Let me take that, please! I want *that*, sir!" Lt. Jean-Louis was too busy to hear or more likely too angry to listen.

Callum prayed harder as the lieutenant asked the tower for clearance. Callum had barely gotten his flight headgear and goggles on when Lt. Jean-Louis pushed Manman to full throttle, released the brake with a jolt, and sped down the runway. In seconds, Callum was aloft and screaming. "Lordy, Lordy, Lordy!" It was about two hours to Hamilton. He had plenty of time to "Lordy" more and more.

Lt. Jean-Louis was a great pilot. The flight along the beautiful California coast was uneventful except for some turbulence. On the way, the good lieutenant sang at the top of his lungs, his voice even audible over the sound of the radial engine. He kept repeating "Wongolo, Wale!" in a perfect baritone register. It was a traditional Haitian folk song celebrating a sixteenth-century Angolan king. He varied his singing cadence from slow, almost weeping, to quick and rhythmic. Still praying out loud, Callum was somehow calmed by Lt. Jean-Louis's voice.

As they approached Hamilton, the field was shrouded by clouds. Cal heard chatter between the lieutenant and the tower. He assumed they were cleared to land. Instead, they climbed up hard to a point where Cal thought they would stall out. Lt. Jean-Louis then rolled Manman over, and screamed down through the clouds below the ceiling. At the last moment, he pulled hard, trimmed, and lined up the now-visible runway. Then he cut power and pinpointed the landing.

Afterward, Callum staggered down off the wing and vomited.

"Wongolo, Wale," Lt. Jean-Louis sang in a whisper. They climbed into a waiting jeep and drove to Hamilton headquarters.

After entering a large building, they were ushered into a room with a huge conference table with all but two of the twelve seats occupied. Callum thought he recognized the figure at the head of the table. The bald, wide lieutenant colonel puffing on a cigarette slowly stood up after Lt. Jean-Louis said, "Attention!", his hat half on. Salutes were exchanged. Major C. J. Laughlin held his salute for Corporal Ward. "Welcome to Hamilton, Corporal. Welcome back, Lieutenant Jean-Louis. Safe flight?"

"Yes, sur. Sava, sur!" Jean-Louis replied.

"At ease, y'all. Did the lieutenant do his patented roll/dive/land for y'all, Corporal?"

Callum belched. "Yes, sir. He did, sir!" This brought laughter from several USAAC folks sitting along the walls around the table.

"Ward and Jean-Louis, y'all be seated up here."

They took seats at the front, flanking Lt. Colonel Laughlin on both sides. Some of the uniforms were unfamiliar to Callum. Lt. Jean-Louis was not surprised. Air forces from France, the Soviet Union, and Britain were represented. Laughlin let fall a large front/side blow-up schematic of a Bell P-39 Airacobra attached to a blackboard. "Gentlemen, as most of you know, this is the Bell P-39D Airacobra power plant, the Allison V-1720. It's a V-12, liquid-cooled, y'all. Unique design. The Allison is behind the cockpit. It has a ten-foot driveshaft. It also has new heavy armor, 256 pounds, two M2 .50 cal. Browning machine guns mounted in the nose, and a 37-mm Oldsmobile (AAC) cannon, around which the aircraft was originally designed. Corporal Ward, will you detail the Allison for us?"

Callum was speechless and breathless at the same time, certain there were men in the room who were more qualified to do that than a seventeen-year-old corporal.

"Corporal Ward?"

"Uh, yes, sir. I will do that, sir." He stood at attention as the major set down a schematic of the Allison.

"Y'all at ease, Corporal!"

"Yes, sir. At ease." This brought more snickers from the audience. "Sirs, this is the Allison V-1710. I believe this one is an E18 design, slightly different than the one I've worked on. It has twelve pistons in a V alignment. It's liquid cooled and has reduction gears. This model supersedes the original with 1,150 horsepower at 2,950 revolutions per minute. This engine does not have a displacement or alloying material turbo-supercharger, either of which would increase its performance at higher altitudes, though both would require more technical maintenance. They also would present fuel-air mixture problems. This engine is reliable and easy to maintain. It would be better protected and be easier to access positioned as it is here mid-fuselage.

"In summary, sirs, the V-1710 is a tough, reliable engine. Fuel mixture and oil pressures must be checked between flights to prevent lock-up. These challenges can be manually addressed in flight, if necessary. It's been said the Allison's oil pressure is like an old lady's temper: one minute's she's running even, the next moment she's through the roof!'"

The room erupted in laughter. Callum's audience was stunned. What was that?

"Gentlemen, please join us outside for a demonstration of the P-39's capabilities." Laughlin motioned to the door. Callum had noticed Lt. Jean-Louis's departure at the beginning of his presentation (perhaps a passive-aggressive payback for the "bucket of bolts" insult?).

Outside in the cockpit of a modified experimental P-39, its engine turning, sat Lt. Jean-Louis. The plane appeared to have been upgraded with increased armor and a drop tank. The lieutenant taxied and took off. He performed limited aerobatics while flying over the field (rumors of the aircraft tumbling end over end later proved false). He climbed out, rolled, dived, and returned to low strafing/close bombing levels above the field over and over again. On the whole, the performance was described by one of the Brits as "just adequate." It was, however, enough to convince the Brits, the French, the Russians, and the USAAC to place orders for the Airacobra. The Russians and the Brits did so under President Roosevelt's Lend-Lease program. The French order was never delivered after their armistice with Germany in 1940. Callum was kept at Hamilton for two months to help train more mechanics on the Allison engine.

He flew back to March in late November, stuffed in the bowels of a B-18 Bolo (nicknamed the "Digby"). Callum had another name for it: the "Dudby." He'd often and unwillingly been lectured (well into the night) by his brother on the merits and deficits of several bombers. Convinced Gordy was right about the Bolo, he wasn't happy when the plane hit heavy weather along the coast. Tossed and turned, he remembered his first flight with Lt. Jean-Louis. The constant sensation of his stomach dropping through the bottom of his feet made him long for his Haitian tormentor.

He tried in vain to remember Jean Louis's song. He sang "Wongolo" to himself, to no avail.

****

Gordy and Callum both concluded that Sgt. Wang had bet on the wrong horse by choosing the radial Curtiss power plant for the P-36 and its successor, the P-40. The Allison won out because of its profile, which better fit the Warhawk's sleeker and more aerodynamic nose. They were unable to say "We told you so" though because Wang was in the Pacific and China helping train pilots, mechanics, and flying hot "training" missions.

In time the boys were allowed to travel on leave in Southern California. They had a cousin, Francis Ward, in Fullerton and often spent weekends at his orchard farm. He and his wife, Leah, supplied fresh fruit for many of the commercial pie makers in Orange County.

Frankie was an entrepreneur who had established a frozen dessert company. He was working out how to sell fresh flash-frozen pies. Gordy and Callum helped with picking fruit and delivering pies.

Frankie and Leah loved to go to the beach. So did the boys. At Laguna Beach one day, Frankie convinced the boys they should start a car battery business. "Batteries will be in high demand and short supply when war comes," he said. Frankie seeded the money for them to do so. Since their leaves weren't consistent, he also ran the business in their absence. Callum and Gordy thought about returning to Southern California someday.

The boys were still spoiled with Private Lundgren's superb cooking. They often thought he should open a Swedish restaurant in the Inland Empire. That was unlikely to happen. He was sequestered at March at their behest. He seemed content with his lot.

As 1940 loomed and Christmas came, the boys received leave to travel back to Texas. They were grateful for the opportunity to visit their siblings.

# CHAPTER 19

# EVERYTHING'S BIGGER, NOT SO MUCH BETTER

Gordy tried to convince Callum that they should fly to Kelly Field on a military transport, but after Callum's experiences with Lt. Jean-Louis and the Digby, he was having nothing of it. They took the train to Dallas instead.

There was more reading and study time for Gordy. He annoyed his brother by reading Moliere in French. "Oh comme c'est bien de savoir une chose ou deux, Callum."

"What?"

"Oh comme c'est bien de savoir une chose ou deux."

"OK, I'll play. What's that mean?"

"Oh, how fine it is to know a thing or two! Ce n'est pas seulement pour ce que nous faisons que nous sommes tenus responsables, mais aussi pour ce que nous ne faisons pas."

"Are these just gonna get worse...and longer?" Callum complained.

"It's not only for what we do we are held responsible but also for what we do not do."

"Please stop! I'm buckin' for sergeant."

"What, servicing P-39 Peashooters?" Gordy retorted.

"We could do worse. You and me at Hamilton working for Major 'More Beers for Him.'"

"The plane's got issues," Gordy countered. "What exactly is a mid-altitude fighter? I think it means it's got 'mid-limitations.' It's fodder for any aircraft that is faster or flies higher. Rumor has it there's an upgrade coming to the P-36 Hawk. By comparison, that's likely to be way better! I'd be inclined to wait to work on it."

"I know the Allison, Gordy. I know it so well I can teach it in my sleep. Either way, we win. We should look into what Hamilton could hold for us."

"You think Major Pearson and Sergeant Wang might have something to say about that?" Gordy asked. "You know, they just might not let their two best mechanics/trainers go that easily, don't you think? I don't believe so. But we'll see. And you, as always, should pray about it."

"OK."

Callum continued to study the Airacobra well into the night; he fell asleep doing so. When he awakened, the train was passing into Texas. He was a Texan and a proud member of the United States Army Air Corps. He was also one of the best mechanics in the Air Corps, and he was praying he could convince his brother to go with him to Northern California. For the first time in his life, he realized they might be separated, and that frightened him more than anything (even flying).

****

As the boys' train pulled into Dallas, they were reluctant to go directly home. To their surprise, Izzie and Conn were there to meet them outside the depot in their dad's old Model T.

"What are you guys doin' here?" Gordy asked.

"Mother, she checked the train schedules and figured this was the only train you'd be on," Izzy replied.

"Who drove you here?" Callum asked. "Please don't tell me it was Conn!"

"Nope. I did." The brothers looked at each other and then at Izzie, realizing that at age twelve, he looked like he was sixteen or seventeen.

"You do know you need to have a license to drive in Texas, right?" Gordy queried.

Izzie smiled confidently. "I pray before I start the car. I'm a good driver, and I practice practically every day. Conn comes with me. Nobody ever checks."

"That doesn't instill great confidence, Izzie! Conn has never driven!

Izzie shrugged. "Well, I sort of have that under control."

"Uh, under control?" Callum said. "How's that?"

"I kinda changed my birth certificate date to 1923." Izzie pulled out his birth certificate and showed it to Gordy.

Gordy chuckled. "What? You, the Baptist preacher boy?"

"I'm not a preacher boy! If I get stopped, I'll just tell 'em I'm on the way to get my license."

Callum smiled. "Yes, be sure to do that!"

Gordy looked around. "Wait, Conn? Where'd he go? Conn!"

Around the corner in the alley, they heard a commotion—trash cans being overturned. The three brothers ran to the alley. There was Conn, gleefully kicking over every can he found, his arms flailing like chicken wings. "Cluck, cluck, cluck!" he yelled as he went.

"Conn, stop! Stop it! No cluck!" Izzie, aware of the "cluck incident," as told by Mary Mother, took Conn by the arm and led him across the street to an ice cream parlor. The boys picked up the cans and the garbage, then went for a malted milk with their uncle and brother. They agreed they'd keep the garbage can incident between them. Callum drove home.

The house at 927 Oak Park had never looked worse. Brambles and weeds had overgrown the yard, and trash was strewn about. Then there was the outhouse, smelly and close to falling down. They realized everything at home in Texas was bigger, including the messes, and not so much better.

****

Mary Mother was happy to see the boys, though unable to afford a Christmas dinner, so the boys bought the turkey and fixings. They were disappointed to know that Miri and Tim were still in Itasca. So, on Christmas Eve, they took the Model T down to retrieve the kids. This angered Mary Mother because they likely would not make it back to attend services at First Baptist.

Upon their arrival at the Presbyterian home, their hearts sank. In the front yard was trash. It was almost as unkempt as their mother's home. Several children were perched on the front steps. It was cold. Out through the front door rushed the home's director, Helga Schneider, shooing the children inside.

"Ja, who are you?" she asked.

"Frau Schneider, you may not remember us," Callum replied. "This is my brother, Gordy, and I'm Callum Ward."

"Ja, ja, ja. Wards! How is your mutter?"

"She's well, Vielen Dank," Gordy replied.

"Sprichst du Deutsch?" (You speak German?)

"Ja, ein bisschen. Ich lerne." (A little bit, I am learning.)

"Hereinkommen!" (Come in!)

The boys followed her through the door. Inside, it was almost as cold as it was outside. About fifteen to twenty kids sat on the floor or leaned on the walls. They appeared clean, but they were dressed in shabby clothing.

Then, from the end of the long hallway came shrieks of joy. Miri and Tim ran to their brothers and hugged them wildly. "Brothers! Brothers! Oh, brothers!" they screamed. Miri refused to let go of Gordy. As she held on for dear life, he explained they were taking their siblings home to celebrate Christmas.

"Ja, eest goot!" Frau Schneider replied. "I git thur coats."

Still in Miri's death grip, Gordy asked how she was. She broke into tears. "Oh, Miri Anna, don't cry, we're here!" He leaned over to wipe her tears. She tightened her grip.

"You're here, Gordy! You're here Callum! You're both here!"

Gordy welled up. "Yes we are."

Frau Schneider brought their coats and a shabby pair of shoes for Tim. For his part, a frown was all he could muster. He said nothing.

"Are those Tim's shoes?" Gordy's ire with the director was apparent.

"I am sorry, misters. Da church been limited w' da monies. We make do. We make do."

"How many children are here, Frau?"

"Eest thirty-eight, Herr. We make do. We feed. The church hast small monies for us."

"Pardon a moment, Frau, bitte?" Gordy, with Miri still attached, huddled with Callum. "Mother!" he whispered in exasperation. "We must do something!"

"How much cash do you have, Gordy?" Callum asked. "I have sixty dollars."

Gordy checked his wallet. "I have eighty-five. How about we give it all to Frau Schneider as a Christmas offering?"

Callum added, "On the condition she buys food and shoes for the kids?"

"Yes! Ja, ja, ja!"

As they left, they put the money in her hand. She burst into tears. "Christus sei mit dir! Christus sie mit euch beiden!" (Christ be with you! Christ be with you both!)

As they turned around to head back to Dallas, they noticed the children had returned to the front steps. They didn't wave goodbye, just watched forlornly for the next car to arrive.

****

The Model T provided little warmth, save that from the engine. Gordy drove with Miri nestled against him. Callum shivered in the back with Tim. He covered Tim's shredded shoes with the corner of his service coat, his hands in the pockets. Gordy whispered some lines from Robert Browning to Miri.

> *Small feet were pattering, wooden shoes clattering,*
> *Little hands clapping, and little tongues chattering; and*
> *like fowls in a farmyard when barley is scattering,*
> *Out came the children running: All the little boys and girls,*
> *With rosy cheeks and flaxen curls,*
> *And sparkling eyes and teeth like pearls,*
> *Tripping and skipping, ran merrily after*
> *the wonderful music with shouting and laughter.*

"Say it again, brother! Say it again!" Miri pleaded over and over. By the time they stopped in Ft. Worth for gas, they all had memorized it and repeated it over and over on the way to Dallas, their "rats extermination Christmas carol."

By the time they reached First Baptist for the post-service Christmas supper, they were full of joy. Mary Mother was not. She shamed them for missing the service. Joined with Izzie at the church, they laughed at her rebuke. She was confused and unamused. They were grateful for their first Noel together with their siblings.

On Christmas morning, the "men of the house" refused to go to church again, though Izzie argued that they should. Instead, they cleaned the yard and made the outhouse new with a lye coating. After Mary Mother returned home, Gordy confronted her in the kitchen.

"What have you done, Mother?"

"What? Whatever do you mean? Other than try to keep everyone alive after your father died?"

"No. What have you done to Miri and Tim?"

"How dare you! I've done my best with so very little!"

"Do you know that the Presbyterian home is without adequate funds?"

"I was assured by Mrs. Schneider—"

"Frau Schneider is barely holding on. She's the one doing without. She's desperate!"

"She's a good woman, I have nothing against her."

"She has thirty-eight children, Miri and Tim amongst them, and practically no money to support them. She can barely keep them fed. What can you do through First Baptist to help?"

"I can do nothing! They're Presbyterians; we're Baptists."

"And there you have it, denominations of Christians separated by their names and tenets. Are you all not followers of Jesus, believers in His mercy and grace?"

"Bite your tongue, child! Of course we are, but we're not all the same."

"I will not be quiet, Mother. 'Suffer the little children.' You need to approach Dr. Truett and the elders. Either that or we need to bring Miri and Tim here to live with you."

"I cannot. We cannot. You know how little I make at the cemetery! They will be worse off here."

"Callum and I are doing well. We send money to support you, Isaiah, Laurence, Conn, and the kids. How much more do you need to bring them home?"

"We are barely scraping by." She thought for a moment. "At least one hundred dollars more a month." Gordy realized that he and Callum combined made a little over $140 per month.

"I'll talk with Callum about that. Or we'll be supporting the Frau down at Itasca."

"You'll *not* give me an ultimatum! I'm your mother!"

Gordy became incensed. "You are 'the mother,' but you are not our mother!"

"You impudent boy! You'll not talk to me this way!"

"I'll talk with Callum. By the time we go back to California, you need to decide."

"Out! Get out! No more of your rebellion. I won't have it!"

"No...no, you won't. You will decide though."

Gordy walked out and found Callum working in the garden. "I need to talk with you. Now."

Sadly, by the end of their leave in the second week of January 1941, Mary Mother refused to move Miri and Tim back to Dallas. Gordy called Frau Schneider and asked to meet with her. They drove the kids back down to Itasca. Miri was screaming and ranting as they went into the orphanage.

In Frau Schneider's small office, the door always open to monitor the kids, Gordy detailed how Callum and he were committed to sending one hundred dollars per month to the orphanage. They only had three provisos. One, that the children be well fed. Two, that the children each receive a new set of clothes by year's end. Three, that each child receive new shoes in the same time frame.

Frau Schneider agreed. Then she got up and closed the door, turning to face them. "Sid sind beide ein Segen fur die Kinder und mich." (You are both a blessing to the children and me.) "Entschuldigung (Pardon), Herr Callum. I forget you do not speak the German. I have to tell you both something."

"Of course, Frau Schneider. What do you want to share with us?"

"I am, how you say, a 'completed Jew.' My parents sent me here from Cologne three years ago. They know a Presby minister in Dallas. Dey send me here to him and his wife. I pray fur my parents' safety in Germany. They still there! The Nazis hate de Jews; they kill de Jews. The Presby minister tell me 'bout Jesus. I become Christian. I ask dis favor. I try to get my parents out. I have done savings. May I wire dem ten dollars per month to come out, please?"

Gordy and Callum looked at each other. Then they nodded in agreement. "You are a good director, Frau, a good manager," Gordy said. "We know you make do with very little. If you can find ten dollars per month from our contributions to help your parents, please send them the money."

She stood up, stomped her foot, and raised her hands together in prayer. "Dank, Jesus! Dank, dank Jesus!" She hugged them tight and then opened the door. Miri and Tim were waiting in the hall. Callum and Gordy knelt down and hugged them. "We'll be back! We promise. Teach Frau Schneider about tripping and skipping, running merrily after the wonderful music with shouting and laughter. We're coming back!"

The train ride back to Los Angeles seemed shorter than the trip home. Gordy didn't cite foreign playwrights or languages. Callum closed his eyes and visualized the Allison in his mind's eye. He slept more. They missed their brothers and sister. They knew that Izzie could take care of himself and would do so at the cemetery and at the CCC camps with the help of Lefty Burress. They were going back to March to work for their siblings, a kind German Christian woman; her Jewish parents, and some very needy kids in Itasca, Texas.

# CHAPTER 20

# PUH-KHAN, PEACH, AND <u>NOT</u> SWEET POTATER PIES

Gordy and Callum's return to March afforded them the opportunity to work on several P-40 Warhawks. The Air Corps brass had made the Allison the golden boy of fighter engines for the time being. The P-40 was quickly becoming a premier fighter aircraft. At medium to high speeds, it had turning and strength advantages over the Japanese AM6 Zero and the Nakajima Ki-43. Later known as the Kittyhawk, the P-40 was in heavy production. March Field was home to the 9th Pursuit Wing, which was composed of the 14th and the 51st squadrons. The P-40 quickly became their preferred fighter. Full squadrons were preparing for potential operations in the Pacific. Air Force Command, pilots, mechanics, and armorers were coordinating war games over the Mojave Desert.

Sergeant Wang was back, only now he was Lieutenant Wang. He became heavily involved in P-40 training. The boys couldn't ask about his exploits in the Pacific or China. They surmised that he was a catalyst for aircraft deployment and training happening there. Early every morning, he flew a Warhawk west over the ocean. It was his chi (life's breath). He spent precisely one hour and twenty minutes in the air every day. On his return, he taxied in front of Callum and Gordy's hangar to check in on their activities. He conveniently arrived in time to enjoy Lundgren's Swedish breakfasts with the boys.

"What are your thoughts on the Warhawk?" he asked one morning while enjoying Swedish gravlax with Private Lundgren's own mustard dill sauce and deli bagels.

"Seems like a vast improvement over the P-36," Callum replied.

Lt. Wang nodded. "Yes, yes, it is. Stronger and more maneuverable. Easy to learn, easy to fly, turns on a dime."

Gordy knew never to ask the lieutenant a direct question about his work. Instead, he made a statement. "There are so many P-40s streaming through here, so many for only two squadrons, sir. I assume they're being deployed elsewhere."

"Good assumption, Corporal. Lots of planes, lots of pilots, and lots of training. It's good, and the more experienced, the better."

"How about the Airacobra, sir?" Callum's question drew a disapproving glare from the lieutenant.

"I trained on them at Hamilton." Lt. Wang paused, drew a breath and looked contemplative. "Have flown a couple. Like the design. Good pilot's plane. Convenient to maintain. Not bad."

"So, 'not bad' isn't good?" Callum asked.

"Not bad is *not bad*. The Allison engine is good. There are some aircraft that it's better in though."

With that, Wang stood up. "Make sure she's ready again for me tomorrow morning. Thanks."

Callum and Gordy were left to ponder if he meant that the P-40 with the Allison was superior or if there was another aircraft.

The pilot training line at March extended beyond the 9th Pursuit Wing. There was another group of pilots who didn't wear standard-issue USAAC uniforms. Gordy had noticed one of them leaving Private Lundgren's kitchen. He visually tracked him back to a barracks considerably larger than theirs.

Then, within moments, he saw twelve pilots drive out in four jeeps past the active tarmac around the mountain. From an auxiliary runway there, he'd seen P-40s take off. Soon he heard the sound of Allisons firing up, and shortly thereafter he saw six and then another six P-40s ascending aloft. They flew east toward the Muroc Dry Lake bombing range. Gordy later witnessed rotation of several sets of pilots manning the same P-40s. He and Callum were not maintaining those aircraft. *If we're Special Projects,* he thought, *they are some other special something, ergo, none of our business.*

Behind the scenes, Lt. Wang and his colleagues associated with "Old Leatherface," USAAC Retired Captain Claire Chennault, who had quietly recruited pilots with interceptor/pursuit experience to build a mercenary air force for the nationalist Chinese. In 1939, Chiang Kai-Shek sent him to the US to find planes, pilots, and mechanics. Chennault was Kai-Shek's chief air advisor. His efforts with Banks and the US government failed, but key flight personnel began traveling to central and western China, posing as "tourists or adventurers."

Lt. Wang took off as expected the next morning. The boys were concerned when he didn't join them for breakfast and didn't roll up to the hangar. Hours later, he finally arrived. Gordy greeted the lieutenant and invited him to dinner. Wang agreed on one condition: he wanted nose paint for his P-40. He had a template made up with the Chinese character 氣 (chi). He wanted it in red on both sides. They ate together and invited him to join in the markings. The lieutenant made sure it was installed right side up! He reveled in doing so.

****

It was nearly two months before Callum and Gordy got a weekend leave. They were anxious to see Frankie and Leah. They invited Private Lundgren to join them in Fullerton. He was excited to go along.

The train followed down through the Santa Ana Canyon, which was full of fragrant orange orchards. Lundgren hadn't ventured farther than Riverside, close to the base.

Arriving at the Wards' house, Lundgren was ecstatic. First, there was an amazing aroma—Leah was busy baking in the kitchen, and in her enormous double oven were pies. Surprise!

"Vad händer...er...Whut's cookin'?" Lundgren practically shouted after introductions from Callum and Gordy.

Leah pulled out two pies. "Puh-khan and peach pies, Erik."

"Puh-khan?"

"That's right, Erik, dear. Never let me hear you say, 'Pee-can,' understood? We're southern people."

"Ja. Sure, ma'am."

"Also, never call me 'ma'am' again. It makes me feel like I've become my mother. Old, don't you know?"

"Ja. OK. Will never, fur sure. Callum and Gordy have tolt me 'bout yur pies."

"You betcha they did, and if we have anything here, it's lots and lots of pies!"

"I'm from Minnesota, don' ya know?" Erik proclaimed proudly.

"Oh, we've heard all about you, Mr. Chef, the Swede! They've raved about your cooking since they first visited us here. Perhaps you'll give me your thoughts on our pies?"

"Ja, visst...Wait, no! They're *your* pies, ja? No one should tell you about your pies!"

Leah laughed. "Well I like that! Frankie's *never* satisfied with my pies!"

Leah pulled out eight pies to cool. Frankie led the boys out behind the house to an enormous walk-in freezer. "This is where it all happens, gentlemen!"

They put on hooded coats, stocking caps, and gloves, which they found hanging outside. Frankie pulled a large lever on the door, and they walked into the seven-foot-high room, which was kept at a constant thirty degrees. Left and right, back to front, stacked high on shelves seven inches apart were frozen pies. "We're working on flash-freezing pies for distribution here in Southern California," Frankie said. "We're starting here in Orange County with six freezer trucks. We have orders, starting with restaurants, from San Clemente to Newport Beach and inland to here. Leah's working on different crusts that do better when frozen. We're doing apple, cherry, peach, pumpkin, and of course, puh-khan."

"Are those Swedish apples?" Lundgren shouted over the noisy refrigeration motor.

"Actually, I don't know," Frankie replied, flummoxed by the question. Were apple pies Swedish? "You should ask Leah when we go back in."

"You ever made rhubarb?" Lundgren asked.

"Uh, don't think so. Maybe ask Leah."

"Sur will, ja will."

The boys were surprised by all the words flowing out of their private. He'd barely said anything to them at all at the field.

Continuing the tour, Frankie pointed out that they were keeping the labeled cardboard boxes in the back of the freezer so as to have them at the same temperature as the pies. "You're motivated to get them in the boxes before you freeze too!"

The boys and Frankie showed Lundgren the rest of the property, which was rife with apple, cherry, and peach orchards. "We buy pumpkins and puh-khans from local farmers," Frankie explained. "Keeps us in good with our neighbors."

"You grow sweet potaters, eh?" Lundgren asked. "Sweet potaters are better than pumpkin for pies."

"No, no we don't. We're focusing on five kinds of pies: apple, cherry..."

"Sur, rhubarb and sweet potaters make fine pies."

"Yeah, I'm sure they do."

Returning to the house, Lundgren began his interrogation of Leah. "Is your crust Swedish? How about crumble, have you tried sweet crumble? How 'bout molasses for the puh-khan filling? What about rhubarb? Strawberry? Strawberry-rhubarb? Why not sweet potaters?"

Leah was exhausted and relieved when the boys asked Lundgren to accompany them in the delivery truck. Three abreast in the cab was crowded, but at least the private was out of Leah and Frankie's hair.

The truck was a new Dodge with a special frame for the freezer box. Compared to the Model-T and the trucks on the base, it drove like a dream. They went south toward Orange and Santa Ana.

"How'd you end up at March, Private?" Callum asked.

"From Minnesota. Bemidji, to be exact, sur."

"Bud-midy...who? What?"

"B-e-m-i-d-j-i, sur. Home of Paul Bunyan and Babe th' Ox, don't ya know'? Th' statues on Lake Bemidji...in the Cass Lake Chain at the head-waters of the Mississippi, sur."

"You have a statue of Paul Bunyan?"

Lundgren nodded. "And Babe the Ox and the Ax, for sure, sur. Uh, sorry, sur! Built in thirty-seven to attract tourists, they say. They be huge. Paul's eighteen feet tall. Blue's ten feet. Huge, don't ya know."

"Yeah, that *is* big. How about when we're off base we're Gordy and Callum and you're Erik, OK?"

"OK, then...ya shur, sir, er, Callum."

"So where is Bemudgery, was it?"

"Bemidji! North of Rosby, east of Wilton, south of Birchmont, and west of Andrusia.

Gordy chuckled. "Andrusia?"

"Ya, fur sur. Named fur Andrew Jackson!"

"Well, *that* explains it all! How'd you end up in California?"

"I cooked at Joe's Lodge, right there on the lake, ya know, and this fella come in from fishin'. He was stayin' at Joe's, and he was a majur in the Army, and don't ya know, he liked my meatballs and macaroni with lingonberries and—"

"Was that Major Pearson?"

"Oh ya...fur sure, but I didn't know him, don't ya know. Not because he's Swedish—Pearson ya know, it's Swedish. Well, he said he thought I'd make it in the Army, don't ya know."

"Yeah, Pearson...Swedish name. So Major Pearson recruited you to be a cook in the Army?"

"Oh no, sur—I mean Gordy! He drove me to recruiting station at Fargo—that's where he's from—and they recruited me. They said I had an aptitude for navigation an' such. Went to school at March while I cooked, and don't ya know..."

"Know what?"

"I kinda, you know...flunked out, kinda. Which I kinda...uh, don't ya know, wished I hadn't."

"You wish you didn't go through nav school, or you wish you didn't flunk out?"

"Both, don' ya know?"

"No, no, I don't."

They pulled down an alley behind Watson Drug Store and Soda Fountain in Orange. Callum and Gordy were in stitches with Pvt. Lundgren's antics. They unloaded thirty frozen apple, cherry, and peach pies.

As they did, Lundgren sat at the soda fountain counter. He ordered a piece of peach pie a la mode with a vanilla malt. *If this is Leah's peach pie, it's stupendous!* he thought. The boys wondered where he'd gone. They found him at the counter talking up the lady soda jerk. "What kinds of pies do you sell? How about cherry or apple and sweet crumble? What do you think sweet potater pie; you serve that? Way better than pumpkin. How's 'bout rhubarb? Strawberry-rhubarb crumble? Like pie with ice cream? I like it on pie an' in a malted. How's 'bout whipped cream? On top of malted?" On and on it went, to the soda jerk's dismay.

They drove farther south, to Corona del Mar, where they delivered eight pies to the Hurley Bell, which had just opened. Matilda MacCulloch, the owner, invited them in. Gordy and Callum declined, but Pvt. Lundgren was entranced by the recreation of Ye Old Bell, an old English inn at Hurley on the Thames. Once again, he resumed his pie cross-examinations. Thanks to another scheduled stop at the Arches Diner in Newport Beach, they cut short their stay. While in Newport they stopped to pick up prawns, fresh tuna, and smoked salmon, at Lundgren's request.

The ride home was filled with a fishy smell.

****

After making their rounds, they were happy to be back at the Wards in Fullerton. Lundgren volunteered to make dinner. With Leah's help he made Smörgåstårta (Swedish sandwich cake). Thanks to Leah's garden for the cucumber and chives, he prepared his infamous dill sauce with a tub of mayonnaise. The Wards were not teetotalers. They broke out schnapps in honor of the meal. Gordy and Callum tried some and weren't impressed. Afterwards, in his Texas drawl, Callum confided to Gordy, "Even my 'snopps' tasted like fish!"

They spent the evening sharing family stories, including the "Whoa Santa" episode. The Ward farm, the orchards, and the relationships would become lasting. Lundgren became a member of the family.

Breakfast was a feast. Lundgren was up at 4:30 a.m. to bake Swedish cinnamon buns. He couldn't find cardamom in the spice cabinet, so he made do with extra cinnamon and butter-sugar frosting. He boiled potatoes and eggs and found some leftover ham and smoked salmon in the refrigerator. He was finished cooking by the time the Wards awakened.

Callum and Gordy filed into the kitchen. The table was set, and coffee was percolating.

A cheerful "God aptit," (good appetite) greeted them.

"Got morgan, is it?" Gordy replied.

"*God* morgan. Tank."

"Wow, Erik," Gordy raved, "you've outdone yourself! Vad händer... is that correct?"

"Ja, is right...what's cooking. We have buns, boiled potaters, eggs, lox—cured wit dill—and ham. Also cheese and my sauce from last night. Coffee?"

Frankie and Leah joined the boys. Frankie grabbed the coffee and served it all around. Callum blessed the food, and then they chowed down.

"Is good, ja?"

"Wonderful, Erik!" Leah said.

The Swede took advantage of the silence around the table. "My family is from the Aland Islands, near Finland, don't ya know? My mother, Tuva, ist teacher. Father ist military. He volunteer last November for Finland against Soviet communists. Bad fur Sweden; against invasion. He culled back to Sweden."

Callum frowned in confusion. "I thought Sweden was neutral."

"Ja, neutral! We defend Aland for Sweden. We help da Brits."

"Uh, how do you do that without angering the Germans?" Gordy asked.

"We keep distance; stay careful. We careful. Germany is hope to take over Denmark and Norway. They have need for iron. Must have Denmark to take Norway iron. They also need keep North Sea from Brits."

"Where's your mother?" Callum asked.

"She is in Bemidji with my Aunt Nova, her sister. She teaches high school there."

"And your father?"

"He work intelligens on trade wid Germany."

"Wait, what? Your father is working for Germany?"

"Nej, no! He work intelligens. He's defend Sweden."

"He's a spy? What does he do in trade?"

"He monitor shipments—iron an' such, don' ya know, from Norway. He reports to Brits. Sens reports, wireless."

"Where is he doing this?" Gordy asked.

"I dunno. Never do we know."

Gordy gave him a stern look. "Erik, you should *never* say anything about this to anyone. You could compromise, er...hurt your father. People might misunderstand and..."

The private looked mortified. "Tell only you! And majur! That is all! I say nothing. Nothing, no one, no more!" He began to tear up.

"It's OK, Erik! Your secret is safe with us. We'll pray for your father. You're safe here!"

"Tank! Everyone, tank!"

"What's your father's first name?" Callum asked.

"Is Befälhavare (Commander) Carl Lundgren."

Callum prayed out loud for the commander's protection. Lundgren wept as he did. Leah got up and put her arm around him. Breakfast was a feast and an eye-opener. The Swede had a story. He was not alone.

****

Frankie drove the boys and Private Lundgren to the train station. As they arrived, they heard a familiar sound: a P-40, its Allison singing as it flew west and south. The soldiers and Frankie shaded their eyes to see if they could identify it. The nose art was definitely red, though they couldn't make out the details.

"Lieutenant Wang, maybe?" Callum said.

The train ride back to Riverside was quiet. Gordy and Callum talked about the blessing of Frankie helping them with their battery business. They'd done nothing to make it go, but it was growing nonetheless. Frankie was happy to continue to bankroll them, even after they let him know that most of their pay was going back to Itasca. He said he would be honored to help bring Frau Schneider's parents out of Germany, if possible. On the way, they all enjoyed a piece of Leah's apple pie. It too was stupendous!

# CHAPTER 21

# HERO? I'M NO STINKIN' HERO

It wasn't yet full spring in Dallas, but in late March, the signs were there. Izzie looked forward to the season and even more to turning thirteen years old in June. He rose early to study his Bible and pray. At 6:00 a.m., after his devotions, he dug graves if there was a need. If not, he read. He and his siblings read everything they could get their hands on: books on languages, science, grammar, geography, history, poetry, and fiction. When they finished a book, often because another wasn't available, they would reread it.

Isaiah would make a weekly trip to the Dallas library. There was a three-book limit on check-outs. He was always at the limit. He focused on history and archeology. He was fascinated with the Holy Land. He'd read every book in the biblical archeology section (eighteen books) and was working on the second go 'round. He filled notebooks, cross-referencing the books' histories, and searched the Bible for validating scriptures and prophecies. But something was missing. Izzie felt alone. His mother was pleased that he was focused on his Baptist faith, and he was. He led studies at First Baptist. He also volunteered weekly to help clean the church. He sang in the choir, and he ran errands downtown when he wasn't working. He was a servant. He was blessed to work with the CCC three to four days a week, and still he yearned for more.

Izzie had one vice (not a sinful one per se). He loved the history of the Great War. He read everything he could about it. He had met Col. Bass through Gordy, Callum, and Lefty. He asked the colonel if he could interview him, ostensibly for a high school history paper, but in fact to satisfy Izzie's curiosity about the colonel's experiences in World War I. Col. Bass was reluctant. He agreed to meet Izzie at First Baptist to tell his story on one condition: he would only speak of it once and only once.

"I was born in Big Spring, Texas, in 1890," the colonel began. "I applied to West Point in 1908. I graduated from there, third in my class, in 1912. I was commissioned as a second lieutenant and was posted to Fort Sam Houston here in Texas at San Antonio. I qualified for flight cadet training. The first and only US Army plane arrived at Sam Houston in 1910. For about four and a half years, I bounced back and forth between there and Fort Sill in Oklahoma and San Diego Aviation School. Finally, in 1915, the First Aero Squadron was transferred to Fort Sam. I was promoted to first lieutenant.

"On March 15, 1916, the first Aero was sent by train to Columbus, New Mexico, to support General 'Black Jack' Pershing's punitive expedition into Mexico. We assembled eight modified two-seater Curtiss JN-3 bi-planes—the JN-4 version was called the 'Jenny.' Other than the JN trainers at San Diego, those were the only planes in the US military. Captain Benjamin Foulois, the first military pilot and the leader of the Signal Corps, commanded us. The JN-3 was a two-seater. Though I was a trained pilot, I served as an observer for the Signal Corps. As Pershing extended our lines deeper into Mexico, he employed our planes to spot and track (via flag signals) Pancho Villa's raiders and to communicate with the cavalry on the ground. The conditions were miserable, and the JN-3s were underpowered. Eventually, we lost all eight of our JN-3s to bad weather, the ten to twelve-thousand foot mountains, and darkness. There were violent confrontations with Mexican nationals on the ground. Somehow, we survived it all.

"At the end of the punitive expedition, the new JN-4 'Canucks' (built in Canada) were becoming available. We didn't have them or the funding to buy them at the time. Regardless, the Jenny made the greatest impact on American air involvement in the Great War."

Sam looked wearily at Izzie, "That's enough for today, Isaiah. I'm tired."

"But sir, pardon me, I'm writing about your experiences in World War One. What about that?"

"We'll continue soon. I'm tired now."

"Yes, sir. May I see you Thursday?"

"Yes, Thursday. I'll talk with you Thursday. Good day, and God bless you, son."

"Thank you, sir. Yes, see you Thursday. God bless you too, sir."

****

On Sunday, Izzie accompanied Mary Mother, Conn, and Laurence to church. They prayed faithfully for their corporals in California. Mary Mother worried about the prospect of her boys going to war.

As they left the service, Col. Bass greeted them. "Mrs. Ward, good morning. Y'all, good morning to you too." Conn smiled a corny smile. Laurence nodded. The colonel nodded to Izzie as he addressed Mary Mother. "You have a fine young man here, Mrs. Ward, a very fine young man."

"Thank you, Colonel. How do you know Isaiah?"

"He's been interviewing me for a history paper, ma'am."

"Is he now...about what?"

"My experiences in France in the Great War."

"Oh, dear no, Colonel! My Isaiah is in love with Jesus, not war. He wants to be a biblical scholar, don't you, Isaiah?"

"Yes, I want to study the Bible, Mother," Isaiah replied reluctantly, "but with Gordy and Callum at March Field, I'm also interested in military history."

"Not in lieu of the Bible, my son. You know your brothers are in California, but they'll be back. And they'll be with us here at First Baptist studying under Dr. Truett—Jesus willing."

"We're closer to war every day, Mother!" Isaiah said, feeling emboldened. "Callum and Gordy are training to be warriors. Someday, I want to join them."

Mary Mother turned to Col. Bass. "Did you put this nonsense in my boy's head, Colonel Bass? Shame, shame on you!"

"Oh no, Mrs. Ward. Honest, I didn't put anything in his head. He's a bright young fella interested in the military. I never—"

"It's clear to me, Colonel Bass, that you have corrupted his thinking!" Mary Mother said. "I forbid you to come near him!"

"Mrs. Ward, please, be reasonable. I helped your boys get into Baptist Military. I have no ax to grind—"

"I forbid you to contact my Isaiah again, Colonel, ever!"

Col. Bass was dismayed. "As you wish, ma'am, but may I at least help him complete his paper, please?"

"I'm unaware of any such assignment," Mary Mother shot back, "but I'll talk to his history teacher, and if she agrees, maybe."

Izzie's stomach was in knots. His mother had ruined everything.

Led by Mary Mother, he, Laurence and Conn began the five-mile trek home. At a little more than halfway there, Izzie slipped away from the group. He knew where his history teacher lived. He ran to her door and knocked. He told her about his situation and pleaded for her to allow him to write the colonel's story. She agreed on the condition that Col. Bass would allow her to publish the information in the school paper. *Do all adults have their own selfish agendas?* he wondered.

As the Ward clan reached 927 Oak Park, Mary Mother finally noticed Izzie's absence. "Where's Isaiah?" she asked, looking around.

"As far away from you as possible, sister!" Laurence replied. C'ain't you see you humilitated him at church?"

"That's 'humiliated,' Laurence! And I know what I know. That colonel is a bad influence on Isaiah!"

"The boy udmires the captain, sister. They're friends."

"That's 'admires,' and Sam Bass is a retired colonel, not a captain. Besides, what do you know about being friends?"

"Well, la-tee-da, sister!"

 "That's 'lah-di-dah.'"

"Mary Clover...la-tee-da...lah-di-hah!" Conn said.

"What! What'd you say, Conn?"

Laurence answered for him. "Didn't hear nothin', sister. Conn, did you hear somethin' or nothin'?"

"Nothin'," Conn replied. "Lah-di...nothin'."

****

That Thursday, Izzie arrived to meet Col. Bass. They both arrived precisely fifteen minutes early. They sat together in the back of the sanctuary. There was silence. When they spoke, their voices echoed in the empty space.

"Grateful to see you, boy! Wasn't sure you'd be able to come. Please convey my apologies to your mother for our misunderstanding last Sunday. I was out of line."

"Blessed you're here, sir, and you have nothing to be sorry for. She should apologize to you, sir. She was rude to you."

"No, Isaiah. You'll learn soon enough to stand aside of a woman's ire. Nothing good can come of it."

"I still don't understand, sir. Why apologize?"

"There's no venom in the word 'sorry.' Say it, mean it. She's your mother. Respect her."

"I do respect her, but sometimes she's unreasonable. My brothers suffered from our half-brother's beatings and then joined the National Guard to get away. She wanted to send them back to him. How can I respect that?"

"Ultimately, you can question her judgement, but until you're a man, she's in charge. Your brothers made the decision to become men. She may not have known until they left that they were not safe with your half-brother."

"We all knew it, sir! It's possible she would've sent me to Wichita too. She has terrible judgement sometimes."

"She's doing her best. We all make some bad judgements. She may not recognize hers. Forgive her as Jesus forgave us and then move on. Speaking of moving on, how about we get to your assignment?"

"Still don't understand, but OK, let's do it."

"Where were we? I believe I talked about the Mexicans and the introduction of the Curtiss JN-4 Jenny. After the Communist Revolution took the Russians out of the war, in early 1917, the Germans reinstituted an unrestricted U-boat warfare policy to break the British blockade in the Atlantic and turn the tide in their favor. Then the Mexicans were exposed by the Zimmerman Telegram in which the Germans offered Mexico land in the US southwest if they (the Germans) prevailed in the war."

"Pardon me, sir, but Mexico again? What do they have to do with the Great War? What about you?"

"Patience, son. It's important that you learn the importance of context. Many factors lead to war. You cannot understand a war without looking at the specific contextual factors that led to that war. May I continue?"

"Sorry, sir, yes, sir."

"Pancho Villa was upset that President Woodrow Wilson supported his rivals in Mexico. The president supported two Mexican regimes—Huerta the "government of butchers" Carranza and even Villa at one time. When Wilson threw support behind Carranza, Villa felt betrayed. He conducted a raid on a Mexican train, singled out eighteen Americans, and murdered them. Then Villa brought over one thousand raiders across the Border to Columbus, New Mexico, and brutally murdered seventeen people and set fire to the town. That led to General Pershing's punitive expedition, which you already know I was in. Pershing, by the way, never found Villa in two years!

"America was not in favor of joining the European conflict. Under President Wilson, the country was isolationist. Before the communists took over in Russia, Germany sank both passenger and merchant ships at will. After the sinking of the luxury British passenger ship Lusitania in 1915, which resulted in the deaths of one hundred and twenty-eight Americans, Germany apologized and pulled back from their unrestricted submarine warfare strategy.

"Shortly thereafter, British cryptographers intercepted and decoded the Zimmerman Telegram, which offered US territory to Mexico if they joined the Germans and declared war against America. Based on Germany's unrestricted U-boat policy and the treachery of the Zimmerman Telegram, President Wilson declared war on Germany on April 2. Congress voted the declaration resolution on April 6, 1917. Context, Isaiah, context."

"All interesting, sir. Understood, context! How'd you end up in France then?"

"We were ordered back to Columbus, New Mexico. Only two JN-3s were operational. They were in such bad shape that Captain Foulois ordered them set on fire."

Izzie sighed. *What is it with this guy and Mexico?*

Sensing his frustration, Col. Bass continued. "The Secretary of War, Newton Baker, asked the US Congress for five hundred thousand dollars for twelve Curtiss R-2s fitted with Lewis guns, cameras, bombs, and radios. Though approved, when the new aircraft arrived at Columbus, they were not R-2s but JN-8s. Worse, there were only eight of them. All of the JN-8s' engines and propellers had to be altered to fit the higher altitudes. When two R-2s did arrive, they also needed retrofitting. It wasn't until late August 1916 that six of the planes actually flew in the first air review in US history for General Pershing."

*OK, outta Mexico, please...please!* Izzie thought.

"More context, Isaiah. The First Aero was called back to Fort Sam. Foulois basically built the beginnings of our Air Force as the aeronautical officer for the Signal Corps. From spring to fall 1916, he became responsible for all aviation operations and personnel. He built an aerodrome that became Kelly Field near San Antonio. He testified before Congress to increase budgets. He also climbed the ranks from captain to brigadier general. At the beginning of the war, the new American Air Service (AAS) consisted of sixty-five officers, twenty-six of whom were pilots, and I was blessed to be one of them. Only fifty-five airplanes were in service, and fifty-one were obsolete. The US aviation industry had delivered only sixty-four of the three hundred and sixty-six planes ordered by the government. The planes that were being produced were not a strong fit for combat operations in Europe.

"War was upon us. Pershing wanted General Foulois in Europe. He was still busy building the framework of the AAS and its specific aircraft at least for the next six months. On the recommendation of the Aircraft Production Board (Major Bolling), it was decided *not* to build pursuit planes—that is, fighter planes. Instead we would mass-produce British-designed two-seat de Havilland DH-4 reconnaissance bombers with an American-built Lincoln Liberty V-12 engine. The aircraft was wood-framed with cloth covering. For the wood, Sitka spruce was ideal because of its strength and light weight. Production began immediately at the Army's Spruce Production Division (ASPD) facility in Vancouver, Washington. The first DH-4 Liberty Plane rolled out in late October 1917. Over twelve hundred would follow it to France.

"I was one of the first pilots to train in the DH-4 Liberty. The plane was a pleasure to fly! Then I trained others. By spring 1917 we sent the planes over. But it wasn't until August that we shipped out with the First Aero Squadron to England from New Jersey. We arrived at Liverpool. Then it was on to the British rest camp at Le Havre, France."

The Colonel sighed. "That's it for today, Isaiah."

"But you *still* haven't talked about what happened after you arrived in France!" Izzie objected.

"Think about that for a moment. If we continue, your mother could enforce her 'not see the colonel rule' immediately. If we spread this out, and you tell your teacher I'm an old soldier who takes his time, we'll be able to enjoy each other's company more and longer. What do you think?"

"I see your point, sir. I'd like that. How about next Thursday?"

"Next Thursday it is, Isaiah. Give my regards to your family."

"Yes, sir."

****

At Itasca, things were improving. Miri and Tim had new shoes and coats. Their fellow orphans were better off thanks to the two corporals in California.

Frau Schneider was hopeful and anxious at the same time. The children at the Presbyterian home were her family, but her parents were too.

After many cash wires and planning, via Scotland, the presbytery made a back-channel contact with a man in the Confessing Church in Germany. He was friends with a contact working with German intelligence. Gerta and Hans Schneider were surprised and suspicious when they were contacted at church about fleeing their home in Cologne for America. Based on questions from the contact, they were assured he had been sent by Helga in Texas and not from the Gestapo. He said they would need to leave that night. They were now representatives of the First German Presbyterian Church with the perfectly forged papers necessary to emigrate from Germany to New York.

In 1934 a Presbyterian minister attended a German-speaking service in London. Dietrich Bonhoeffer, author of *The Church and the Jewish Question*, was the pastor he heard that day. The Presbyterian, David Leigh, had read and admired the discourse. They became friends. After Bonhoeffer returned to Germany in 1935, they stayed in touch, exchanging letters regularly. Bonhoeffer joined the resistance to the Nazis. A friend, Hans von Dohnanyi in the Justice Ministry, helped him forgo military service and get assigned to the office of Military Intelligence. Dietrich's brother, Klaus, was also a resistance operative.

The phone call from New York came at 1:00 a.m. The children were awakened by Frau Schneider's cries. "Dank, dir Jesus! Danke, dass du meine eltern befreit hast! Danke Gott!" (Thank you, Jesus! Thank you for my parents' liberation. Thank you, God!) She shouted it over and over. Morning brought special hugs of joy for every child under her care. Her parents were safe with the church.

The how, where, and who of Greta and Hans Schneider's exodus out of Cologne remained unknown to Helga. Her parents both passed before the end of the war. Save their *dankbarkeit* (gratitude) for those in Scotland, they never spoke about their rescue for fear of exposing those still in Germany to the Gestapo. Dietrich Bonhoeffer, his brother, Karl, and von Dohnanyi were imprisoned in Berlin and then sent to Buchenwald before being moved to Flossenburg Concentration Camp in 1945. They were hanged just days before the camp's liberation.

"Love never fails..." (1 Cor. 13:8)

****

As agreed, Izzie met Col. Bass the following Thursday. The colonel dove into his story immediately. "There wasn't great organization of our pilots into squadrons. Despite having experience with General Pershing in Mexico, we were not thrown into combat in France immediately. After crossing the Atlantic to France, we were billeted at Avord Aerodrome, the French aviation school. And yes, before you ask, we were being trained all over again. Our DH-4s were being used elsewhere. They had this 'flightless' ground trainer, a Blériot Penguin, that simulated flying. We were frustrated; most of us were experienced pilots! We trained on three different models of Nieuport fighters. I was promoted to captain. We were still not an American air force.

"The French continued training us. We flew Avion Reconnaissance-1 (AR-1s) trainers at two more aerodromes. We even endured French ground machine gun and radio training by some of their snooty officers. Then, to add more insult to injury, they replaced the AR-1s with the French SPAD S-XIA fighter, of which we only had eight in total. Along with a couple of other officers, I was sent to the front-line trenches for more training. We still hadn't seen combat.

"From October 1917 to April 1918, Generals William 'Billy' Mitchell and Benjamin 'Benny' Foulois were duking it out as to who would be in charge of the Air Service (AS) for the American Expeditionary Forces (AEF) under Pershing. Foulois was named chief of the Air Service. What a contrast. Billy was a blue blood, the son of a US senator. Benny was middle-class and would get dirty with the mechanics. For me, a guy from Big Spring whose dad worked in the Texas oil fields, Foulois was a better choice. Shows what I knew!

"Mitchell ended up commanding the AS Zone of Advance on the front, eventually becoming chief of the Air Service I Corps. He complained about the glut of officers, flyers, and personnel at Foulois's disposal. Mitchell was outwardly insubordinate to Foulois. Pershing intervened, and Foulois asked to be relieved. I ended up reporting to each of them at different times in the war. Context, Izzie, context.

"We started as the Observation Group I Army, flying the two-seater French Salmson 2A2. It had the same limitation as the DH-4 two-seater. The distance between the pilot and the observer/gunner made communication between them difficult. We had more pilots than planes, so we cross-trained as observers and gunners. Lieutenant C. J. Laughlin was my pilot, and I was his gunner.

"We saw our first action in April flying deep over enemy territory taking pictures. Three German planes dove at us. Laughlin didn't hear me screaming for him to pull out. Finally, when I fired our dual Scarff-mounted .303 Lewis machine guns, he realized we needed to get out of there. He turned and flew higher. I was able to hit one of the planes. Smoke began pouring out of the engine, and the pilot dove down to land. That was enough to send his comrades down to help him on the ground. We'd survived our first combat, or so we thought.

"As we returned to land at Ourches Aerodrome, the inside wire wing support snapped and hit Laughlin across the face—perhaps due to an enemy bullet? To his credit, while we approached the field, he controlled the unstable plane and landed us safely. After I saw his bloody face, it was a miracle he did! Perhaps that's a good place to stop, Isaiah."

Izzie knew that when the colonel said that, there would be no argument. "Yes, sir. See you next week. Same time and place?"

"Absolutely, Isaiah!"

The meetings continued for more than a month. Mary Mother was suspicious of Col. Bass's motivation. In time, it became clear that Izzie's teacher was in cahoots with her student and Col. Bass. As the colonel continued his World War I "memoirs," he detailed a number of other events.

In June, during the Chateau Thierry Offensive, the 1st Army lost men and machines. Col. Bass had flown sorties and tried to defend Saints

Aerodrome from attack. In the same day, he chased the Germans after they bombed the field and manned his machine guns on the ground to repel another attack.

In late August to September 1918, during the St. Mihiel Offensive, as the Americans advanced on the German lines, they helped with observation to pinpoint artillery fire, sending the enemy into further retreat. As the campaign continued, Bass, now a major, led the 1st Aero Squadron in low-level strafing and reconnaissance sorties that aided the 1st Army's advance. He was also credited with his first two air victories—the plane he'd shot down over Thierry and another in the Mihiel Offensive. Both enemy pilots survived.

Finally, in late September came the Meuse-Argonne offensive, the bloodiest of the war for the 1st Aero Squadron. After another move to Remicourt Aerodrome near the Argonne Forest, the 1st became the premier squadron in the theater. They also became the primary targets for the German air force. Known as "Bloody September," eighty-seven American planes were shot down. Almost all of their casualties, including sixteen pilots killed and three missing in action, were lost at Meuse-Argonne. Now Col. Bass led the squadron. He scored two more air victories for four of the thirteen total, missing ace status by one. It was more important to Bass that the 1st was awarded thirteen Maltese Crosses.

After the three subsequent meetings, Izzie was convinced that the colonel was a hero. Bass wouldn't allow that label. He said the real heroes were buried in France. "Greater love hath no man than this: to lay down his life for his friends," he added. "Luke 15:13."

Col. Bass agreed that Isaiah's accounts could be printed in the school paper but with no reference connecting him to the word "hero." And so it was published. Izzie became an accidental journalist through his abiding role model. He would remember him for the rest of his life.

****

Mary Mother was surprised when she saw three of Izzie's articles about Col. Bass published in consecutive issues of the school paper. After reading them all, she was astonished. "What will you do next?"

Izzie didn't respond. He knew exactly what he was going to do. It would take time, but he began to plan for it.

# CHAPTER 22

# THE SNORING HAMILTON

**JUNE 3, 1941**

Callum had known this day would come. He wasn't happy. Maj. Pearson had ordered him to Hamilton to be the chief mechanic/trainer for the Curtiss P-40 Warhawks and Bell P-39 Airacobras based there. Gordy would not be coming with him.

"Go see the major," he pleaded with Gordy. "Ask for a transfer!"

"Sorry, brother, I can't."

"Why not?"

"Because for now the major and Lieutenant Wang need me here."

"I don't know if I can do this without you!"

"Of course you can. You're the best Allison mechanic in the Army Air Corps."

Callum was stunned by Gordy's statement. "What'd you say?"

"You're the best Allison mechanic in the Army Air Corps. Don't make me say it again!"

Callum was embarrassed. He knew his brother was the best overall aircraft mechanic he'd ever known. On the other hand, since they'd learned and been together forever in isolation, he knew no other mechanics to which he could compare him. He only knew he'd miss Gordy. That made everything else irrelevant.

Gordy was devastated, but he couldn't show it. He put his arm around his brother. "Be the best. Be better and better than the best. I love you, Cal. Be safe!"

****

At Hamilton, the Warhawks were shuttling through quickly to destinations unknown. Not so much the P-39 Airacobras.

When Callum arrived, Lt. Jean-Louis and Lt. Col. Laughlin—both of them recently promoted—were there to greet him. They approached and he saluted. In Laughlin's hard were Callum's new sergeant's stripes. The Lt. Colonel swore him in on the spot.

"Congratulations, y'all, Sergeant," Lt. Col. Laughlin said.

"Uh, thank you, sir."

"Vous (you)!" Lt. Jean-Louis said. "With a' moi!"

Laughlin nodded in agreement with Jean-Louis's order and then turned back toward headquarters. So much for ceremony.

The lieutenant and the new sergeant got into a jeep and drove to the other side of the field. Behind a large hangar were eighteen new Warhawks and four Airacobras.

"We do work to'geder to mak' a perfect, mais qui?"

"Yes, perfect, Lieutenant. Perfect they will be."

"Sergeant, 'vill be best, d'accord quis?

"Yes, sir, we will be the best." Callum realized he was now reporting to the "death dive and maybe land" lieutenant. "Where are my barracks, sir? I need to unload my duffle bag, and then we can get to work."

The lieutenant pointed to a small outbuilding behind the dreaded ol' Manman A-17. There it was, Lt. Jean-Louis's pride and joy and Callum's worst nightmare. *Maybe not?* Callum thought as he entered the shack. *This is my worst nightmare!*

The lieutenant motioned to the only unoccupied bed and plopped down on the other. There was an old woodstove for heat. "C'est toi. C'est ton lit." (That's yours. Your bed)

"How do you say, 'I don't understand,' sir?"

"Je nes comprends pas."

"Pardon, Lieutenant, Je nes comprends pas. Is this my bunk?"

"Mais, qui, Yes."

"And whose is that?"

"E-est mine."

"Lordy, Lordy!" Callum whispered. He was trapped.

"What dis Lordy, Lordy is meaning?"

"Nothing. Means nothing, sir." He gulped, "Absolutely nothing. Where do we start, sir?"

"We need to exam-een my Manman first. She eest running rough."

Callum pointed to the hangar behind them. "Is that ours ?"

"Ha ha, you make the joke, no? Pardon, non...er, no! E-est for new plane—Spe-ceale Prujects. Is no hangar ours, Sergeant. Eest 'Spe-ceale Pruject, n'est pas? We work here on ground."

"Outside? With no protection from the elements, sir?"

"Mais, qui. Is good here, Corporal—pardon, Sergeant Vard. C'est la vie."

Callum remembered his first time at Hamilton. It was cold, and it seemed to rain quite often.

"C'est la vie, sir."

They worked the kinks out of Manman. Then Callum worked on two Airacobras. The lieutenant retired to the shack for a nap. They ate supper at the general mess. Lt. Jean-Louis summarized Callum's thoughts out loud. "Eest slop, Corporal, excuse...Sergeant! C'est slop!"

Immediately, Callum missed the luxury of the Swede's food. "C'est slop, sir, indeed."

✳✳✳✳

On the first morning after Callum's departure, Lt. Wang joined Gordy for breakfast. He asked Pvt. Lundgren to join them. Something was up. That had never happened before.

"Lundgren...your Swedish eggs—superb!" Wang said.

The private was as surprised as Gordy that Lt. Wang had called him by his last name. "Thank you, sir."

"Corporal, Major Pearson will be here momentarily. But before he arrives, I have something to ask. What do you think about Lundgren working with you?

Gordy didn't comprehend at first and then realized what the lieutenant was saying, "Uh, sir, he's a great cook. I consider him good...uh, a great cook."

"Yes. I would call him a chef, wouldn't you?"

Gordy was wary. "Uh, sir...a chef he is."

"We're short of mechanics who can work on P-40s," Wang continued. "As you've noticed, we have many of them coming through for overseas posts. We need more permanent March-based mechanics to work on them."

*Then why'd you allow my brother's transfer?* Gordy wondered. "Sir, I understand. We have several qualified folks I could recommend—"

"You're going to need an assistant, Ward. You're great, but you won't be able to keep up with the volume that's on the way."

"Sir, as I understand it, you want me to train Private Lundgren to work on planes as my assistant?"

"Precisely, Corporal."

Gordy turned to Lundgren. "Have you ever worked on a plane, Private?"

Lundgren shook his head. "No, sir, don't ya know."

"I'm afraid I *do* know," Gordy replied sarcastically. "Have you ever worked on a car engine or a tractor?"

"Neigh, neither. I did help pull a car outta a ditch with a tractor once though."

Gordy turned to Lt. Wang. "All right. Sir, I'd like..."

Just then Major Pearson arrived, and the others stood and saluted. "Private, where are my eggs?" Lundgren rushed into the kitchen and returned with a good portion. Then Pearson turned to Wang. "Are we settled on what we discussed yesterday, Lieutenant?"

"Yes, sir, I believe we are. Aren't we, Corporal?"

Gordy acquiesced. "Yes, sir. I believe we are." Gordy couldn't believe it. He didn't want to think about it, but he did. How would he train a cook who had flunked out of navigation school the intricacies of an Allison V-12 or the complexity of retractable landing gear?

Pearson finished his breakfast and stood up to answer Gordy's "What am I supposed to do with this?" expression. "Sergeant Ward, Private First Class Lundgren, Lieutenant Wang has your new stripes. Congratulations, men! Let's get you sworn in, Sergeant Ward and Private 1st Class Lundgren."

Gordy's training of his assistant began that afternoon in the hangar. "This is the P-40 Allison, Erik."

"Pardon me, sir, that's Private First Class Lundgren, don't ya know."

"You're right, Private. Let's make a deal to save time, OK? I won't call you that unless I'm angry or annoyed with you."

"Yes, Sergeant."

It wasn't very long between the incessant questions about "Why four valves per cylinder? Why not two or six?" or "Why a gear-driven supercharger? Why not a turbo supercharger?" became as annoying as those about rhubarb pie. Gordy referred to his student as "Private First Class!" more often than not.

★★★★

It was the snoring. The beyond-any-tolerable-decibels snoring! How could one person make that much noise and not wake himself up? Lt. Jean-Louis slept deeply. Callum did not! There wasn't enough cotton in the world to plug his ears, and the snoring was taking its toll.

Every morning the lieutenant would take Manman up for his pleasure. After his flight check and departure, within the hour of his flight, Callum tried to catch up on his sleep. Then one morning, to his dismay, Lt. Jean-Louis returned thirty minutes early. He urgently needed the latrine (no sweet potatoes and buttermilk involved). He shut down Manman at the end of a taxiway and sprinted to the loo. Upon his return, she failed to start. Jean-Louis ran to the shack, opened the door, and found Callum sound asleep.

"Sergeant, wake up! Are yooo eest steel sleeping?"

Dazed, Callum popped to attention in his skivvies. "Very sorry, sir! Dozed off. Won't happen again, sir! Sorry, sir. Can't sleep at night, sir."

"Whut? Pourquoi, er, why?"

"Sir, I can't say..."

"I order yoo, Sergeant."

"Lieutenant, you snore." He snorted to demonstrate. "So loudly... with all due respect, Lieutenant."

"Oh, ah, le ronfler—snore. Theses 'snore' is a prolemm how?"

"You sleep deeply. You only stop snoring for a few moments, and then you start snoring again all night. I plug my ears with cotton balls." He put his fingers in his ears to demonstrate. "But it doesn't work, Lieutenant. Without sleep, I am unable to perform at my peak."

"C'est nes pas bien, Sergeant. This eest not good."

"Lieutenant, I don't want this to be an issue. I'll get by."

"Mais no! Whut can we do?" Jean-Louis paused as he searched for a solution. "Aha!"

Callum frowned in confusion. "Uh, what?"

"Get dressed, Vurd, and cum with me."

Reluctantly, Callum did so. Jean-Louis was an athlete and ran everywhere. Callum dutifully ran after the lieutenant to Manman. There, from under Manman's pilot seat, Jean-Louis pulled a ratty, old leather flight cap. "You try, no?"

Callum looked at it, wanted to say no, but he put it on. It smelled like engine oil, exhaust, and who knew what else. The decrepit ear covers were crumpled and worn but very thick. He got a glimpse of his reflection in the canopy and chucked. He looked ridiculous!

"Hulp me start her, Vurd!" Lt. Jean-Louis shouted. There was no response from Callum. Jean-Louis yelled louder...nothing.

Callum didn't realize the lieutenant was screaming at him until he looked directly at him in the cockpit. He took the headgear off and heard, "Hulp me start, Manman, Vurd! C'est bon, No?"

"Yes, Lieutenant Jean-Louis. C'est bon, yes."

That night Callum slept deeply with the WWI flight cap fastened around his chin. The lieutenant wasn't as crazy as he thought. And perhaps he was not as arrogant either.

****

Back at March, Gordy realized what Callum was best at: training. Lundgren was having all of his "moments" at once: Questions, questions, and more questions. Progress was as slow as Gordy's patience was short.

With ten to twelve P-40s to be pre-flighted every day, Lundgren needed to learn quickly. Since the checklist was the same, Gordy decided to limit Lundgren's responses to a single word: "check." As they went through the steps, Gordy would have Lundgren "watch one, do one, and teach one" back to him. Lundgren's response on each step was "Check." No metaphors or similes necessary.

At lunch or dinner (burgers and fries, way less spectacular than Swedish cuisine), Gordy reviewed binders and specifications, drilling the private. They worked until midnight every day. Thankfully, neither of them snored.

Then in mid-July, Maj. Pearson and Lt. Wang appeared at breakfast (something important usually was up when that happened). After finishing their meal, they briefed Lundgren and Gordy on the importance of completing their checks and double-checks.

The P-40s at March were being sent to undisclosed locations in the Pacific. Some were being flown, some dismantled and shipped. The Warhawks were on their way to war.

"Where do you think the Hawks are going, Corporal, er, Sergeant Ward?" Lundgren asked as they bedded down that night.

"I honestly don't know, Lundgren. But you know the major."

"Oh, yeah, fur sure I know the major. Where d' ya think?"

"Guessing the Philippines and China, knowing that Lieutenant Wang is part of the operations there. Believe he's some kind of Special Projects guy in logistics with the air forces there."

"Oh yeah, fur sure...But, what d' ya think he does?"

"He fits the planes to specific area combat needs," Gordy replied, annoyed. "For example, a P-40 is a better fit to close-support strafing in China. A P-39 isn't as fast, but it's easier to maintain. Might be a fit for low-level bombing of islands. Bombers aren't part of the mix for him. He leaves that to bomber logistics."

"Do ya think he's fightin' there?"

"Perhaps. He's never returned Chi with battle repairs. Either he's not in combat or he's the best pilot in combat."

"Chi? What's Chi, eh?"

"It's what he calls His P-40."

"Oh, yeah. Then think he's gotta be the best, ya know?"

"True. The other possibility is that he's helping build the Pacific pursuit strength. We both believe we can be more effective with the right fighter power."

Lundgren nodded. "Oh yeah, sure. We can't bomb without fighters protecting the bombers."

"Right you are; we're going to make sure they have plenty of protection. Goodnight, Private First Class."

"For sur, goo'night."

****

By the end of November 1941, 152 pursuit aircraft had been moved and had taken up stations at Hickam, Wheeler Bellows, and Ford Fields at Oahu, Hawaii. Ninety-nine were P-40Bs & Cs, thirty-nine were P-36As, and fourteen were P-26s. Many of these had passed through March Air Field and were under Gordy, Callum, and Lundgren's maintenance. Countless other fighters that found their way to the Philippines and China had been serviced there too, not to mention their mechanics and crews who also trained there.

# CHAPTER 23

# MARY, MARY, QUITE CONTRARY, HOW DO YOUR HERMENEUTICS AND GRAVES GROW?

Teachings at First Baptist Church continued with Izzie doing some Sunday school classes. He studied deep into the night on Friday and Saturday in preparation. Mary Mother was very proud of his biblical knowledge, especially when other parishioners complimented his lessons.

"Sister Lila said she was excited to hear your instruction on the Sermon on the Mount this morning," Mary Mother said. "Did you consult Dr. Truett's sermons to prepare?"

"I did my own research, Mother," Izzie replied. "I explored a copy of Cruden's Concordance, which I checked out from the library."

"I do declare, you are growing in the Lord!"

"I spent time researching the lesson. I tried to look at the passages from the perspective of the receiver."

"You what?"

"Yes, as Sister Lila might have mentioned, I asked everyone in the room to close their eyes and imagine they were at the mountain listening to Jesus deliver the message. Instead of having them read sections out loud, I asked them to listen as if they were hearing the words for the first time."

"But those folks have read it many times before."

"Exactly. That's why I wanted them to experience it."

"Sounds awfully worldly to me. That's the Holy Ghost's responsibility! First Kings 3:9 says, 'Give therefore thy servant an understanding heart to judge thy people, that I may discern between good and bad.'"

"We're saying the same thing, Mother. We prayed for the Holy Ghost's guidance to come before we started. In sections, we covered the passages as new to us. Stopped between verses and let the message sink in."

"Isaiah, this is not how you were taught. Dr. Truett's teachings are based on scriptures without it 'sinking in.'" She held her Bible high. "This is the divine Word of God, uncorrupted and true! It stands on its own. It needs no sinking in!"

"Mother, we only got through the 'Blessed are' passages, and most of the people said they were glad they'd gone through it as if new. They said they felt the verses in their hearts for the first time."

"Felt? Who felt? Lila said nothing of felt!" She held her Bible up again. "This is the Word of God, uncorrupted—"

"And true, Mother. I know the rest...and that it needs no feelings."

"Oh, no! You did not just mock your mother, did you?"

"No, Mother. The Scriptures are the Word of God and inspired. The Holy Ghost helps instruct us and guide us in God's will. He is well pleased, but that doesn't mean we have to hear God's Word in a stilted way."

"Stilted? Who is possessing you Isaiah! Do you think my beliefs are dull?"

"No, Mother I didn't say that! We both believe we all can experience God personally through Jesus. That can encompass different ways He wants us to hear his Word."

"Well, I don't like it! I don't like it one bit!"

"I can hear you don't. Just know that people can receive the Word in lots of different ways. It can be in silence. It can be in loud, forceful preaching. It can be hearing it as if you'd never heard it before. I don't want to argue about it. I love you and your strong, abiding faith."

"I still don't like it, but—"

"Let's pray. We can agree on that, right?"

"I guess."

After Izzie prayed for peace between them, she said, "My boy! You always can make me feel better."

The moment came when Izzie realized he and his mother would never agree on doctrine or hermeneutics (interpretation—he'd learned that word from a library book too). That was OK though.

"Blessed are those who hunger and thirst for righteousness, for they shall be filled." (Matthew 5:6).

At age fourteen, Izzie's discernment and heart were growing faster and further. He longed for more.

****

After nearly five months, the family received their first letter from Callum at Hamilton Field. They didn't immediately notice the postmark came from Northern California. The contents of the letter revealed that he and Gordy were now separated and that he missed his brother terribly. He mentioned he'd made a pilot friend from Haiti.

Mary Mother was aghast and asked Izzie, "Haiti? Where's Haiti?"

"In the Caribbean, Mother. It's on an island in the Caribbean."

"Oh...oh, yes. Isn't that a slave colony?"

"It *was* a slave colony. It's on the island of Hispaniola—you know, after Columbus came to the New World and discovered it. Spain ceded the western part of the island to France. Haitian slaves rebelled in the late eighteenth century. It declared independence from France in 1804 after the most successful slave rebellion in history."

"So do you think this pilot Callum writes about is a darkie?"

"Mother, please! Yes, he's most likely a Negro."

"But the military is segregated. I've read about it."

"Yes, officially, it is. But there are Negroes in the Army, Navy, and the Marines."

"Robert E. Lee wouldn't be happy."

"Lee's amusement is irrelevant! Slaves are no more, and if this fellow is from Haiti, he's a remarkable soldier. It's very difficult to become a pilot, much harder if you're colored. He has to be an exceptional pilot! God doesn't care what color people are anyway."

"Well, it's still good to know there's separation," Mary Mother persisted.

"Why? Did you hear what I just said?"

"I did, but it's not natural."

"God made us all in His image. Nobody's seen Him. Who knows, maybe he's Negroid."

"Bite your tongue!"

"I'm just saying our understanding of the persona of God is very likely not him. Paintings of him as white were painted by white men. He made a great deal of different races. Perhaps they're all like him?"

"What have you been reading now? Lord help us, it's the devil's work."

"The Lord doesn't countenance hate. What if the thief on the cross were a Negro? Surely, to paraphrase, he's in Paradise with Jesus."

"Never paraphrase Scripture, Isaiah. It's 'Verily, I say unto thee, today shalt thou be with me in paradise.' It doesn't say he was a Negro anywhere."

"It doesn't say he wasn't either."

"Enough! Your uncle, the senator and governor of Mississippi, would be shocked! He has kept the blackies in line there. As an example, they have their own churches and facilities, as it should be."

"And the whites have the Ku Klux Klan, who lynch Negroes and burn crosses on their properties. How is *that* as it should be? Is that what Uncle stands for, hate?"

"No! It's just that they're different. *We're* different."

Izzie paused and thought about what he would say. It would "stand in the way of a woman's ire," but he said it anyway. "I don't believe that, Mother, and I wish you didn't believe that! We're all children of God... all." He turned and walked out.

When they met at the cemetery later, there was nothing more to say. His words had created a schism between them. It wasn't an argument for Izzie; it was about speaking truth and upholding justice. That day he realized Mary Mother would remain filled with her prejudices regardless of what he said. He was disappointed but still committed to letting God mold him into what He wanted him to be. He prayed continually to know exactly what that was.

****

Laurence and Conn continued their antics at 927 Oak Park (or anywhere else, apart or together, for that matter). When Laurence was away for a long freight-train trip, Conn waited at the cemetery for his return. He was strong and could dig a grave in minutes (an asset that Izzie found valuable). Charming he was not (his mud-caked "overall hugging," particularly the women, was downright embarrassing). When clients were about, Mary Mother would remove him from the premises or make sure he was supervised by Izzie (not all that charming for Izzie).

One hot day Conn dug a grave under a live oak tree and decided he'd jump in, lie down, and cool off in it (after all, he "done dug it"). Conn quickly fell asleep. The mortuary delivered a casket on time and began preparations for the graveside service as planned at 4:00 p.m. Izzie was frantic. Where was Conn? He was supposed to set up ten chairs across from the hole. Alas, Izzie completed the task on his own.

It was a small gathering of four people, perhaps mourning a relative of little inheritance worth to anyone; who knew? As the family filed by the open casket, and a pastor stood greeting them, offering condolences, a long set of resounding farts rumbled from the hole followed by an overpowering concomitant smell. A moment went by, and the sound blew out again, as did another putrid odor. (Perhaps Conn had eaten some of Laurence's beans.) Izzie looked down in the hole. Conn smiled up at him with great satisfaction and glee.

"Conn! Outta there, now!"

"Ladies and gentleman," the pastor interjected, "forgive the small inconvenience. A moment please. Very sorry."

The mourners were holding their breath and coughing into handkerchiefs intended for tears. As Conn hoisted himself out of the grave, he giggled and then let loose again—longer, louder, and with the most prodigious smell ever. One of the ladies fainted. The reverend nearly caught her, but instead she fell into Conn's embrace. He bear-hugged her with delight until she regained consciousness, peering up at Conn's silly, toothless grin. Then she blacked out again, adorned in ceremonial burial coverall filth. The pastor pried her out of Conn's vice-like clutches.

As she came to again, this time in the reverend's arms, Izzie exclaimed, "Ladies, sir. I am *so* sorry! This has never happened before! He's my uncle, Uncle Conn! He digs graves. That's all he does! I'm so sorry! Can I pray for you? For your loss?"

"That better be a really good prayer!" the man replied. "Better pray *you ever* get paid!"

"That's sort of my job, son," the pastor said. "Why don't you take your uncle somewhere, anywhere, else, OK?"

"Yes, sir, I will. Conn, let's go!" Izzie grabbed his arm and pulled him away.

Conn looked at the "fainter" with longing. "Love you so!" he shouted. "I does mean it!" Then he pointed. "I dun digged this here hole!"

Back at the cemetery office, Mary Mother was working on monthly billings. She'd been joined by Laurence, who was back from a trip. Conn bolted in, smacking the door nearly off its hinges.

"Hey, Connie boy, what's you been doin'?"

"He's been digging a grave for me," Izzie answered for him.

"Y'all been diggin' a grave this afternoon, brother?"

"Love her so..." Conn replied proudly.

"No, no, no, Conn!" Izzie protested.

"What, Conn?" Mary Mother asked, looking up from her paper-work. "What on earth is bothering you, Isaiah?"

"Nothing. Nothing at all! Conn fell into a grave and...it doesn't matter. It really doesn't matter."

Mary Mother's curiosity was piqued. "Fell into a grave? Are you alright?"

"You done digged a grave and falled in it, Connie?" Laurence asked.

Conn nodded enthusiastically.

"It was nothing!" Izzie pleaded. "Nothing, I tell you! Please, can we just forget it?"

"Alright, then," Mary Mother said. "Was there a graveside this afternoon? Who do I bill?"

"It was a mistake! Conn dug a grave and then fell in and got out. It was a mistake."

Laurence winked and looked at Conn and Izzie. "That was some dang good huggin', huh, Connie boy? Betcha you done a good job there, done diggin' that there grave."

Conn winked back. Laurence had seen it all while walking back from the railyard.

Izzie sprinted out to fill in the hole. As he did, he thought of what the reverend had said about praying being his job. *My job is to keep a loveable imbecile from having to go back to the asylum*, he thought. *I don't want my job anymore.*

As the day finished, Laurence and Conn helped Izzie position a surprisingly large grave marker. The dedication read, "The Sweet Smell of Heaven is Mine Forever." Izzie prayed for the decedent's eternal soul.

# CHAPTER 24

# FIGHTERS, FIGHTERS, AND MORE FIGHTERS

March Airfield began to transition from pursuit to bombing groups in 1941. The 17th Pursuit became the 17th Bombardment Group. Then on June 10, 1941, the 14th and 51st pursuit groups arrived at March. Both were activated at and came from Hamilton Field in Northern California. Both squadrons were equipped with capable fighter aircraft.

Gordy and Lundgren were assigned to the 14th. They were maintaining and training on Curtiss P-40 Warhawks, Republic P-43 Lancers, and P-38D Lightnings. The Lancers were powered by Pratt & Whitney 1830 radial engines, which Gordy brought Lundgren up to speed on. He was getting more proficient with "check only" response training. Wang came back to March as a captain. He was likely again training pilots for the Flying Tigers.

While the Lightnings were new, their twin Allison engines were familiar to Gordy. Most pilots were trained to fly single-engine fighters. A comparable twin-engine trainer, the Curtiss-Wright AT-9 ("the Jeep"), was still in final development. Most pilots flew their Lightnings for the first time without twin-engine experience. Also at March were two unarmed/modified RP-322 ("castrated" P-38 sans turbochargers) two-seaters for "piggyback" training, but most pilots never trained in them. This increased the potential for disaster. On Gordy's minimum "avoid a catastrophic failure" checklist were the following points.

1.  Twin 1,600-horsepower Allison V-1710 liquid-cooled engines—rods, valves and plugs, intercoolers, turbocharger regulators, and radiators

2.  Twin nine-foot three-bladed Curtiss electric-powered propellers

3.  Ducted engine intakes for heat in the cockpit

4.  Generator and gun heater switches

5.  External tank valves

6.  Gauges/lights for RPMs, auto-rich, combat-on, manifold pressure, general flight indicators

7.  Toggle switches for outboard tanks

8.  Tricycle landing gear; front gear stability

Gordy remained worried by the plane's complex mechanisms. He memorized the controls, thinking about what they activated, then backwards by what they shut off. The only simple devices were the left/right rudder pedals. He spent late evenings with Lundgren and new pilots going over the instrument panel, which was arrayed with levers and out-of-sight toggle switches. The pilots were incentivized to attend to learn and enjoy Lundgren's Swedish cuisine.

Early mornings were spent with Major Pearson and Captain Wang. Finally, at the end of July, they announced that Gordy and Lundgren would be exclusively assigned to the Lightnings. The pilots were younger and younger, the mechanics and crews less and less experienced. Twelve-hour days turned into sixteen- to twenty-four-hour days. Coffee, coffee, and more coffee.

****

Late one afternoon, Captain Wang came to the hangar and pulled Gordy aside. "Need you with me tonight."

"Uh, yes, sir," Gordy replied. "We still have two Lightnings on the ramp that we haven't gotten to though."

"Lundgren will have to take care of that. Come with me."

They walked farther down the tarmac to a P-38, which was being fueled. "Hop in."

"Sir, I know you're aware the Lightning is a single-seat—"

"It's castrated—a two-seater, Sergeant."

"Beg your pardon, sir, and no offense, but you're checked out in Lightnings, right?"

"Sort of. I flew piggy-backed once. I believe in this trainer."

Gordy was aghast. "Sir, it's not that I don't trust your experience, but this is the most complicated aircraft I've ever worked on, Captain, sir."

"Ha ha ha! You trust me but not in 'your' Lightning? Think about what you're saying, Ward."

"Sorry, Captain, sir. Sorry, you're the best pilot I know—"

"And you're the best mechanic I know. So, what could possibly go wrong up there if we both do our jobs? And if something does go wrong, both of us are best equipped to handle it, don't you think?" The captain had two very good points.

"Sir, actually, I've never flown, Captain Wang."

"First time for everything. Get in. That's an order, Sergeant."

After fueling, Wang fired up the Allisons and then taxied out to the runway. He released the brake and barreled forward. As he took off, the front landing gear (a giant spring) bounced. Gordy knew what would happen next: the Lightning would nose up, pushing the tail down to scrape the runway. Fortunately, Wang flattened their trajectory enough to compensate.

Gordy tapped his shoulder and gave him a thumbs-up.

"What'd you think, Ward?" Wang shouted over the engines.

"Amazing, sir! Pardon me, sir, where are we headed?"

"Hamilton! Thought you needed a break and a day with your brother."

"I don't know what to say, sir. Thank you. Does he know we're coming?"

"To my knowledge, no! Believe his lieutenant does though. He'll be surprised to see a P-38 land, if he's looking. Officially, we just moved all of them to March. I can radio ahead if you like."

"No, sir!" Gordy shouted back. "I'd like to surprise him, sir."

"Then, surprise him we shall."

On their approach at dusk, the skies were full of pursuit trainers. Wang received clearance to land.

Gordy couldn't help himself. "Sir, you're aware this bird is tricky to land?"

"Yes, Sergeant I've landed one—once!"

"The twin power requires—"

"Three-point perfect. Keep her flat, Sergeant?"

"Yes, sir, keep her flat, sir!"

The crosswind was a challenge. Capt. Wang slightly crabbed the nose, barely pushed up the power, then cut it, touching the rear wheels and nose gear almost simultaneously.

Gordy was impressed and gave him another thumbs-up. "Perfect, sir! Three-point perfect."

"Thank you, Sergeant. Coming from you, that means a lot."

Gordy wasn't sure which side of Wang's hand the "compliment" came from.

They taxied off the ramp to the holding area. Gordy noticed the enormous hangar. They pulled through a ramp beside it. Another large piece of tarmac was behind it. On the ramp were P-40s galore and a few P-39s. As twilight set in, he wondered what was in the hangar.

As they found an empty spot to park, Gordy saw the infamous Manman. He remembered Callum's disgust with it. Behind it, he noticed a disheveled shack. Wang climbed out of the Lightning. "Off to meet with Laughlin." He headed toward headquarters. "We're only here tonight and tomorrow morning, so enjoy."

Scanning the rows of P-40s, Gordy saw three sets of mechanics working. He recognized one of the mechanics on a roller-scaffolding bent over the cockpit.

Callum looked up for a moment and was confused to see a P-38 taxi and park near Manman. *Should've parked behind the hangar,* he thought. He continued his work with a pilot in the cockpit. Moments later, he heard someone say, "Bad oil pressure gauge?"

Callum didn't look down. "Trick question. The Warhawk only has a manifold pressure gauge. Who's askin'? People are busy here."

"Hey, numbskull! Who do you think's askin'?"

In that moment he recognized his brother's light Texas drawl. He turned abruptly and almost fell off his perch when he saw Gordy.

"Watch your step there, clumsy," Gordy chided. "Wouldn't want to lose the best Allison mechanic in the world falling off a P-40!"

Callum ducked under the top railing, grabbed on, swung over, and leapt down. The brothers embraced. "Sergeant? They made *you* a sergeant. Who made that mistake? Congrats, brother." He followed up with a salute. Callum's jumpsuit covered his stripes.

"Hey, Vard," a voice from the cockpit said, "thees plan-a no fix e-et-self, mais qui?"

Callum waved Jean-Louis over to join them. "Lieutenant Jean-Louis, come down and meet my brother, Gordy, sir. Why are you here? Please tell me you've been transferred."

"Sorry, Cal, no. Captain Wang flew me up from March in that Lightning trainer. He has a meeting with Major Laughlin today. Said he wanted me to be with him here to take a break and spend the day with you."

Jean-Louis stepped down the scaffold, saluted Gordy like a Brit (Gordy wondered why he'd done so), and held out his hand. "Allo, 'am Lieutenant Amos Jean-Louis. I am pilot. Am superveese Sergeant Vard repair for dees planes."

"Sergeant?" Gordy replied. "Excusez-moi, avez-vous dit que Ward est un sergeant, sir?"

"Ah, bon. Tu parle Français, si? Qui—Vard a été promu par le Major Laughlin au sergeant." (You speak French? Yes—Ward was promoted by Major Laughlin to sergeant).

"Um, what?" Callum asked.

In response, Gordy erupted in pride. "Congratulations, Sergeant Ward! Couldn't see those stripes under that suit. Looks like you're sporting your own personal deployed parachute. You need Lungren's cooking. So proud of you!"

"Thanks, Gordy!"

"Stay humble, brother. Martin Luther said, 'True humility does not know that it is humble. If it did, it would be proud from the contemplation of so fine a virtue!'"

Callum chuckled. "And there you have it. Lieutenant Jean-Louis, now you've truly met my brother!"

Gordy translated the Luther quote and his brother's response. The Haitian didn't seem to find the humor in any of the banter, which tickled the brothers even more. They smirked, trying to hold back their laughter.

"Vil we work?" Jean-Louis asked. "We no play the games, sergee-ants?"

Callum chortled. "Gordy, grab a jumpsuit. Extras are in the shed. Then grab a wreench or zee rit tool, vee neeed to vurk!"

Insulted, Jean-Louis pointed dismissively to the shed and to Gordy. "Vous, go, go! Va là-bas! We neeed tu vurk, nu-ow."

Gordy ran to the shed. He was stunned at its tiny size and meager décor. *What a dump!* he thought.

As he ran back to the planes, it began to rain. "How can I help, and why are we outside in the rain?" he asked.

"You'll get used to it," Callum replied. "Final-checking the instrument panel. Hand me the voltage meter, there in the tool box." It began to rain harder.

"No. No, I don't think I will."

"What? Why not hand me the meter?"

"No, I meant I won't get used to working in the pouring rain. Why not in the hangar?"

"Oh, that. Up until about a year ago, they used it for B-17s. The runway here was too short for them. They transferred the Seventh Bombardment to Utah. They have four Lightnings in there now."

"How do you know?"

"I snuck in and looked. It's OK. Lieutenant Jean-Louis was with me."

"Why the secrecy, do you think?"

"We're sending planes to the Pacific. Maybe they don't want the Japanese to know we have P-38s here. Rumor has it they're heading to Alaska. I don't know for sure."

"We've got a bevy of them at March. Training and flying them every day. They probably know."

"Then that's all I know, brother!"

They worked together until 1800 and completed four more P-40s. They were still the best team. Dinner in the general mess, on the other hand, was far from the best. Lt. Jean-Louis had nailed it the first time: "Slop!" No translation required.

✳✳✳✳

The night was miserable for Gordy as he tried to sleep on the floor of the shack. Lt. Jean-Louis continued his "freight train" snoring, and Callum had the only protection from it. Capt. Wang slept well in the officers' guest quarters.

After enduring a barely tolerable breakfast, Gordy and Callum were summoned to headquarters with Lt. Jean-Louis and Capt. Wang for a meeting with Lt. Col. Laughlin. Callum prayed it was a transfer for Gordy to Hamilton. After salutes were exchanged, Laughlin got to the point.

"Welcome, y'all. Great to see you again."

*When did More Beers meet Captain Wang?* Gordy wondered.

"Soldiers, we have asked Captain Wang to indulge us here and keep Sergeant Ward here for the rest of the day. He's agreed, y'all. We need you to pre-flight the captain's Lightning and four more today. Now, y'all."

"Yes, sir," Gordy and Callum replied.

"The first priority will be the trainer," Laughlin continued. "Lieutenant Jean-Louis needs an introduction to the P-38 with Captain Wang. Understood, y'all?"

"Yes, sir," Callum replied. "We need to get to the hangar now, sir. The 38s are complicated; we need to get to work."

Laughlin smiled proudly. "That's what I've always admired about you boys, your work ethic. Captain Wang and Lieutenant Jean-Louis can escort you fellows to the hangar, the contents of which, Sergeant Callum, I believe you've already seen."

"Sorry, sir," Callum replied sheepishly.

"Y'all never apologize to me for looking ahead to next steps. Dismissed."

On the way to their work on the Lighting trainer, Callum turned to Gordy. "How'd you think he knew the lieutenant and I peeked in the hangar?"

"Not yours to wonder. Old 'More Beers' seems to know everything about us. Kind of creepy."

The trainer was pre-flighted and with Lt. Jean-Louis at the controls and Capt. Wang in the rear seat, it took off for the day. The boys worked on the other four Lightnings past lunch and dinner, finishing by 2300.

They returned to the shack and were surprised to have "le bad" food available from the mess. Wang and Jean-Louis were also there. They reviewed their day. Jean-Louis had done well in the cockpit according to Wang.

Callum and Gordy reported that other than fueling, the hangar P-38s were flight-ready. Gordy's reward was to sleep in the guest barracks. Callum's was to have Lt. Jean-Louis invite him to spend the night in the officers' guest quarters. He slept like a baby sans the flight helmet.

The next morning, Callum was up at 0500 anticipating Gordy's one more "check and double-check" review of the four Lightnings in the hangar. As he ran there, he heard a Lightning revving for takeoff. It was the trainer with Gordy and Capt. Wang on board. He stood and saluted them. They were returning to March, perhaps to enjoy Lundgren's breakfast in lieu of slop.

****

By late November, P-40s were scarce at March. The Lightnings and their trainers were gone. A few P-39s came through. For the most part, Lundgren and Gordy were working on planes piecemeal. They were blessed to visit Frankie and Leah more often. They spent Thanksgiving with them. Lundgren baked a strawberry-rhubarb and a "puh-can" pie as his contribution to the desserts. Where he'd procured the rhubarb and pecans remained a mystery. Leah served an aged Muscat wine with them. They were all superb.

Late in the afternoon of December 7, 1941, Gordy and Lundgren were summoned to Maj. Pearson's office. That rarely happened. An hour earlier, they'd heard about the Japanese attack at Pearl Harbor on the radio. America was at war.

Of the ninety-nine P-40s at Pearl Harbor, many of which had been serviced at March, seventy-two were destroyed or damaged in the attack. Of the 152 fighters there, 95 were destroyed or damaged. Only twenty-seven remained combat ready. Twelve B-17 Flying Fortress bombers arrived as the attack was ongoing. Two were destroyed on landing, and ten survived the attack. They had stopped at Hamilton Field on their way to the Philippines.

Within days, Lundgren was transferred to Hamilton. Gordy was left at March to maintain the only P-40 Warhawk that remained on the West Coast. It flew observation missions up and down the coast from San Diego to Ventura. It stood alone as the only pursuit/interceptor defense against a Japanese invasion of the southern California coast.

# CHAPTER 25

# GOTTA GIT AND OTHER STIPUDEOUS WONDERS

After their hard work on Saturday at the Cleburne CCS Park Project, Laurence tried to convince Izzie to travel down to Itasca to visit Miri and Tim at the Presbyterian Home.

"And how are we going to get down there, Laurence?" Izzie asked sarcastically. "We rode down here on the CCS truck, and they're headed back to Dallas."

"Maybe we could hitch-like a ride. A farmer or rancher. Maybe we can hop a train. I done it before. It done run right through here. Yur a prayin' man. What's He say?"

"That's 'hitch*hike*,' Uncle. He probably wouldn't answer prayer to help us commit a crime. Isn't hopping freight cars illegal? And then how would we get back home?"

"Yur soundin' jus' like yur mean ol' mama. Sometime she be cat mean. No worry—we gitter back easy. No worryin' boy."

Just then a voice hollered at them. "Gordy, Gordy Ward! It's Lefty! Lefty Burress. Gordy!" Izzie looked back and was surprised to see a man in uniform with a shriveled hand running after them, waving like he was his best friend.

"I'm sorry, sir. Do we know you?"

"Gordy—"

"That's my brother's name," Izzie clarified. "He's in California."

"Sorry," Lefty said. "You're the spittin' image of him. I'm Lefty...Lefty Burress. I'm a friend of his from Gilder Oil. He's a fine young fella."

"He spoke highly of you, Lefty. Pleased to make your acquaintance."

"And yours. You workin' here at Cleburne? I'm in charge of Dallas CCS. You goin' back?"

"To answer your questions, yes, we've worked there, and yes, we're headed back."

"Ah dang an' all to heck, nephew!" Laurence said. "We got to git down to E-tas-ker. See dem kids."

Lefty introduced himself to Laurence. "Did ya mean Itasca? What kids are in Itasca?"

"My Sister Miriam and brother Timothy are at the Presbyterian Orphan...er, Home there," Izzie said. "We're not going down there. We have no transportation. We're going back to Dallas."

"What if I drove you fellas down?" Lefty asked.

Izzie raised his eyebrows. "You have a car?"

"No, but I have the CCC truck. It's mine sort of, you know because I'm kinda in charge...sort of."

"Aren't you supposed to use that vehicle for official CCS business only?"

"As I said, I'm kinda in charge, and I may have official business down Waco way. Just might."

"O-ffici-eal," Laurence quipped. "That's some sorta important busyness, nephew. If I knowed it, *very* important!"

"Truck's right there, fellas. Jus' gotta gas her up. Hop in. It's 'bout twenty-five miles down there. I gotta go back to Dallas anyways."

Izzie jumped in the back of the truck. "Thanks, Lefty! Thanks a lot. Er, Laurence you sit up front!"

He knew Laurence would talk poor Lefty's ears off. He was grateful for the ride and the solitude in the back of the truck. It was a beautiful early December night in Texas. He sent up a prayer of thanks for the ride south.

Sure enough, Laurence peppered Lefty with questions. "Tarnation, you in the Army? Where'd you git that messed-up hand? How'd you be chief of them Cs? Where's Tyler at? Is you goin' there after E-task-er an' Dallus? Where'd you git them boots? Them's some fine good boots..."

****

Lefty was a patient man—a kind, patient man. Upon their arrival at the Presbyterian home he declared, "Isaiah, I'll take you back to Dallas tomorrow on one condition: Laurence rides in the back, OK?"

Izzie chuckled. "Uh...yes, sir!"

"I'll wait outside, fellas. You catch up."

"No, you come inside, please," Izzie insisted.

As they all waited in the foyer for the kids, Frau Schneider had an old gramophone playing. It was the most beautiful music Izzie had ever heard. He hardly recognized Miri. She was a beautiful fifteen-year-old young woman. Tim was a strong, handsome young man of thirteen years. Both were polite and shy and had intense stares that penetrated the soul. Each had a book in their hands.

Miri hugged Izzie. "Who hears music feels his solitude peopled at once!"

Izzie shuddered at her words. A tear fell down her cheek. Indeed, they were "peopled."

"Ah, Vards," Frau Schneider greeted them. "How wunderbar to see you! And to meet you too."

"Dang good to see youse too, Frau-ee Lady," Laurence said.

"I meant that gentleman, sir." She pointed to Lefty and invited him in.

"Pleasure, ma'am. I'm Lefty Burress. Friend of Gordy's."

Frau Schneider's eyes twinkled, "Ya. Eeest. Yu vill enjoy visit, ya? Apology, ve have no extra beds. My parents sleep guest room."

"I, er, we can sleep on the flatbed of the truck. We're used to it, huh, fellas?"

They nodded in agreement.

"What music is that?" Izzie asked. "It's beautiful."

"Liszt, Franz Liszt's first piano concerto in E flat major," Tim replied. "My favorite."

"Ve play music of oppress-ed peoples by Nazis," Frau Schneider added. "Da Polish, da Hungary…"

Lefty could see her sadness, hear her words of compassion. He was smitten. *You are wunderbar, Frau,* he thought.

His moment of infatuation was interrupted by Laurence. "Where's the crapper?"

"Wha'eest dees, crap-per?" Frau Schneider asked.

"He means the toilet, ma'am," Izzie replied.

"Ah die toilette. Eeest just there." She pointed to the end of the hallway.

Laurence ran to the door. "Gotta pee like a racehorse!"

"Wha' eest—"

"Don't ask, Frau," Izzie said.

They spent the evening in the sitting room, the boys and the ladies exchanging stories of their lives, extraordinary stories from all. Frau Schneider's parents joined the clan to tell of their remarkable escape through her translation, and the music played on in a moment for all of "peopled at once."

****

Bedded down on the truck bed under the stars and CCC-labeled blankets, the boys exchanged ideas about their situations. Izzie was troubled. How much longer would his family be separated? What could be done to bring them together? He felt responsible for the answers.

Lefty looked up at the star-filled Texas sky. "So big, eh? So wide. 'A wonder to behold and to wonder about,' eh? So my mom used to say."

"Job 12:12," Izzie replied. "'Wisdom is with aged men (and women). And with length of days, understanding.' Wonders indeed, Lefty! May I ask you something?"

"Of course."

"Why do you think our family has been separated? I've asked God for His answer. He seems to be asking us to be patient. What do you think?"

"Patience is a virtue and all that, but in all honesty, I don't know why, Isaiah."

"I'm growing impatient, Lefty! I'm thinking about doing something about it."

"Like what?"

"I've promised myself I'm going to take Miri and Tim away from here."

"To where? Where would you take them?"

"Away," Izzie said in a desperate voice. "Anywhere away from here."

"And how would you do that? How would you support them?"

"I don't know. I'm a hard worker. Tim's strong. Miri's smart. I don't know."

"What we yearn for isn't always what's possible right now," Lefty said. "My mother also used to say that."

"I can't stand the thought of not being with my family any longer. Gordy and Callum are so far away."

"You're OK to want that, Izzie. But think of what it would mean for Miriam and Timothy. They're safe here. Frau Schneider's keeping them safe."

"Cal and Gordy give her money to do so. And she does keep them safe. I'm thinking I could ask my brothers to send the money to me at home. Laurence and I could work more. Tim's strong; he could work. I just think—"

"Pray for guidance, Izzie. Don't think it's the right timing, son."

"I have prayed and will pray again now. Please, you pray too?"

"Of course I will. Don't do somethin' stupid though, OK?"

"I'm not stupid!" Izzie replied.

"No, you're not stupid. You need your family; that's all."

"Thanks for listening," Izzie said remembering Gordy's description of Lefty's kindness and compassion.

Lefty fell deeply asleep. Laurence's feet stuck out the open driver's door. He was not sleeping. He exited the cab and snuck back to jostle Izzie. "Ya ready?"

"Wha...Laurence, what do you mean, ready?"

"Ready to take dem kids back home?"

"What...how?"

"That there what's I calls, 'dead to da world.'" He pointed to Lefty's mouth dripping with drool and then poked him hard in the ribs—nothing.

"What are you thinking?"

"We takes in the candy I brung for the kids—back door's open. Only two floors. You goes to the boys' floor, and I go to the girls' an' git Tim and Miri. We brings 'em back to da truck, puts in the frunt. I switcheroo with you in the back. You drive, and we git outta here."

"What if Frau Schneider or her parents wake up?"

"They's on the other side of the main floor. When I went to the loo next to the sittin' room, I made some pritty loud satisfaction and strainin' sounds. Y' didn't hear them in there, did ya? If-in we're real quiet, we gits the kids in th' truck, and off we go! "

"They'll hear the engine start."

"Fur all they'd knows, we're a-takin' off early to git back t' Dallas. By th' time they's up we be gone. It'll be dang pur-fict!"

"Uh, just dang *perfect* to get us in trouble."

Izzie had prayed for a way to get the kids home. Now Laurence had a plan. Had God provided this avenue? He looked at his uncle and thought of the many well-meaning misadventures he'd perpetrated. He rationalized that Laurence was being used by the Lord to accomplish a good deed.

"OK, but I'll go get Miri on the girls' floor. You're likely to fart or belch and wake everyone up! Take those old boots off; they squeak worse than the floors in there!"

The plan was afoot. Laurence had awakened two boys on the third floor, mistaking them for Tim, then bribed them with candy to remain silent. Tim recognized his uncle's squeal of "Ooo, dang and tarnation!" as he stubbed his bare toe on a bed frame.

Izzie's role was easier. Miri was reading a book by flashlight under her covers and welcomed her brother and the candy. She gladly grabbed her shoes and coat when Izzie suggested, "We're on an adventure; want to join us?" All went well as Miri and Izzie made their way to the truck. Still reeling from his swollen toe, Laurence limped down the stairs and outside with Tim.

He got as far as the flatbed before he exclaimed, "Ee-oh-oh, me toes!" That produced a snort from Lefty, but he stayed asleep.

"Quiet, Uncle!"

As Izzie loaded the kids into the cab (they barely fit), he noticed that Tim had no shoes or coat. "Where's his coat?" he chided his uncle. "Where are his shoes?"

"I dunno. Me toes was smartin'. Sorry!"

"Get back up there, and get a coat and shoes for him!"

"How'd I know which is his?"

"Tim, what color's your coat? Where do you keep your shoes at night?"

"My coat's grey, and it's on the first peg to the left. My shoes are at the end of my bed."

Izzie ordered Laurence to retrieve them both. Again, it seemed that the plan was on track for success, except as Laurence snuck down the stairs past the kitchen, he heard the creak of the floorboards in the hallway. As he was pulling the door shut, lights came on in the kitchen, and there stood Hans Schneider, Frau Schneider's father. Laurence threw the shoes and coat into the backyard.

"Hallo. Guten abend, Herr Laurence," Hans said. "Uh, Guten tag evenings. My Engiish eest not so goot."

"Howdy," Laurence replied. "Er, goodie-tag, yourself."

"Was ist los? Er, Why you here?"

"Uh, 'just gittin' some water." He stuck his head under the faucet and gulped.

"Ach ja, Wasser...water, yes?"

"Whut? Wass...Huh? Oh, you mean—Wha-tur! Or wash yur what? Er...Hansie, Piece of advice for ya: don't never eat sweet potaters and buttermilk! 'Pologies, 'gotta git. G'night."

"Was ist po-taters? Uh, gute nacht...Eest goot night, ya?"

"Uh, yeah sure is goot...Gootie naughty."

Uncle Laurence gathered the shoes and coat and ran to the truck.

"Fire 'er up, Izzie! That Germun father guy is up. Gotta git right now!"

The sound of the International was shout-out loud on ignition. Laurence barely was able to jump in the back as Izzie gunned the engine and then spun out violently and lunged forward. Then the truck let loose with two huge backfires.

****

How Lefty slept through the chaos was a miracle, and Izzie needed one. The plan was a success. The word "kidnapping" wasn't in it. They found their way to the main highway and headed north toward Dallas. Izzie had to think. He realized it was early Sunday morning. He slowed the truck to a snail's pace to plot what to do about the First Baptist Mary Mother routine and what he'd tell Lefty when he awakened. *Uncle Laurence is nuts. Why would I listen to crazy Uncle Laurence? What was I thinking?*

****

It was just after sunrise when Conn realized Izzie and Laurence weren't back from CCC. He ran to the cemetery to see if they were there. He checked the office, the maintenance shack, and the storage shed: no sign of anyone. Just as he was about to run back home, he heard a car idling near the locked front gate and ran to investigate. Outside the gate sat the most "stupideous" (his description) car he'd ever seen: a four-door 1937 Chevrolet Master Deluxe. Conn didn't know that; he just knew it was "stupideous." He'd seen a car of similar grandeur, but that was a hearse. In the driver's seat was a man dressed in his Sunday best smoking a cigar.

Conn pressed his head against the bars of the gate, grasped them as if a prisoner in a cell, and flashed his toothless smile. "That there is a stupideous car, Mister!"

The car's occupant rolled down the passenger window. "Pardon me?"

"That there car, it's stupideous!"

"You mean, stupendous?"

"Yeah, stupideous."

"Don't I know you? Aren't you Laurence...Laurence McDougal?"

If Conn knew anything, he knew his McDougals. "Nope! Ain't my brother."

"Oh wait, you're Connell! We've met at church, I'm Colonel Sam Bass. Remember me from First Baptist?"

"Nope! Er maybe. You friends with Izzie?"

"You mean Isaiah? Yes, we're friends."

"Can I see the inside of your stupideous car, Mr. Bass?"

"It's Colonel Bass, and sure. How're you going to get over the gate?"

In a moment Conn was over the bars, ripping the bottom out of his coveralls on one of the pointed posts. "What in heck or heaven is that there?" Conn asked as he pointed to the water cooler attached to the back window.

"It's a swamp cooler for the summer heat. Hop in, and I'll turn it on."

Conn jumped in, depositing a week's worth of grave-digging filth on the front seat. "Amazin'! Feels jus' like a cool spring breeze in here, Mr. Bass. Stupideous!"

"Stupend...that's Colonel...oh, never mind."

At that moment the CCC International truck pulled up in front of the gate. Conn was surprised and excited to see Izzie, Miri, and Tim crammed into the front seat. Lefty popped up in the truck bed, looking very irritated. Izzie jumped out and greeted Col. Bass and then introduced him to everyone.

"Colonel Bass and I know each other through James and Junior Gilder at Gilder Oil," Lefty said.

"Sorry to call you so early this morning, Colonel," Izzie said. "As I explained on the phone, we're in a spot, sir!"

"We? Don't you mean *you're* in a spot?"

"Well, My Uncle Laurence—"

"Isaiah, have you been missing your brother and sister?" Sam asked.

"Yes, sir."

"And you shared that with your uncle? and Lefty?"

"Yes and yes. But sir—"

"No buts, Isaiah. Part of being a man is taking responsibility. Now how do you intend to take responsibility for bringing your kin up here without checking them out of the Presbyterian Home and getting your mother's permission?"

"I don't know, sir. I missed them so much. What'll I do? Mother will be furious!"

"We don't want that, do we?" the good colonel said.

"No, sir, but they're here, and it's Sunday, and I'm teaching Sunday School. What a mess. Lord, why'd I listen to Uncle Laurence?"

"Responsibility, Isaiah," Col. Bass said. "Responsibility."

"Yes, sir. I guess I'll have to fess up to Mother and take the consequences."

"And apologize to Frau Schneider?"

"Yes, sir."

"You're ready to do that?"

Izzie lowered his eyes in resignation. "Yes."

"Then I think we have another solution."

"Pardon me, sir?'"

"I've wanted to go down to Baptist Military for a while now. Good drive in the Master Deluxe. On the way I could drop a couple of Wards at Itasca."

"Oh, would you, sir? Would you please?"

"On one condition."

"What's that, sir?"

"That you go to the church now and call Frau Schneider from the rectory. She's expecting your call."

"I don't understand, sir. How's that possible?"

"I spoke to her after you called, before I came here to meet you."

"Oh...Oh, thank you, sir! Thank you!"

"Miri, is it? She and Tim can ride down in the back seat. Believe Connell has left quite a mess in the front. Will that be OK?"

"Oh yes, sir!"

"Might could I ride along in this stupideous automobile?" Conn asked.

The colonel said no, but he did explain to Miri and Tim that when Christmas came, he'd make sure they could ride up to Dallas with him again then.

Izzie went to change into his "church shirt" and then ran to First Baptist. He went directly to the rectory and called the Presbyterian home. Frau Schneider answered. "I was vorried sick! I am vhat grateful to Jesus; huv yuu be wit Miri and Tim. Thank yu for culling, ya?"

"Frau Schneider, I'm so sorry!"

"Ya forgive. An' eest furgottin nuw. Yu cum at Christmas, ya?"

"Yes."

There was a click on the line. The colonel was already driving south.

Izzie's Sunday school lesson was on Ephesians 4:32: "Be kind and compassionate to one another, forgiving each other, just as Christ forgave you." Izzie struggled. How could he forgive himself or his crazy uncle?

There would be little time to think about that question going forward. That Sunday evening the Wards received the news of the attack on Pearl Harbor. There were bigger issues to pray about.

# CHAPTER 26

# FLIPPIN' AND FLOPPIN'

Maj. Pearson's face was stern as Gordy entered his office, and they exchanged salutes. "You're reassigned to Hamilton, Ward. Your transfer papers are signed. You have forty-eight hours to get there. They're ferrying some pilot named Jean-Louis down here to fly you up there in our last Lightning trainer."

Gordy grimaced. "Lieutenant Amos Jean-Louis? I don't know him well, but my brother certainly does. I do know he's checked out in the P-38."

"You'd better hope so. Heard he's a Negro. Is that a problem?"

"Oh, no, sir! He's got a reputation for being an excellent pilot. According to Sergeant Ward, he likes aerobatics."

The major chuckled. "Then you'd better definitely hope he's been checked out in the Lightning!"

A knot was forming in Gordy's gut. "Yes, sir. Guess I'd better—"

"I know that your successors won't be able to fill your shoes. Proud to have had you here. Don't know where we'll all end up. Good luck and Godspeed."

"Proud to have served under your command, sir," Gordy replied.

"Thank you, Sergeant. And oh, say hello from me to your brother and my favorite Swedish chef."

"Yes, sir. Yes, I will." They saluted each other. Gordy ran to the pay-phones in the mess and called Leah and Frankie. He couldn't tell them where he was going, but he wanted to see them before he left. He jumped on the train for Fullerton. It would be almost four long years before they saw each other again.

****

Lt. Jean-Louis arrived earlier than expected the next morning. Gordy had fully packed the night before, as was his habit. He greeted his brother's nemesis with a salute followed by coffee in the kitchen. He'd prepared his own version of Swedish eggs and offered a portion to Jean-Louis.

"Quand partons-nous (when do we leave)?" Gordy inquired.

"Ah, qui. Yur mechani-x auwr, how we say, are pre-flight now, yes?"

"How many flights have you done in a Lightning?"

"Er, ah vols? J'ai fait trois. Three flights." Not what Gordy wanted to hear.

"How did the P-38 perform in your roll-in dive?

"Shee wus, how you say, sluggeesh?"

Gordy was more concerned. "Sluggish? She was sluggish? Did she shudder?"

"Mais no. She...was hard to flatten; niveau."

"Niveau? She was hard to level. Did you deploy the dive flaps?"

Jean-Louis looked perplexed. "Qu'est-ce que' 'dive flaps?'"

"Les volets de pongee aident à réduire la compressibilité. They reduce compressibility, mais qui? Very, very important in a dive, sir—critique, critical! Excuse me, sir, I need to check on something with our mechanics, er, mécaniciens. This might take a couple of hours, sir. Vérifiez et revérifiez...Check and double-check, sir."

Jean-Louis seemed incredulous. "Deux heures?"

"Mais qui, Two hours. I want to make sure she's perfect for you!"

"Ah! Parfait...perfect...pour moi. Qui!"

Gordy ran to the hangar to find his last dive-flap kit. He personally installed them on the trainer. Then he checked and double-checked to make sure they worked perfectly. He wasn't leaving the ground with the lieutenant any other way.

At the end of the runway, in the cockpit with Lt. Jean-Louis, it was almost impossible to hear. As the trainer strained against the captain's hold on its brakes, Gordy thought he heard, "Autorisé pour le décollage, nous allons ici." Had he just heard "Cleared for takeoff?"

The plane bounced forward with a jolt and was soon airborne. *Did we reach air speed rotation?* Gordy wondered. Instead of a steady climb, Jean-Louis pulled her up hard. *That's it; we're going to stall and plow into the San Bernardino Mountains.*

Jean-Louis turned hard right and then leveled off. He waggled the wings as they passed the tower. Gordy looked down on March Field for the last time and thought of Bob Hope's visit there. *Thanks for the memories.* His reverie was rudely interrupted by Jean-Louis' singing of "Wongolo Wale" at the top of his lungs. Now *that* he could hear.

The two hour-trip to Hamilton was uneventful, but as they approached, Lt. Jean-Louis slowed the trainer. Traffic was heavy. Gordy noted their altitude was 13,000 feet. As soon as he looked at the altimeter, Jean-Louis pushed the power and rolled left. Gordy had more to pray about.

As the plane fell steeply, vertigo set in. Gordy was close to blacking out. At the last moment, Jean-Louis leveled her for landing. Gordy was grateful to have installed the dive flaps and for his old friend Captain Wang's training of Jean-Louis. The landing was three-point perfect.

****

Hamilton was beyond a hectic place. P-39s and P-40 Warhawks were on the tarmac near the large hangar, which was still reserved for the Lightnings. They taxied behind it. There, Gordy gazed upon the largest number of P-38s he'd ever beheld. Twenty-four were arrayed in three rows of eight.

His orders were to report to the commander of the 48th Pursuit, Lt. Col. C. J. Laughlin.

At headquarters, Laughlin greeted Gordy. "Sergeant Ward, we're excited to have you here at Hamilton. Welcome. Y'all had a good flight?"

Gordy nodded. "Uneventful, thanks to Lieutenant Jean-Louis, sir."

"We are reorganizing your group to become the Forty-eighth Pursuit Training Squadron," Laughlin said. "The Forty-eighth will patrol the west coast to protect from a Jap invasion."

Gordy was flummoxed, "Pardon me, sir, but didn't we just deploy the Forty-ninth to San Diego? What's the logic of switching out the Forty-eighth from March to here and sending the Forty-ninth down there?"

"I dunno. Y'all wanna ask Lieutenant General Hap Arnold that? Y'all see where that gets ya!"

"Yes, sir."

"Yes, sir, y'all wanna ask him or yes you see where that'll get ya?"

Humbled, Gordy lowered his eyes. "Yes, sir, no, I don't want to ask the lieutenant general, sir."

"Dang right, Ward, you don't! We need you on the line trainin' mechanics and keepin' Northern California patrols flyin' twenty-four/ seven. You and your brother will be workin' together again soon. Does that suit you?"

"Yes, sir. That will absolutely suit me, sir."

"Grand. Then on with ya! Git to the hangar. Dismissed."

"Yes, sir."

Gordy sensed Lt. Col. Laughlin's frustration with the Air Corps command and control. It was a vexation that would continue throughout the war. Laughlin was circumspect about how air power would be employed to win the war.

****

The days at Hamilton were spent doing training and more training. It was clear the 48th and 49th training squadrons were not going into combat anytime soon. By February 1942 they were both flying defensive missions from the Mexican to the Oregon border. The Lightnings at Hamilton did have a secret assignment: they would first be deployed to the Aleutian Islands to help reclaim Attu and Kiska from the Japanese. Their occupation carried the threat of an invasion of the West Coast. Their capture would allow for the US potential to launch attacks on northern Japan.

****

At San Diego there was much confusion. Lindbergh Field was dedicated in 1928 and named after famed aviator Charles Lindbergh. Lindbergh had test-piloted his "Spirit of St. Louis" there. Immediately after Pearl Harbor, the 49th Training Squadron (soon to be Fighter Squadron) was deployed there to defend the southernmost West Coast. Lindbergh was being expanded by the Corps of Engineers to accommodate larger bombers. The P-38s of the 49th seemed to be an afterthought.

Callum was at his best after finally being assigned to a specific squadron. He and three other mechanics were maintaining twelve Lightnings. He had confidence in them because he'd trained them at Hamilton. He was not, however, happy about the air traffic around Coronado Bay. North Island Airfield was across from Lindbergh. Planes were everywhere.

Early on the morning of his arrival, six P-38s were pre-flighted, armored, and fueled to fly patrols outside of the overtaxed air corridor up and down the coast. Their pilots were young and inexperienced. The crowded skies and crossing flight patterns were a formula for disaster. The second set of Lightnings would be ready for their patrols as the first returned after 1300 hours. While there were landing lights at one runway, they'd been blacked out for a potential Japanese attack.

In broad daylight, a Lightning cleared for takeoff clipped an unauthorized B-18 Bolo Bomber's wing while taxiing onto the same runway. The pilot was able to abort, but his right engine caught fire. He escaped with severe burns.

We can't stay here, Callum thought. We're not safe here. Only weeks later, the squadron was transferred, based again at March Airfield.

Gordy wasn't sure how Lt. Colonel "More Beers for Me" thought he and his brother would be working together again. At least Lundgren was with him at Hamilton with the 48th Pursuit, though there was no hope the Swede would be cooking anything but Allison engines anytime soon.

****

Lockheed had originally nicknamed the P-38 "Atalanta" (the virgin huntress from Greek mythology, translated from the Greek as "unbalanced"). Private Lundgren loved the name. He had a sister by the same name back in Sweden.

The Brits dubbed the P-38 "Lightning Mark" (as in a duped person in a scam) after ordering Model 322 38Es with Allison engines exchangeable with P-40 Warhawks. Those 38s had twin right-hand engines rather than the counter-rotating propellers and no turbochargers. They couldn't reach the promised 400+ mph cruising speed and performed poorly at high altitudes.

The British Royal Air Force (RAF) Fighter Command had 143 P-38s on order after France fell in 1940. After a poor assessment from an RAF test pilot in the summer of 1941, the Brits canceled delivery of all but three P-38s. The contract was worth $15 million to Lockheed, and they held the RAF to its terms. Hostility ensued. Adding insult to injury, after Pearl Harbor, the Army Air Corps "claimed" forty of the P-38Es for defensive patrols of the west coast. Versions of the P-38 lived up to their "unbalanced" and "Lightning Mark" monikers. How different would the Battle of Britain have looked with turbocharged P-38s on the RAF's side?

Regardless, the intrepid Lightning name stuck but not for reasons one might have supposed, and Lundgren's Atalanta, working for her far (far-her in Swedish) in intelligence, remained in Sweden for the duration of the war.

# CHAPTER 27

# YOU'RE A FLOOZIE, I'M A MARINE

In early 1942, Izzie was fourteen years old. In June he would turn fifteen. He was still too young to join the US Armed Services, though he wanted to do so. At 927 Oak Park, Izzie remained the man of the house. His uncles' crazy making and grave-digging drudgery remained the bane of his existence.

Izzie found solace in his daily devotionals, meetings with Col. Bass, and reading about the United States Marine Corps. Col. Bass had provided him with several books, including *War Is a Racket* by Major General Smedley Butler. Butler's book decried industrial profiteering from warfare—an interesting choice from a World War I veteran. Izzie thought Sam might be trying to discourage his zeal for the Marines. He read every book he could get about the history of the Marines, from its founding on November 28, 1775, to the Civil War to the "Banana Wars" to WWI Germany's *Teufel Hunden* (Devil Dogs) name for them. Under top-secret cover, amphibious missions in Micronesia to establish forward bases were underway. The Marines had been preparing for island warfare since 1920.

Izzie's fascination with the Marines was first kindled from a book about the Texas-Mexican War. The Texas Marine Corps were modeled on the US Marine Corps. Republic of Texas Marines' pay was the same as their federal counterparts. They were the enforcers of order on the

Texas Navy's fleet of ships (*Invincible, Independence, Brutus,* and *Liberty* in 1836) and guarded the onshore facilities. Texas Marines were part of the boarding party that captured the Mexican ship *Pelicano.* While not exactly swashbuckling, it was exciting to Izzie. There were even stories of mutiny and pirating.

Col. Bass didn't dissuade his young friend's interest in the Marines. Bass knew Izzie was thinking of joining them, and he wanted Izzie to understand that the Marines' tagline, "First to Fight," meant potentially "First to Die."

"If you were a Marine, what would that actually look like to you?" Col. Bass asked.

Izzie was puzzled at the question. "I would be proud and brave."

"I know you would be, Izzie. What would that look like now that we're at war with Japan?"

"I'd be on the front lines taking back the Pacific from the Japs," Izzie replied, growing irritated.

"Combat isn't glorious, Izzie. It's brutal and indescribable. Men die in inglorious ways. It's not how brave or proud you are; it's whether you can kill or be killed."

Izzie was confounded by Col. Bass's statement. "What do you mean? The Marines are trained to kill the enemy. They're the best of the best."

"The Japanese Imperial Marines are trained to kill their enemy— that would be you and your fellow Marines. They follow 'the way of the warrior' or Bushido. Their code dates back to the eighth century. They believe in unquestioning loyalty to their emperor. Their obedience is absolute. They value honor even above life. They believe they're the best of the best. If you become a Marine you will be fighting them. They will not relent or surrender. They will kill as many Americans as possible."

"They have committed some of the worst atrocities in China and the Pacific," Izzie countered.

"They have no moral code but Bushido. They are doing the emperor's will. As a Marine, you will be their target. Do you understand?"

"They're godless pagans."

"That's no reason to kill people. 'Justice is mine sayeth the Lord.' They believe their emperor is a god."

"All the more reason to destroy them," Izzie said. "After Pearl Harbor they need to be annihilated!"

"I'm not arguing our righteous indignation against them," Col. Bass said. "I need you to understand that war is not a game. It's not just about defeating your enemy. It's personal. It destroys souls. It can take away your ability to reason. You relive it in nightmares, in fits of rage, or weeping. It's worse than you can ever imagine."

Izzie shook his head in confusion. "I don't understand. You're a hero. You fought for us in France. You fought for us in Mexico."

"I did my duty. I'm no hero. Heroes get buried. I just need you to understand that war is not what you expect. And as a Marine, you will have a greater probability of dying or becoming maimed for the rest of your life."

Izzie was not swayed. "Guess you're right. But still, I know I want to be a Marine more than anything in life. I want to be the best. I want to be a Marine."

"OK," Col. Bass concluded, "but don't become a Marine to escape Dallas. That is *not* a reason to become anything. Pray about it, and at least wait until you're fifteen. I know a lot of young fellows are lying about their ages to join. Will you wait until you're fifteen? Do that for an old soldier, please?"

"OK." Izzie stared at the colonel with renewed respect. "Will you show me a proper salute?"

"Of course I will."

****

On April 18, 1942, Jimmy Doolittle led the US bombing raid on Tokyo. The Battle of the Coral Sea, from May 4–8, 1942, was the first major naval battle in which American and Japanese aircraft carriers engaged one another. A month later almost to the day, June 4–7, 1942, the Battle of Midway raged. American cryptographers unmasked Japanese codes that led to an ambush of the Japanese fleet and the loss of four of its carriers. These engagements revealed the importance of "flattop" airpower in the Pacific. The remainder of America's success in the Pacific would depend on the amphibious invasion of strategic Japanese-held islands. The US Marine Corps would distinguish itself in ten significant island bloody battles. During World War II, 41,592 Marines were killed, and 145,706 were wounded.

****

On his fifteenth birthday, June 18, 1943, Izzie arrived at the Dallas Marine Corps recruiting station at 7:45 a.m. After passing his preliminary physical in downtown Dallas, Izzie walked out onto the street with renewed confidence. A prostitute on the corner waved at him. "Hey, big fella!"

"You're a floozie," Izzie replied. "I'm a Marine!"

He was so excited he didn't remember running to the cemetery. Upon his arrival he saw Conn digging another grave. *No more grave diggin' for me,* he thought. Conn looked up from his work and greeted his nephew. "Diggin' is fun. I'm not done."

"Good day to you, Uncle. It is a good day."

"Yup, good day. Where's my pay? Pay today, good day."

Izzie decided he'd miss his Conn's rhymes. "No pay today. Dig away."

"Yup, dig away, good day."

Izzie left for the cemetery office. There he accounted for the meager revenues from two services in the previous week. In the ledger he recorded a total of $4.25 to date for the month of July. On a separate piece of paper, he jotted the number down for Mary Mother. She would not be pleased.

Walking home he noticed the heat and thought, *This place is oppressive in summer.* He remembered reading about San Diego and its "superb coastal climate." He made a mental note to check that book out again from the library before he left.

Mary Mother was in the kitchen upon his arrival. She groused at the figure on the paper Izzie handed her. He prayed silently for provision for her, Conn, and Laurence. Soon, he would be able to help (as his brothers had before him) by sending part of his military pay home.

Izzie went to the church rectory to call Col. Bass with the good news.

"I will continue to pray for your safety until the day you come home," Col. Bass replied.

Izzie broke the long silence that followed. "Are you still there, Colonel?

"It's not Colonel; it's just Sam now. You're a Marine. Be the best of the best. Jesus's blessings to you, Isaiah."

A terrible scream could be heard for blocks around 927 Oak Park. A telegram from Isaiah lay on the kitchen floor. The Western Union messenger assumed it was news of another soldier's death. He was wrong. Her dear and beloved boy was in boot camp in California. He had lied about taking a trip to visit Callum there. Mary Mother's attempts through Col. Bass to inform the Navy of her son's actual age failed. Izzie was a Devil Dog.

Before he left, Izzie had visited Tim in Itasca. He'd sworn him to secrecy about his enlistment. Tim kept his promise to Izzie to read two books: Izzie's dog-eared copy of *Guadalcanal Diary* by Richard Tregaskis (it detailed the 1942 battle, the valor, and the camaraderie of the Marines there) and a San Diego travel guide. (How would it ever be returned to the Dallas Public Library?)

****

Upon his completion of six weeks of basic training at Camp Pendleton, California, and another three weeks to qualify as an expert rifleman, on his only leave, Izzie sought out his cousins, Leah and Frankie Ward, in Fullerton. Izzie prayed for them, his brothers' safety, and someone else they called the Swede. He also put away four pieces of delicious pie.

Izzie was on a troop train to San Francisco the following Monday. Within a day, he boarded a troop transport ship for a 4,782-mile trip to an undisclosed Pacific island. It would be his first trip overseas. He would be on four other transports to four other undisclosed islands before World War II came to an end.

****

"Where are we now?" Izzie screamed. "When do we go?"

"We're in hell now, son!" Marine Gunnery Sergeant Brad Younger screamed back. "Keep your head down!"

The Higgins (Landing Craft Vehicle Personnel (LCVP)) boat they were crammed into bounced and bobbed against the chop, swerving right and left. Ocean spray flew over the armored bow ramp, drenching the thirty-six Marine occupants.

Looking left, Izzie saw another Higgins, empty save for four photographers. *Bizarre,* he thought. *Wastin' a perfectly good Higgins...They're filming this!*

As the boat slowed, Izzie peeked above the gunnels to see stranded amphibious tracked vehicles (ATVs), "Alligators," littering the exposed reef. Strewn among them were countless bodies. Smoke choked him. He could barely see.

"This is as far as I can get you guys!" the driver shouted. "Neap tide... only three feet of clearance. Need five feet. Can't lose my boat to the reef. Good luck! Give 'em hell!"

*We are in hell,* Izzie thought. *What the...*

Japanese artillery opened up at the same time their machine guns seemed to spit from every direction on shore (there were over 500 nests on the island). The boat behind theirs took a direct artillery hit. The concussion of the explosion shook Izzie's boat, lifted it up, and slammed its bow down hard enough to swamp it. Bodies and boat shrapnel flew into their wake and off the starboard stern. The whistle of shells on their way and the continuous whizzing "pfft" of rapid fire and the clunk against the boat's armor was deafening. It seemed like thousands of rounds, and it was.

With an ominous creak, the ramp fell, exposing them to ravaging fire. They were 500 yards from any cover. His comrades fell from raking machine gun fire in the rows they were in before the ramp dropped, unable to get off a shot. He hoisted himself over the starboard side, attempting to take cover, but the Higgins driver gunned the boat's engine to full power and turned hard to port, leaving him exposed.

"Follow me!" Sgt. Younger shouted. "Stay low! Hug the reef! Nobody stand up!"

Izzie followed the sergeant crawling along the reef, tearing his new uniform to shreds. Only eleven of his fellow Marines were able to find cover next to a seawall on the beach, a corpsman among them. He began to render aid to the wounded. Nothing could be done for the dead. They were everywhere. Some were in piles. They were used as the only shields from fire.

Izzie's war had begun on the infamous Red Beach 2, Betio, on the Tarawa atoll in the Gilbert Islands.

★★★★

The Japanese commander of 5,000 troops (most of them Imperial Marines), Rear Admiral Keiji Shibazaki, told his troops that to conquer Tarawa, "It would take a million men one hundred years." It took 5,000

US Marines 76 hours at a cost of just over 1,000 men to take Tarawa. Shibazaki died there when a five-inch US naval artillery shell struck his headquarters.

US Amphibious Commanders Holland Smith and Harry Hill urged 6th Marine reinforcements for Tarawa. Radio messages from Red Beach 2 included "Have landed. Casualties 70%. Can't hold." They described it as an "Issue in doubt." That was the final message from Wake Island when it fell to Japan.

# CHAPTER 28

# I-BOATS AND I DON'TS

In 1942, there were numerous rumors of Japanese plans to attack the continental United States using B-1 (I-class) submarines. These were formidable, sophisticated weapons of war. Each was able to cruise up to 14,000 miles at 16 knots per hour, 800 tons of diesel fuel capacity, top surface speeds of 23.5 knots, 17 torpedoes, one 5.5-inch deck gun, two 25-mm machine guns to defend against enemy aircraft, a safe maximum dive depth of 330 feet, and one Yokosuka E14Y1 crew of four scout float planes (dubbed "Glen" by US Naval Intelligence) housed in a watertight deck hangar with a catapult launcher that could be sea-landed and collapsed back into its hangar.

Originally tasked with finding and sinking the USS *Lexington* aircraft carrier, an I-subs task force was redirected to patrol and attack targets on the California and Oregon coasts. Nine I-9 subs hidden outside the Golden Gate Bridge were ordered to shell (with a minimum of thirty 5.5-inch rounds each) San Francisco on Christmas Day 1941. On December 22, the attack was pushed back to December 27 by the infamous Admiral Isoroku Yamamoto. The delay caused the subs to run short on fuel, and their mission was eventually scrubbed.

On the southern California coast, a single I-sub (19) attacked the freighter *Absaroka* in the Catalina Channel, sinking her to her main deck. A crew member was killed; thirty-three survived. The US Navy sent a Patrol Coastal Yacht Pyc-3 Amethyst that dropped 32 depth charges, to no avail. Then on February 23, 1942, I-17 attacked the Ellwood Richfield Oil Storage facility.

Fear abounded resulting in terrible consequences. The relocation of American- and Canadian-Japanese had begun before the attack. It was a horrific moment in American history: 110,000 people of Japanese descent, 66,000 of them US citizens, were forced into internment camps.

Then there was the bogus "Battle of Los Angeles." An unannounced air-raid drill resulted in an erroneous report of enemy planes sighted, resulting in over 1,400 antiaircraft shells being fired, many of which fell on homes and cars in Santa Monica and Long Beach.

Panic ensued on the West Coast. More antiaircraft installations were installed and manned. Consolidated PBY Catalina flying boat patrols increased. People moved inland to avoid seaborne attacks.

The Japanese had plans to use their Kawanishi H8K "Emily" seaplanes' 4,400-mile attack range and 5,000-pound bomb capacity to target the US interior. From a base in the Gulf of California, they could hit just about any target on the mainland. Attacks on Oregon utilizing a Glen to drop 170-pound incendiary bombs failed due to unseasonably heavy rains.

All of this underlined the missions of the 48th and 49th Pursuit Squadrons to protect the West Coast. Unfortunately, their P-38s were not yet equipped to fly at night. They did watch for surfaced I-subs charging their batteries or oil trails from leaks. There were no encounters with Glens, Emilys, or with the subs. Things were getting boring and tense at the same time for Gordy and Callum. Yes, they were maintaining P-38s for patrols, but they were also concerned about being targeted for attacks (air-raid drills were conducted daily). The routine continued into the summer of 1942. Their August orders to England ended any monotony.

Their separation continued in England. They were restricted to their bases in preparation for Operation Torch. They would not see each other again until late February 1943. They would have no time to correspond. Their mutual consolation was eventually they knew were in the same Mediterranean Theater of war.

# CHAPTER 29

# SURVIVOR, "SCHM-VIVOR"

In November 1943 Tim Ward turned fifteen. He'd been "called up" from Itasca to replace Izzie at home and at the cemetery. He was not pleased with being the next man of the house. Miri returned to Dallas with him. Col. Bass kept his promise to drive them back in his '37 Master Deluxe. Mary Mother would have been furious that the colonel was doing so after, in her mind, he'd "influenced" Izzie to become a Leatherneck. Little was said during the trip. Col. Bass noticed that Tim had brought two books with him: *Guadalcanal Diary* and a San Diego travel guide. He knew who'd given them to him.

"Have you heard from your brothers?" he asked.

Tim shook his head. "No, haven't heard."

"Do you know where they are?"

"That's not supposed to be known!"

"As far as the East is from the West," Miri said.

"Psalm 103:12," Tim added.

The colonel smiled. "What good Bible memories you both have."

"So far, God has removed transgressions from us," Miri added. "I will miss Frau Schneider's Bible studies. Far away from his kind, in the pine, till deliverance come with springtime—so agonized Saul, drear and stark, blind and dumb."

Col. Bass was awed by her poetry memorization as well, "That's some memory you have there, young lady!"

"I have a lot of time to memorize," she replied. "That's Robert Browning, you know."

"No. No, I didn't know. Are you excited to be going home?"

"No, sir!" Tim replied bluntly. "We have no home."

"Your mother will be happy to have you there."

"To have us to work for her there!" Tim said. "She needs us now that the boys are all gone."

"Your mother does what she thinks is right," Col. Bass said, trying to quell Tim's bitterness. "Sometimes that's not right for both of you. Forgive her. She's trying to love you the only way she knows."

"She knows she abandoned us," Tim fired back. "She abandoned Cal and Gordy too. Abandonment isn't love."

"You both have been left; it's true," Col. Bass admitted. "She did what she could to survive, and look at you both...you're survivors!"

*What kind of nonsense is this guy trying to sell?* Tim wondered.

"When I say 'survivors,' I mean it in the best way. You both are stronger because of your experiences versus other people. You're not victims. You can forgive your mother and go on. Perhaps she can't go on. Don't get stuck in bitterness. You and your siblings are survivors."

"We're survivors," Miri said, repeating the colonel's words.

"Survivors survive," Col. Bass said. "It's what they do."

Tim was not impressed. "Survivors *must* survive. They have to."

Sam inquired about the books.

"I've read Guadalcanal Diary five times," Tim replied. "The travel guide's overdue at the public library. Don't know how much the fine will be."

"Remind me when we get to Dallas to take you there. I'll take care of the fine. It'll be fine."

Tim didn't appreciate the pun, but he was grateful for Col. Bass, nonetheless.

★★★★

Miri and Tim's arrival was ignominious. Sam had to drop them two blocks away from 927 Oak Lawn. They walked the rest of the way, telling Mary Mother they'd taken the bus. She was, as ever, critical of their "way home." She greeted Miri with a gentle hug and Tim with an awkward handshake.

"Grateful for your safe trip. No time to waste. I've given you the boys' room upstairs, Miri. Tim, you can sleep downstairs here in the sitting room—I have a cot."

*At least I had my own bed at Itasca,* Tim thought.

Soon Mary Mother had him walking with her to the cemetery. He ignored her admonitions about watching Conn. He had no plans to stay long enough to become entangled in supervising his uncle.

****

November 16, 1943, was a Friday. After digging two graves at Oak Lawn Cemetery, Tim slipped away downtown. He'd prepared his birth certificate to be barely legible. He caught the recruiter at the door of the station as he was trying to leave early for the weekend. It was good timing. He enlisted in the Marines and would be at Camp Pendleton in two weeks. He was a fifteen-year-old survivor who knew all the sights in San Diego.

# CHAPTER 30

# FIELD MANUAL 31-35

## *SNAFU Extraordinaire*

On Valentine's Day, 1943, the Battle of Sidi Bou Zid began, the first and most humiliating US Army ground defeat of World War II. At the Kasserine Pass in Tunisia, German forces routed US troops, pushing them back fifty miles. Several factors (not the least of which was the inexperience of US II Force ground forces and poor leadership) contributed to the success of Irwin Rommel's Afrika Korps. Three hundred were killed, 3,000 wounded, and 3,000 were missing or captured. Tactical support by Ju-87 Stuka dive-bombers and Bd-109 Messerschmitt fighters on US positions bolstered the Germans' offensive.

Since the establishment of the US Army Air Corps Command in 1941 under General Hap Arnold, US strategic and tactical control was in question. FM 31-35 put the control with field ground commanders, most of whom had little training in coordinating tactical use of air power. The American defeat at Kasserine brought changes in the form of FM 100-20 allowing for "centralized control; decentralized execution" tactics that had been effective for the British at El Alamein, Egypt.

Allied air fighter support in western North Africa was hampered by a number of factors. The first was the chain of command confusion, as mentioned above. Second was heavy losses. By the end of 1942, the 14th Fighter Group had lost nearly 60 percent of their pilots and planes, six of which resulted from attempts at night landings. Communication limitations were another factor, including inadequate numbers of radar installations for early warning of impending German attacks and poor communication from ground to air and vice versa. Locations of Allied airfields west of the Atlas Mountains were more prone to rainy weather in winter. Building Marston Mat (pierced or perforated steel planking) proved ineffective to combat muddy runways. Finally, the P-38 Lightning was a complicated aircraft flown by pilots with limited training and meager combat experience.

Major General Lloyd Fredendall, commander of the US Forces in North Africa, bunkered his headquarters eighty miles from Sidi Bou Zid where his troops were deployed. Fredendall positioned his troops too far apart to support each other. Air cover might have been able to bridge those gaps, but it was not employed. General Fredendall's headquarters were close to Tebessa, Algeria, where a US Air Corps airfield was established.

Fredendall was replaced by Major General George Patton on March 6, 1943. Gen. Patton was a proven ground tactician and a "tanker." He was credited (although not documented) to have shouted upon Rommel's retreat at El Guettar, Tunisia, "You magnificent bastards, I read your book!" Patton was not talking about the Luftwaffe's book.

It wasn't until after the invasion of Sicily that Allied commanders began to understand the importance of close air/ground support. P-38s were still mostly employed as protective escorts for heavy bombers.

****

The 48th Fighter Squadron's losses were unsustainable. Missions were scrubbed for lack of pilots and too few P-38s. After Kasserine, everything was in "reorganization" under Patton. Gordy was sent to Casablanca, Morocco, for a short leave. There he was finally reunited with Callum, who'd been maintaining P-39 Airacobras and P-40 Warhawks patrolling the northwest African coast since Operation Torch. They enjoyed a dinner together there before Callum was ordered back to his base. The next day Gordy was ferried back to Tunisia on a B-24 "flying coffin."

Gordy was almost immediately summoned to headquarters. He was unsure why; he had never been called there before. As he entered the command tent, he recognized his former commander, now Lieutenant Colonel Lindell Pearson. Gordy snapped to attention and saluted, a gesture that was not returned. Pearson motioned to him to remain outside and then joined him and lit a cigarette. Only then did they exchange salutes out of earshot of anyone in the tent.

"Good to see you alive, Ward," Pearson began. "Reports are you're still the best with the Lightning. How's your brother—what was his name?"

"Thank you, sir. Congrats on your promotion, and my brother's name is Callum, sir."

Pearson seemed indifferent. "Yeah, Callum. He alright?"

"Yes, sir. 'Got to see him in Casablanca last night and—"

"Cut the crap, Ward. I have a mission for you and some of your crews. We're preparing a counterattack push against the Jerrys—big armor operation. Need you to head a column over the Kasserine Pass to deliver ordnance to anti-tankers at El Guettar."

"Pardon me, sir," Gordy replied, "I'm an Air Corps tech sergeant, sir. What do I know about moving armor-piercing ordnance, sir?"

"What do you need to know, Ward? Deliver thousands of 75-mm shells, deadly to Panzers. Right now, you have too few P-38s to fly effective sorties. Need you to take ordnance over Kasserine to El Guettar—simple as that."

"Yes, sir," Gordy said, frowning in concern. "But we're in a full moon. That will make us easily visible to Stuka dive-bombers. Kasserine is narrow. There will be no space to evade a bombing, sir."

"You're looking at this from an Air Corps viewpoint, Ward. Fact is, we have no other route, and we need the shells there to kill Panzers. No other alternatives. Orders from the general."

Gordy knew, but he asked anyway. "General *Patton*, sir?"

"Yes, *that* general, Ward." Pearson pulled a typed set of orders from his inside coat pocket. "You can read the details if you want. Seven trucks requisitioned. You'll need one driver and two riflemen for protection each. One jeep, .50 cal. mounted. You'll lead the column in that. You can choose your drivers, or they will be assigned to you."

Gordy glanced at the orders, "Sir, I'd like to go on the record, sir. This is a suicide mission with the moon full, sir."

Pearson looked away and put out his cigarette. "Noted, but you're under orders from General Patton. It would be suicide to challenge him, Ward."

"Understood, sir. For the record, I would prefer that Command chose my drivers, sir. I will not risk my crews, sir."

Pearson nodded, avoiding eye contact. "Noted. Everything will be loaded tonight. Your trucks, drivers, and you depart at 2200 hours. Understand?"

"Yes, sir. Understood. May I ask a question, sir?"

Pearson nodded, still looking away. "Yes, of course."

"Whatever happened to Lieutenant Colonel C. J. Laughlin, sir?"

Pearson looked Gordy straight in the eye. "He was relieved by the Twelfth Air Force. Along with the Fredendall replacement, several Air Corps were changed. I'm his replacement."

*Yes, yes you are,* Gordy thought. Any hope of appealing the mission to Laughlin disappeared in that moment. He headed back to his tent and was greeted by Willie.

"You got some extra writing paper?" Gordy asked. "Need to write some letters."

"Sure. What's going on?"

Gordy explained and asked his friend to send his letters if anything happened.

Willie put his hand on his tent mate's shoulder. "Of course I will. But nothin's gonna happen."

"Pray not?" Gordy asked.

"OK, I'll pray." Willie had another idea in mind. He would *never* let his friend go on the mission without him. After all they'd been through, what friend would?

****

In March 1943 Tim arrived in the Pacific on an old towing/salvage scow as a cook for forty-three sailors and marines. His ship was far away from any combat. He was a Marine; he was just fifteen. Somehow everything he'd imagined wasn't coming true. Through an old Navy admiral friend, Col. Bass had made sure of that.

# CHAPTER 31

# SEUL SURVIVANT: MERCI, CROTTIN DE CHAMEAU!

## (Sole Survivor: Thank You, Camel Dung!)

It was March 2, 1943, next to the summit of the two-mile-long, two-mile-wide Kasserine Pass under a bright full moon. Mohammed Eri'Al, a Free French Bedouin, retired to his small black tent behind a large outcropping of rocks that hid his location from the pass. His two camels lay close by. Mohammed finished his evening prayers. Rising up from his Janamaz (prayer rug), he heard the sound of trucks struggling up into the pass, the shifting and grinding of gears. He also heard planes aloft, heard them slowing and then one powering up to invert into a dive.

Suddenly began the terrifying and all-too-familiar whine from Stuka Junkers 87s (from Sturkampfflugzeug "dive-bomber") screaming down at a target, louder and louder, closer and closer. Moments later, an enormous explosion turned the darkness into blinding light. The first Stukas' 550- and two 250-pound bomb payloads found their marks. The ground shook below him. Had they spotted his tent under the bright moon above?

Rocks flew up and then tumbled down seemingly at the same time. Mohammed fell flat for cover. More rocks and pebbles rained down. Then came another jolting blast, this time with a light that rivaled daylight. The camels complained, grunting and growling loudly. In consecutive repetition, more diving Stukas. Again and again, the explosions came louder and brighter until Mohammed could hardly hear or see. More secondary eruptions sent fireworks skyward, propelling rocks and flaming shrapnel in every direction.

In the pass, a commander was screaming orders in English. "Willie, get off! Everyone, off the trucks! Take cover! Get away from the trucks! Get down!"

What Mohammed couldn't see was that forward of the column of seven evenly spaced trucks filled with heavy artillery ordnance (new M62 armor-piercing shells for M10 tank destroyers), was a single jeep fitted with a Browning .50 caliber machine gun on a turret platform in lieu of a rear seat. The sound of its slide cock was followed by bursts of rapid fire. Through the heavy smoke, Mohammed saw tracers going up. Five more Stukas dove in. More rocking explosions followed each, then a final larger and louder explosion sent a huge fireball high into the night sky.

It was followed by an eerie quiet punctuated by smaller explosions and dense black smoke rising everywhere. One Stuka flew back low above the smoke, strafing with its 7.92-mm wing machine guns. After a single pass, it climbed out hard, up and away. There were no screams of agony, no wails from the wounded.

After several minutes, Mohammed checked the magazine of his captured P.08 Luger, took his long dagger, and slipped both into the back of his waistband. He slowly climbed up, around, and over the rocks sheltering him and his camels and peered into the pass. Flames flew up from everywhere, and the black smoke was choking thick. The heat was sweltering. Every truck was alight, engulfed with searing fire. He saw burning figures in the cabs and on the ground. He climbed down, careful to avoid getting close to the trucks. The dreadfully familiar smell of burning flesh assaulted his nose.

Scanning the sky to make sure the dive-bombers were gone, he looked down toward the jeep. Close by lay a body, face down. A trail of blood led from the jeep that indicated he'd been crawling back toward the trucks. Mohammed scurried down the rocky embankment until he reached the soldier. He rolled him over, revealing a deep wound in his left shoulder and what appeared to be shrapnel bulging from it.

"Al-low! Je suis Liber-Francais...I am Free French. Can you hear me?" Mohammed's shouts yielded no response.

He listened for breathing and felt for a pulse. Both were present, but the man was unconscious. He hefted the soldier onto his back in a fireman's carry and began to haul the man's limp body up and over the ridge that concealed his tent. He felt warm blood draining onto his back. As he struggled to keep his balance on the down slope's larger rocks, he lowered the soldier and dragged him by his shirt the rest of the way.

Back in his tent while attending to the shoulder wound, Mohammed used his long dagger to dislodge a large piece of shrapnel. This only opened the wound wider, resulting in profuse, spurting bleeding. He had nothing to close the gash. As he struggled to hold the wound shut, he realized he needed another way. He ran out to where the camels lay and gathered up two large handfuls of dung. Rushing back under his tent, he slung the muck on the wound and pressed. It seemed to begin to stem the bleeding. He ran back out and retrieved another two piles, returned and slapped them on, spreading the rest over the shoulder. Not long after, the bleeding appeared to stop.

The remainder of that night and almost a day passed. The sergeant (shown by his sleeve's insignia) remained unconscious, his breathing steady. Several times he began to come to and muttered something in English that Mohammed didn't comprehend. It was not because he didn't speak English; he knew it well. It was the context of his comrade-in-arm's words he couldn't comprehend.

****

In a moment, there was warm light. A low soothing sound coursed through Gordy's head. He felt increasing warmth but couldn't sense the containment of his body. Gordy was floating comfortably above the tent, smoke and fire below, completely aware and at peace. He felt a pleasant force pulling him up and closer to a bright light. A gentle voice spoke calmly to him. "Do you remember Genesis 32?" Gordy heard the voice recite it clearly. "So Jacob was left alone, and a man wrestled with him till daybreak. When the man saw that he could not overpower him, he touched the socket of Jacob's hip so that his hip was wrenched as he wrestled with the man. Then the man said, 'Let me go, for it is daybreak.' But Jacob replied, 'I will not let you go unless you bless me.' The man asked him, what is your name?'

"'Jacob,' he answered.

"Then the man said, 'Your name will no longer be Jacob, but Israel, because you have struggled with God and with humans and have overcome.'

"Jacob said, 'Please tell me your name.'

"But he replied, 'Why do you ask my name?' Then he blessed him there.

"So Jacob called the place Peniel, saying, 'It is because I saw God face to face, and yet my life was spared.'

"The sun rose above him as he passed Peniel, and he was limping because of his hip. Therefore to this day the Israelites do not eat the tendon attached to the socket of the hip, because the socket of Jacob's hip was touched near the tendon."

Then the voice said to Gordy, "I will bless you by sparing you now. Here where Israel resides is the place that I promised I would prepare for you. However, this is not the time for you."

Gordy struggled to speak. "If this is heaven, Lord Jesus, why does it smell so bad?"

"This is not your time," the voice said again.

"Why?" Gordy replied.

"In time you will be here with me, but now you have much more to do..." The voice was fading.

"I-I'm finished here on earth," Gordy pleaded. "Let me leave!"

"You have more..." the voice faded out completely, replaced by a pounding crescendo. Gordy felt a spinning force pulling him down. Then he felt a thud followed by a searing pain in his shoulder.

"But it smells so bad," he tried to shout, but he couldn't hear himself speak.

****

"Sent si mauvais!" (Smells so bad!) Gordy cried.

*More muttering, now in French,* Mohammed thought. But how could the sergeant know French?

No matter. Mohammed took out his map to confirm his most recent understanding of the Allied lines. The Americans would send up a reconnaissance plane when their convoy didn't reach its destination in a reasonable time. He would need to be ready to send up a distress signal, but not there. His location and his role in the planning for the Battle of El Guettar could only be known to Allah and the highest-ranking Allied officer. He would have to use his camels and a tent pole litter between them to move the sergeant to safety and much-needed medical care.

The journey was fitful. The sergeant would come to and let out wails of pain, which could betray their position to the enemy. Eventually, Mohammed chose a stick-gag as the best way to prevent the outbursts.

Gordy would regain consciousness but could not hear as a result of the concussions of the bombs in the pass. Looking up, he could see the stars. He swayed back and forth in a hammock litter between the camels, covered as if a load of grain. And the disgusting smell! In a moment of clarity, he peeked over at his left shoulder and realized it was covered by a camel dung poultice. He'd been rescued by a maniac.

Mohammed stopped periodically to check on his comrade and to offer water. Finally, he found Gordy conscious and awake.

"Je suis Libre-Francais. Je suis fidèle au général Henri Giraud. Je m'appelle Commandant Eri'Al," he said. (I am Free French. I am loyal to General Henri Giraud. My name is Commander Eri'Al.) Gordy could hear little other than a loud thumping in his ears. He muttered, still gagged.

"Pardon, Sergeant?" Mohammed removed the stick and cloth. Gordy motioned to his ears and shook his head. "Sergeant Gordon Truett Ward, Serial number—"

"Mon ami, I have all that from your dog tags! I am Free French! We are close to your lines. I will show a white flag, get you to hospital."

"Je nais c'est pas." (I don't know) Gordy replied again, pointing to his ears. "Can't hear you!"

"Vous parle Francais? Tres bien!" Mohammed shouted. "Sur nous allon!" (On we go!)

On we go, Gordy thought. So, on we go. So too went the oppressive smell. You might be able to wrestle with God, but you can't wrestle a vile smell. Camel dung and heaven must be mutually exclusive.

Finally, he fell fast asleep. He awakened often from nightmares of the pass. He wept for the loss of Willie and the men for whom he'd been responsible. There would be little sleeping from then on.

# CHAPTER 32

# K(NO)W NEWS

It was a fine spring day in Dallas. Eleven-year-old Andy Bliss, the Western Union delivery boy, hopped off his bicycle and checked the address for his delivery, 927 Oak Park. He'd been there before. Had it been bad news then? He couldn't remember. He was used to delivering bad news. He often prayed that no one would be home. But that only meant he had to go back. He knocked on the screen door lightly. At first there was no response. He knocked again and then began to retreat from the front stoop. Then a voice came from the open upstairs window.

"Who's there?" Miri shouted. "Conn, this better not be another one of your knock-knock jokes! No more giggles for nickels, you sod!"

"Ma'am, I have a Western Union telegram for a Mary Ward!" Andy shouted up.

Miri was embarrassed. "Pardon me. I thought you were my uncle. She's not here. She's at Oak Park Cemetery."

"Ma'am, would you please sign for this? I have to get back to the office, and it's not near the cemetery."

Miri was frightened and curious. She ran down the stairs and out the door to where Andy was standing. He was holding the telegram in his left hand and a clipboard in his right, indicating she couldn't have the message without signing for it.

"Sign here, please!"

Miri hesitated, then signed. As soon as Andy left, she ran to the cemetery.

"Mother, I have a telegram delivered to the house."

Mary Mother's heart sank. *Please no, Lord Jesus, please!*

"Do you want me to open for you, Mother?"

"Yes, please...I can't!"

Miri unfolded the telegram and read it out loud. "The Secretary of War desires to express his deep regret that your son, Sergeant Gordon Truett Ward, has been listed as missing in action since March twenty-three in North Africa. If further details or other information are received, you will be promptly notified."

"Gordy! Lord Jesus, no! Gordy!"

Miri held her. "Mother, he's missing. Let's pray they find him alive!"

They prayed out loud that Gordy would be found alive and safe. They continued to pray for almost a month.

****

Four days had passed. Gordy was now fully conscious and also fully aware of the pain from his wound. His ears were still filled with a sound that could be described as a loud banging, then louder banging.

It was almost sunrise when Gordy felt the camels come to a halt, his litter swinging between them. What was it, another check-up from Mohammed? Yup, there he was.

"C'est bon, mon ami Sarge?"

Gordy screamed (he couldn't hear how loud his voice was). "I'm deaf! Jes suis sourd, Commandant!"

Mohammed frowned and held his index finger to his lips. He pulled a notebook from his pocket and wrote a message: "Quiet! Close to your lines. No mistake us for German patrol, comprendre?"

Gordy nodded. He winced as the camels lay down, and his back hit the ground. He motioned to Mohammed to hand him the notebook. "White flag," he wrote. "Lt. Col. Pearson = Mission Commander. Field

Hospital = Dr. Bosnick, Pass Question: What was Hopalong Cassidy's horse's name? Answer: Topper."

Mohammed gave him a thumbs-up.

Just then they both were alarmed by the distinctive sound of a German Bayerische Motoren Werke (BMW) R75 motorcycle winding up behind them. It was a Jerry scout patrol.

Mohammed pulled the tarp over Gordy and took cover behind the forward camel, pulling out his Luger. The motorcycle slowed and crept toward the camels. The soldier in the sidecar cocked his rifle, jumped out, and cautiously approached the resting camels. His driver stopped, dismounted, and pulled his pistol. The front camel grunted, and the rifleman drew a bead on it. Below the camel's head, Mohammed rolled to the ground and shot the nearest German dead.

Gordy tried not to move but twitched under the tarp, drawing a shot from the driver. That was enough distraction for Mohammed to get a second shot at him. He fell backward into the sidecar. Within seconds both Germans were eliminated. Mohammed checked the Germans' pulses, grabbed their weapons, then listened as he scanned the horizon for another motorcycle. Silence. Then Mohammed ran to see if Gordy was hit. The bullet that the driver had fired at the tarp had ricocheted off the ground. Mohammed pulled the tarp up to find blood under Gordy. He rolled him over onto his wounded shoulder, producing a pain-filled screech, only to find a wound in Gordy's left buttocks. The round had passed right through and was resting in the blood beneath him.

"Vous êtes un sergent chanceux! Vos fesses vous ont sauvé!" Mohammed joked as he dressed the wound. (You are a lucky Sergeant! Your butt has saved you!)

Gordy couldn't hear the quip. He only knew that Mohammed had saved his life yet again. He gave a thumbs-up and then pressed his hands together in thanks. Then on they went.

As they approached the Americans' forward-most lines, they were held at gunpoint by a US patrol. After giving his "Topper" answer and showing his identification, Mohammed was escorted to command headquarters, and Gordy was taken to the field hospital. He had slipped unconscious again. When he awakened, his eyes focused on the eyes of a beautiful surgical nurse. Finally, despite some residual rumbling, he could hear somewhat again. He pointed to his ears and asked her to speak louder.

"Welcome back!" she shouted. "You've been in and out. You've also been complaining about a bad smell. We've taken care of that and your wounds, soldier. You're gonna be just fine."

Gordy smiled. "Bet you tell all the guys that, don't you?"

She laughed. "You all smell pretty bad! But I must say, *nothin'* like you did!"

That brought laughter from another patient in the tent.

"You're going to be just fine!" she assured him.

"Where's Commander Mohammed Eri'Al?" Gordy asked. "I want to thank him for saving my life...twice."

She thought about it for a moment. "Sorry, don't know anyone by that name. Is he with us?" Gordy asked her to repeat her question. "IS HE WITH US?"

"No, ma'am!" Gordy shouted back. "He's the Free French Bedouin who brought me here."

"So sorry, Sergeant, but no one's inquired about you. I'll see what I can find out. You rest now."

Meanwhile, Mohammed had already returned to the desert. He was needed north of El Guettar to help direct artillery fire at German tanks attempting to break out in Tunisia. Patton would win the day.

After Gordy had been in the hospital tent for two days, Lt. Col. Pearson came to visit him. At his bedside, he awarded Gordy a Purple Heart and a Bronze Star "for meritorious service in a war zone."

As Pearson was about to pin them on, Gordy stopped him. "Sir, may I speak, please?"

"Of course, Sergeant Ward."

"Sir, I am refusing these medals, sir."

Pearson looked at him in surprise. "Why, Sergeant?"

"These awards belong to the twenty-one men, including my counterpart, Willie Edson, who died in the Kasserine Pass. I respectfully refuse them, sir."

"Sergeant Ward, this is unheard of."

"Sir, I was responsible for those soldiers. I am not worthy to accept these. Please accept my decision."

"Alright, but this won't look good on your record."

If Gordy could have, he would have shoved the medals down Pearson's throat. It was a blessing that his butt wound kept him bedridden. *My record? Who cares about my stinking record?* he thought. *You Patton kiss-ass!*

"So be it, sir," Gordy said, "and no thank you, sir."

Gordy held Gen. George Patton and his sycophant, Lt. Col. Pearson, in contempt for the rest of his life.

Within two weeks, Gordy returned to duty. He cleaned out Willie's footlocker. There, on top of everything, were the letters he'd written in case something happened to him. He wrote a poignant letter home to Willie's parents in Alabama extolling his heroism and character. "God has promised we will all see Willie again," he concluded. "He was my comrade in battle, my confidante, and my friend. 'Greater love hath no man than this: that a man lay down his life for his friend.'"

✳✳✳✳

Three and a half weeks went by. Miri prayed that no news was good news. She prayed they would hear that Gordy had been found alive.

Andy Bliss returned to 927 Oak Park to deliver a telegram that detailed that Gerome Ward had been found and returned to duty with the 48th Fighter Squadron. Who was Gerome? How many Wards could there be in the 48th? Who cared! It had to be him. The ladies were ecstatic!

****

On the day Pearl Harbor was attacked, only 69 Lockheed P-38 Lightnings were in service. The Battle of El Guettar was a decisive armor victory, finishing off the Germans in North Africa. The Brits drove north to Tunis, the Americans to Bizerte. At El Guettar, the Americans introduced their new M62 rounds with their M10 tank destroyers. It was complemented by the mobile M3s. Thirty German tanks were destroyed at a cost of twenty M3s and seven M10s. Their deadly ordnance was delivered in broad daylight on March 15, 1943, by a convoy of twelve trucks covered by close P-38 air support. The dwindling Lightnings were repurposed as such for the remainder of the North African and Italian campaigns. Rommel had returned to Germany before El Guettar began. Gen. Patton served as commander in North Africa for only sixty-nine days.

By May 1943, the Afrika Korps was defeated. The number of German POWs at the end of the North African Campaign totaled over 150,000—ironically, about 50,000 of them ended up in seventy POW camps in Texas.

# CHAPTER 33

# DOIN' THEIR DOODY

Summer 1943 was busy for Laurence. He was pulling double duty on the Southern Pacific Railroad. Trains were essential to the war effort. Transport of troops, equipment, and food (especially Texas beef) was ceaseless. Laurence was passionate about helping soldiers in every way he could. He secured a small American flag to each engine he drove.

Between the two-week intervals of work, Laurence spent time at home with Conn. He was exhausted but willing to help around home and the cemetery. Conn was his same, comic self. He took charge of the ice cream shop "brigade" to downtown. It was a small respite for Miri, Mary Mother, Laurence, and him from the rigors of work and war. They would walk there and back twice a week, though never on Sundays.

Because of the August heat, Mary Mother refused to go and sent Miri and the uncles on their way. "Don't waste time and money. No dilly-dallying, Conn."

"No time or money," Conn replied. "That's not funny."

"You forgot to include 'fine,' which rhymes with 'time,'" Miri said. "*Not* fine and not funny."

Connie laughed and repeated his version of the phrase over and over as they walked downtown. "Yup, not fine but funny. Not fine but funny!'"

As they walked, they passed a house known to Laurence as "Jerry's Place." It was the home of Ludwig Bishcoff, a German national. Herr

Ludwig had suffered great ridicule even before the war began. It was rumored that he was part of a large spy ring encompassing the entire US. Germans and Japanese were already being rounded up for internment. There was a German camp outside of Crystal City and another southeast of San Antonio. Bischoff kept to himself and avoided confrontation with those in the neighborhood, making him a "suspicious character."

As they passed Herr Bischoff's open detached garage, Laurence spat. "You son of Hitler, die! Die, die, die!"

Miri stopped him. "Laurence, he's German. Not all Germans are Nazis."

Bischoff turned away in an attempt to ignore Laurence, but Laurence persisted, becoming even more agitated. "Sausage eater! Nut-zi! Git on back there to Germany!"

"It's Naat-z," Miri interjected, "not Nut-zi. Let's go, Uncle."

Herr Bischoff turned and stared at Laurence in disdain. "Off with you, peasant. Go on, now!"

"Jerry, die!" Laurence yelled. "Die, ya dirty Jerry, die! I'm a watchin' you!"

Conn held Laurence back as he threw in one more insult. "Dang, yur E-V-U-L, an' you knows it!"

Bischoff closed his garage doors and walked toward his house. As he did, Miri apologized for her uncle and his atrocious spelling. The Wards walked on.

"LUD-week Bish-cough," Laurence said. "Somethin' like that, be his name. He's a spy, Miri, I done knowed it."

Miri wondered how her uncle "knowed" Bischoff's name. She had no idea that Laurence had snuck a look at the mail in the mailbox one night on the way home from the railyard.

✳✳✳✳

As they neared the ice cream shop, Conn bolted across the street to the Rialto Theater. Laurence and Miri chased him. Was he going to repeat his "Cluck Alley" performance of 1941? Instead, he ran to the billboard and jumped up and down. "Mickey, Mickey! Mickey Mouse!" Connie had been a sucker for cartoons since Mickey Mouse premiered in 1928.

Ever the kid, Laurence shouted after him. "Mickey Mouse!"

Miri read the bill title to Conn. "Mickey, Pluto and the Armadillo."

The swamp-cooled Rialto was more than inviting in the heat and humidity. Conn had three dimes to pay for the show. Miri nodded reluctantly. The ticket booth was empty, so they left the money in the change slot and went inside.

The theater owner, Benjamin Weber, was a World War I veteran and the projectionist at Naval Station Dallas (training for Marine and Coast Guard pilots). Ben was previewing a new service cartoon that had been written by Dr. Seuss and voiced by Mel Blanc of Bugs Bunny fame. It was intended for the military only to promote security. Not realizing there were patrons in the theater, he viewed the three-minute short, *Private Snafu: Spies*, four times before he heard, "Mickey! We want Mickey! Where's Mickey?"

Ben shut off the projector, brought up the lights, and ran to the edge of the balcony. "Who's there?" he yelled. He couldn't see the Wards sitting below the overhang.

"We left our money at the booth," Miri said. "My uncles wanted to see Mickey, Pluto and the Armadillo."

"Show yourselves!" Ben yelled.

They moved to the aisle and down to where they were visible. Conn smiled and waved.

"How long y'all been down there?" Ben asked, irritated. "We don't open today until four o'clock. It's on the sign outside. We only have matinees on the weekends."

"Sorry, sir," Miri said. "We came in when you were showing the first Private Snafu. We didn't realize—"

"You saw it all four times? That's a classified movie—not for the public. It's for the military only."

"Sorry again," Miri replied. "We kept waiting for Mickey, Pluto and the Armadillo. You must admit, Private Snafu's a little childish—creative but sort of churlish too. We have four brothers, er, these fellows' nephews, two each in the Army Air Corps and the Marines."

"There's nothing childish or churlish about it, young lady. It's intended to educate soldiers. We have to keep them safe."

"You mean dumbed down, don't you? Is it intended to be nice?"

"What do you mean? Of course it's nice." Ben was becoming more irritated.

"My brother Gordy, one of the two in the Army Air Corps, is a linguist. He taught me that the derivation of the word 'nice' is from the Old Latin 'nescius,' meaning ignorant. So is Private Snafu meant to be... stupid?"

"Enough!" Ben replied. "Maybe it's meant to be understood by soldiers who aren't snooty linguists. OK, look, y'all have seen a movie just now that's not for public consumption. Tell y'all what, I'll spool-up Mickey, Pluto and the Armadillo if you promise you won't tell anyone about Private Snafu."

Miri agreed to the terms. "Sort of like the good Private Snafu couldn't keep his secret?" she asked.

Despite her sarcasm, Ben showed *Mickey, Pluto and the Armadillo*. In Miri's literary-critical analysis, she was certain that the film was not worth the price of admittance.

The Private Snafu series totaled twenty-eight movies by the end of the war. While Miri wasn't impressed with either movie, *Private Snafu: Spies* had a profound impact on Laurence: He had work to do.

****

The Abwehr (pronounced ab'ver, derived from the German word for "defense") was the German Military Intelligence Service. It was the lead German organization conducting covert operations in and against the United States. Headed by Admiral Wilhelm Canaris, it was responsible for subversion, espionage, and sabotage on American soil.

One of Abwehr's strategies was to foment Nazi support amongst the 10.8 million German-Americans in the US. The internment of people of German descent had begun in World War I. Then after Pearl Harbor, 1,260 German nationals who had been under surveillance were detained and arrested. Abwehr believed that, out of fear, German communities would rise up in resistance against the US government. They did not. After Hitler declared war on the US, Nazi organizations like the German-American Bund became anathema. Abwehr landed saboteurs from U-boats in New York and Florida who failed their missions.

Abwehr seemed to have shot itself in the foot at every turn. But then there was Simon and Marie Koedel. Simon, a World War I veteran with the US Army, a naturalized citizen, and later a German soldier, had turned to spying on Britain for Germany. The Brits deported him to the US. Not wanting to change his spots before World War II, he lobbied Abwehr to become Agent "A2001" in America. His cover was that he was a member of the US Army Ordnance Association (AOA). Astonishingly, the FBI and the Office of Strategic Services (OSS) allowed him access to Army ordnance production and storage facilities.

Koedel's adopted daughter, Marie, became his accomplice. She became engaged to Republic Aviation's John Walters (of P-47 Thunderbolt fame), then quickly broke off the betrothal, telling him that she and her father were German spies. Walters went to the FBI. The Koedels were already under surveillance.

With Marie's translation help (Simon Koedel wrote poorly in English), he filed some 600 reports to Bremen until 1943. He was hiding in plain sight as a projectionist at the Lyric Theater in Manhattan.

Koedel's handler was Johannes Bischoff, head of the Abwehr Bremen sub-branch. Koedel proved his value again by uncovering a flaw in the walled and direct phone line security between President Roosevelt and Winston Churchill. Abwehr was able to work around the technology to eavesdrop on the two leaders' conversations.

****

Miri walked far ahead of her uncles on the way home. It wasn't until she was almost there that she was aware that her mischievous uncles weren't behind her. It was hot. She wasn't going back to find them.

Laurence pulled Conn aside as they left the ice cream shop. "Gotta git to that Bit-coff's house, Connie!" he whispered.

They ducked into the alley as Miri walked on.

"Gotta git, coffee bits?" Conn asked.

Laurence grabbed Conn by the shoulders (as if that would make a difference). "No, Connie! Bit-coff! That Jerry! He's hidin' somethin'! You knows it, and I knows it!"

"You an' I knows it. Dig a pit?"

Laurence didn't have time for this. "Listen, or I'm gonna bury your sorry butt in that pit. Listen!"

Conn put his hands behind his ears. "Listen. Listen."

"Here's the plan. We git to the Jerry's house and break into the garage. You keep watch whiles I does the searchin' for *evi-dance*—how's that sound?"

"Yup. Listen. Loud sound. Yup."

"Ahhh-Errg! No loud sound! You watch fur Bit-coff, savvy? Let's git."

As she applied an ice cube to her forehead and sipped on a cold glass of lemonade, Miri's senses returned to her from the muggy heat. *Wait, what have I done?* she thought. *Conn and Laurence! They're on their way to Herr Bischoff's house! I've gotta stop them!*

With a pit in her stomach, she ran next door to use the phone to call the police. Halfway there, she ran to Bischoff's house instead.

She was too late. Laurence had used his "railroad strength" to pull the ventilator cover off the back wall, crawled through, and began his "investigation." Conn was stationed around the side of the garage to watch for Herr Bischoff. He whistled "Comin' Round the Mountain," which raised Laurence's ire in the garage, prompting several knuckle raps on a window and silent "mouth zips." Connie loved him some "Comin' Round the Mountain."

The garage was a mess, filled with piles of dusty boxes. Only one caught Laurence's eye. It was not dusty. As he opened it, he heard a commotion outside of the garage.

"Was ist das? Yoo, again?"

Miri had arrived. She thought quickly on her feet. "So sorry, Herr Bischoff! I believe I dropped my antique rhinestone hairpin when we walked by earlier today. It was a gift from my grandmother. Can you help me look, please?"

In her peripheral vision she caught a glimpse of Conn peering around the corner of the garage. He smiled his silly smile and waved his pinky finger at his favorite (only) niece.

Herr Bischoff was not convinced. "I whud have noticed somethin' shiny in the durt. Why ur you here?" His demeanor became more threatening. Just then, Connie whistled "Comin' Round the Mountain" as he appeared from around the side of the garage.

All of this gave Laurence just enough time to exit through the vent and hide in the bushes to watch what Bischoff might do. He was ready to "jump and whump" the Jerry if he came near Miri.

"Get off my property!" Bischoff shouted. "I vill call police! Off da property! Off an' keep off!"

"I just remembered," Miri said, "I left my hairpin at the ice cream parlor, so sorry."

"Go off, now! You go off! And take das whistlin' ee-diot wid you."

Connie smiled; he'd been called worse.

"Let's go, Uncle. Take my hand."

Conn was a hand crusher. Miri squealed as they walked away. Bischoff thought he'd been made fun of again. It was all Laurence could do not to whack the German "real good." He followed Miri and Conn.

"What were you thinking, Uncle Laurence? If that man really is a Nazi agent, he could be dangerous to you and all of us, including Mary Mother."

Laurence pondered the prospects. "How'd that be bad?"

Connie half burped and laughed.

Miri wasn't amused.

Ludwig Bischoff reconnoitered the garage. Nothing seemed to be missing. As he closed the door, he heard a loud clunk from around back: the unsecured vent cover falling off. To file an insurance claim, he called the police to report a garage break-in. He could only describe the two crazy uncles and the woman vaguely. He didn't have time. He had to get some documents across town.

After a German agent in Brazil was arrested by the FBI, a search of Ludwig Bischoff father-in-law's garage in Dallas, Texas, found four checks to the German, one with the notation "By order Johannes Bischoff." Was he a relative or a cover name? The check was enough to get him arrested. Five months had passed before the FBI got the search warrant. In the long-term, it was helpful evidence in the prosecution and conviction of Simon and Marie Koedel. Marie claimed she had only joined her father in espionage because it was "fun and exciting."

What was Laurence's comment when the *Dallas Morning News* reported the arrest of Ludwig Bischoff? "I knowed it...I done knowed it!"

Again, he got to "a ponderin." "What about that snooty projectionist fella at the Rialto, hmm? Gotta git!"

****

Wilhelm Canaris, the head of Abwehr, was appalled by the atrocities committed by the Nazi Army in Poland. He protested even to Adolf Hitler. Despite that he became the Fuhrer's confidante. In several different situations, he fed Hitler information that was either incorrect or false. For example, he provided inflated estimates of the RAF's strength in the Battle of Britain, and he underestimated the probability that the Americans would invade North Africa (the German high command was "totally surprised" when they did so). Still, Admiral Canaris remained in control of German military intelligence for most of the war.

After the war, papers revealed that Canaris was part of several conspiracies to kill the Fuhrer. In the end, his personal diary sealed his fate when it was shown to Hitler. He was humiliated (stripped naked) and hung the same day as Dietrich Bonhoeffer on April 9, 1945, at Flossenbürg Concentration Camp.

# CHAPTER 34

# PANTELLERIA E SICILIA

## (Eh and Eh!)

Under Benito Mussolini, the forty-two-mile Mediterranean island of Pantelleria was transformed into a fortress "rock" like Gibraltar. The Italians built artillery, anti-aircraft bunkers, and underground hangars for war planes. After Mussolini invaded Ethiopia in 1935 and it later allied itself with Germany in the "Pact of Steel" in 1939, Pantelleria became a strategic stronghold for Italian/Luftwaffe airpower and U-boat and Italian naval operations. It was critical to the protection of the Mediterranean—what Il Duce called "Mare Nostrum" (translated: "Our (Italy's from the time of the Roman Empire) Sea."

General Dwight Eisenhower knew that taking Sicily was a critical step to conquering mainland Italy. Army Chief of Staff George Marshall was not happy about the "lack of boldness and adaptability" he saw in Eisenhower. "Ike" chose air power to conquer Pantelleria. Occupation of the island would provide the base for naval and air raids on Sicily. Operation Corkscrew was born.

After deliberation among North Africa Allied Air Command, it was decided that devastating the island with heavy bombing would be the path to victory. From May 8 to June 11, 1943, they flew 5,285 bombing sorties over Pantelleria, dropping 6,313 tons of bombs on the 12,000 Italian and German troops there. Historically, Operation Corkscrew was so successful that when the British 1st Infantry landed at Porto di Pantelleria, the Italian commander had already surrendered. It was the first time in history that a ground force had surrendered because of air power alone in lieu of a landing assault.

****

From Feb. 28 to May 5, 1943 the 48th Pursuit Squadron was assigned to Médiouna Airfield outside of Casablanca. While still being flown to Tunisia to help with a small group of P-38s, Gordy was grateful for his respite from the constant pressure of daily sorties while in Morocco. He was happy to help Callum and his crews with their P-40 Warhawks and P-39 Airacobras.

Callum was concerned about the American loss at Kasserine Pass. "What do you think, Gordy, are we going to win here in North Africa?"

Gordy pondered his answer. "I don't know, Cal. Believe we need to use our air power better. We can push the Germans out if we use close bombing and strafing support. Our infantry and armor are vulnerable to Afrika Korps' 88-mm guns and Panzer tanks. We don't seem to have a counter on the ground. If we used close-support bombing with Lightnings, P-40s, and Airacobras to take out the 88s and tanks, we'd have a better chance to advance to Bizerte. What do you think?"

"Our planes here aren't being used that way. Wish they were."

Just then, a familiar figure entered the maintenance hangar. "Bonjour, Sergeants. Comment allez-vous, tous les deux? (How are you both?)." Now promoted to Captain, Amos Jean-Louis stood before them, receiving their attention and their salutes.

"Captain Jean-Louis," Callum said. "Congratulations, sir."

"Congratulations, sir!" Gordy echoed.

"Merci, gentlemun. Merci. I come to you buth with a request."

"Sir, what can we do for you, sir?" Callum asked.

"I am the Commandeur de la Formation of the Ninety-ninth Pursuit Squadron. We are the 'Tuskegee Airmen,' named so for our base in Alabama."

Gordy's eyes crinkled with curiosity. "Aren't you stationed at Casablanca Airfield? What brings you to Médiouna, sir?"

Jean-Louis looked sad. "I am, how you say, frustrated? We are best piluts, but we are separated at Casablanca."

"Frustrated, yes, sir," Gordy said, incensed. "If you're training your pilots, they are surely the best, sir. Sergeant Ward and I do not believe in segregation in the Air Corps, sir."

"Mais qui. Merci. We are limuted in mechanucks; trainurs maintenunch for our P-40s. You ur...the best, both you. Yes?"

Callum was too embarrassed to know how to reply to the compliment. "Do you need us to help train your tech sergeants and crews, sir?"

Gordy was not surprised by his brother's response. Callum always had a heart to help though. Captain Jean-Louis looked at him. "We need butter trainung, sergeants. Can you ask? Can hulp?"

Gordy looked at Callum. He knew the answer before they could ask: no. He had another suggestion. "What if after we're finished with our day here, we jump in a jeep and come over to Casablanca? Then we can spend a couple of hours in the evenings training your mechanics and crews."

Callum raised his eyebrows at his brother. He knew that breaking the segregation line could have consequences for them. "Yeah, we'd need to get past your sentries. Can you arrange that, sir?"

"But of course, sergeants. Merci, merci! I can do. Eeest risk for you. What aboot that?"

"We'll take the risk, sir."

"Gud blus yoo buth!"

"By the way, sir, whatever happened to Manman?" Callum asked.

"Shee eest en Haiti, Sergeant, waitung mon return."

So began Callum and Gordy's relationship with the tech sergeants and crews with the 99th Pursuit Squadron. The Tuskegee Airmen would distinguish themselves in their Warhawks and Airacobras in North Africa and eventually go on to legendary status in their P-51 Mustangs. On July 28, 1948, Executive Order 9881 ended segregation in the US Armed Forces. President Harry Truman issued the order, knowing that like legislation would not pass the Congress.

****

By summer 1943, the 48th and 49th Pursuit Squadrons were moved back to Algeria and then in less than a month to El Bathan Airfield. The 99th ended up at Farjana Airfield. Both bases were in Tunisia.

Gordy and Callum were working together again. The 48th was almost at full strength thanks to transfers from other squadrons. A limited number of P-38s were fitted with "droop snoots" (for a bombardier) in the central nacelle. All available Lightnings were loaded with their maximum 4,000 pounds of bombs. The fighters had been transformed into medium bombers.

Sorties to Pantelleria began in early May. Air Command's strategy was to use heavy bombers like B-17s at the highest altitude, P-38s as medium bombers, and P-40s to fly cover, to low-level strafe and bomb targets of opportunity.

In early June it became apparent to Gordy (due to the high number of missions and bomb tonnage) that there would be little left of Pantelleria or its smaller Pelagie Island chain counterparts, Lampedusa, Linosa, and Lampione, based on his P-38s' sorties alone. Callum was also under pressure to keep his P-40s and P-39s flying over the islands. On June 10, consecutive heavy bomber and Lightning runs dropped 1,571 tons of bombs on Pantelleria. Smoke from the resulting fires scrubbed some missions because of no visibility to targets.

****

Captain "Wongolo Wale" Jean-Louis prayed to have his 99th Fighter Squadron in the fight at Pantelleria. He had to fight racial bias to get them in and keep them there. The group commander of the 99th, Col. William Momyer, kept the African American P-40s in reserve until late June and July 1943. Cpt. Jean-Louis was elated to speak to his pilots.

"Gentlemen, we ur en de fight!" A roar went up from his men. "Be red-eee for sorties on July first."

As their Warhawks were armed, Capt. Jean-Louis personally visited each of his twenty-four crews and airmen.

"The eyes of the world are un us. Be yur beest. Be th' Ninety-ninth!"

On July 2 the squadron escorted medium bombers to targets in Sicily. The formation was jumped by German fighters. After the bombers delivered their loads, three Focke-Wulfs that were trailing them attacked. Lt. Charles Hall of the 99th flew between them and their targets, turning into one and firing long bursts.

"Hull tern out, we're un ur wey hume!" Cpt. Jean-Louis called to him.

The lieutenant didn't respond, perhaps because of poor radio contact or he couldn't understand his wing captain's broken English. Jean-Louis called again. "Doo nut breek furmation!" Again, there was no response.

Hall continued to turn and fire. One of the Fw 190s plunged to the sea. The Germans pursued Hall toward Tunisia for some time. Then they turned back to Sicily. Hall returned to Farjana unscathed. Capt. Jean-Louis met him upon landing.

"Yoo disopeyed urders!" he screamed, furious.

"I didn't hear your orders, sir. Sorry."

Capt. Jean-Louis thought for a moment. "Congrutulations, Lieutenant, yoo scoored the Ninety-ninth's first vic-tery!"

"Thank you, sir! You can confirm?"

"Qui!"

Lt. Charles Hall's victory earned him the Distinguished Flying Cross from General Eisenhower. His escape from the German fighters was bittersweet though. Two of his fellow pilots, Lts. James McCullin and Sherman White, died in a mid-air collision.

****

Despite the heroism of Lts. Hall, McCullin, and White, the 99th's group commander, Colonel William Momyer, reported to the North African Air Force (NAAF) commander that the Tuskegee Airmen were incompetent and cowardly. A commission to force the disbandment of the 99th failed. They went on to distinguish themselves in combat throughout the Mediterranean and European campaigns. In their P-51s, the Red Tails were true American heroes—Wangolo and Wale.

****

Pantelleria was a critical staging area for Operation Husky, the invasion of Sicily. Before Husky, the British executed Operation Mincemeat in which they dressed the corpse of a tramp as an RAF airman, placing documents on him that indicated the invasions of Greece, Sardinia, and Corsica were imminent. The body of the fictitious Captain Martin washed ashore at Huelva on the southwest coast of Spain. The Spanish government agreed to a request from Wilhelm Canaris, director of Abwehr, German Military Intelligence, for the fake documents. The information reached Hitler, who ordered Greece, Sardinia, and Corsica to be defended at all costs. Winston Churchill had said of the choices for the invasion of southern Europe before Mincemeat, "Everyone but a bloody fool would know [it was] Sicily."

# CHAPTER 35

# CRUISIN' TO THE BOOT

After the fall of Sicily and the negotiation of the Cassibile Armistice (Italy's switch over the Allies side), the covert Office of Strategic Services (OSS) helped plan the establishment of the Italian Co-Belligerent Army to be populated with vetted Italian Prisoners of War (POWs). Stretched for resources, the OSS sought the help of any Army forces in Tunisia to transport the POWs to the Boot. They accepted an offer from the Air Corps to assist from Lt. Col. Pearson. He had reared his ugly head again for Gordy.

Gordy was ordered to Bezerte. He had refused Lech Marcin's request to accompany him. As he arrived at the dock, he was expecting further orders.

"Sergeant Ward, sir! Good to see you, don't you know, sir!"

Gordy turned and was surprised to see Private First Class Lundgren (his Swedish cook from March Field), "Lundgren? What are you doing here?"

"Got orders, don't ya know, sir. Have 'em right here."

"What orders do you have?"

Lundgren held the folded page out to Gordy. "Says we're taking Italian POWs to Italy, sir."

Gordy gasped in disbelief, "We're taking *prisoners* to Italy?"

"Uh, don't ya know, just us, sir. Says right here."

Gordy read the orders, which said only the two of them would be on the ship with thousands of Italian soldiers. He smelled a Lt. Col. Rat.

The Swede saw the anger in Gordy's eyes. "Sir, they're harmless. They want to get home as much as we do, sir."

Gordy reread the orders. "What in thunder's name…"

"Ya should know, sir, I don't know what or who you calling 'thunder,' Sarge?

"Never mind, Erik—no Norse offense intended by the word 'thunder.' You take the stern; I'll take the bridge. See if supply here can spare a bullhorn; we're going to need it. And make sure your rifle is fully loaded. You still have your sextant?"

"A bullhorn—yes, sir, can do. A bullhorn it'll be…and my rifle loaded. I…don't you know…And yes, still have my sextant, don't you know, sir."

"Get all the ammo you can for my pistol and your M1. And Erik, stop calling me 'sir.'"

"Yes, sir…Sergeant Ward, er Gordy."

Gordy double-checked his Colt .45 M1911 sidearm and his extra magazines. He had a bad feeling about the upcoming trip.

# EPILOGUE

The Allies needed a victory. The Brits needed the Nazis to focus on another front in addition to Operation Barbarossa in the Soviet Union. The Americans needed to prove themselves effective against the battle-hardened Germans. They achieved all of these objectives in Morocco, Algeria, and Tunisia in 1942 and 1943.

Air power had begun to come of age. Fighter squadrons would be the key to defeating the Luftwaffe.

US history would focus on D-Day, Midway, the Bulge, and Iwo Jima. The sacrifices of young men and women in the battles in North Africa would bring about "firsts ever" in war. They soon would be forgotten.

For the Greatest Generation, there was so much more to do.

# ABOUT THE AUTHOR

George Vardaman, Jr. spent 42 years of his successful career in pharmaceuticals, home health and specialty pharmacy. He was born and raised in Denver, Colorado by college professor parents. 30 years of his career were spent in Southern California where he met his wife, Karin, the author of the Children's Book Series, Gary the Gargoyle.

He began his 13 years of service in Africa with Saddleback Church in 2007; established Eye Care, Africa! (ECA)/Clean Stoves in 2012: The 501(C)(3) charity teaches basic eye care; teaches women to build stoves that eliminate 90% of eye/lung damaging CO emissions. ECA Projects must be sustainable; economically empowering, replicable and scalable.

When he was 8 years old, George told his father, George, Sr. (author of 14 text books on Business Communication) he wanted to be a writer. Given his Father's experience in having to have his books adopted for curriculas to sell any books, Dr. Vardaman replied, "You can't make any money doing that." Years passed. George Jr.'s passion for writing never left and thrives in the BATTLES FORGOTTEN Series.

Five years ago, Karin and he moved back to Indian Hills, Colorado where they currently live with their dogs, Padraig, Oakely and Snuggles.

George, Jr. holds a Bachelors of Arts in Political Science/History and a Masters in Business Administration from the University of Denver. He is the Past President of the Laguna Niguel LIONS Club. 2 TIM 1:7